Native Peoples of the Americas

Compton's by Britannica®

ENCYCLOPÆDIA Britannica®

CHICAGO   LONDON   NEW DELHI   PARIS   SEOUL   SYDNEY   TAIPEI   TOKYO

Learn & Explore series
Native Peoples of the Americas
Compton's by Britannica

Library of Congress Control Number: 2007908762
International Standard Book Number: 978-1-61535-330-9

Printed in Malaysia/Times Offset
01-012010

Britannica may be accessed at http://www.britannica.com on the Internet.

Front cover (left): Victor Englebert—Time Life Pictures/Getty Images; (right): Wayne R. Bilenduke—Stone/Getty Images;
(bottom): Lucas Ian Coshenet—The Daily Times/AP; back cover (top): Mauricio Duenas—AFP/Getty Images; (left) William
Fernando Martinez/AP; (right): Joe Cavaretta/AP; table of contents (far left): North Wind Picture Archives; (center left,
center right) The Granger Collection, New York; (far right): William Fernando Martinez/AP

www.britannica.com

EDITOR'S PREFACE

Native Peoples of the Americas joins the Compton's family as the fourth title in the *Learn & Explore* series. The subject of American Indians continues to be a popular one with our online audience as well as a prevalent course of study within school curricula. Over the years several different plans have called for some type of product to address this popularity. With the creation of the *Learn & Explore* series, we have found an ideal match.

While neither a dictionary nor an encyclopedia of American Indian peoples, *Native Peoples of the Americas* is of special interest because of its treatment and organization of the subject matter. Unlike many other books on the subject, this volume discusses native peoples throughout the Americas, from the Arctic North to Tierra del Fuego, at the southern tip of South America. The introduction was written by Elizabeth Prine Pauls, who also served as reviewer and advisor. Pauls, a former state archaeologist of Iowa, holds her Ph.D. in anthropology from the University of California at Berkeley. Her assistance, guidance, and advice as to the organization of this material proved invaluable. Following her introduction is an overview and a key (more on the key below) followed by Part I. Part divisions were created to organize the content in chronological order. Part I addresses prehistory, the beginning of the story. Part II covers traditional culture in the Americas. It includes articles on the 15 culture areas—geographic regions in which peoples lived in a similar way—as well as overviews of some of the more important aspects of traditional life, such as language and religion. The Key to the Native Peoples on page 2 is provided for the reader's convenience and serves as an "at-a-glance" reference guide to the culture areas and the peoples who lived in them. Part III discusses the impact of European contact on American Indian life. And finally, Part IV takes a look at contemporary Native America.

The story of native peoples in the Americas is further illuminated with the use of more than 160 pieces of media, including sidebars, maps, and photographs. A full page of further resources and a two-page index complete the volume. We are confident that this book will prove to be an invaluable resource that, in the Compton's tradition, will inspire, stimulate, and inform.

TABLE OF CONTENTS

INTRODUCTION

This introduction was contributed by Elizabeth Prine Pauls, Ph.D., state archaeologist of Iowa (2002–06), coeditor of Plains Earthlodges: Ethnographic and Archaeological Perspectives, *and author of scholarly and popular articles on indigenous cultures and histories. The articles in this book have all been critically reviewed by Elizabeth Prine Pauls.*

If you were asked to close your eyes and picture an American Indian, who would you see? Would it be a bare-chested young man astride a horse? Perhaps a comely young woman offering up food? Maybe you see an older man, walking through a wasteland, a tear falling from his eye. If your vision is like these, you are not alone—but you are thinking of the past. When I envision Boston or Washington, I do not assume that the panorama will include rebellious colonists in tricorn hats, I think of people in 21st-century garb going about their business. Likewise, a more accurate image of a Native American would be someone who looks like your neighbor, your grade school teacher, the rancher down the road, or the person who gets on the commuter train a few stops after yours.

To say that Indians have changed since Columbus's 1492 arrival is not to say that they have lost their traditions and cultures. Far from it; to paraphrase Mark Twain, rumors of their demise have been greatly exaggerated. Indigenous Americans never became extinct, although they suffered terribly at the hands of European conquerors. Nor have they assimilated completely into any of the Americas' majority cultures. Instead, like people all over the world, they adopted some new ideas from foreign cultures, rejected others, and innovated even more, all the while figuring out ways to make a living, see their children have children, and muddle through the innumerable crises and triumphs of everyday life.

Was the American Indian past characterized by gentleness and plenitude, a sort of pre-Columbian Garden of Eden? Alternatively, was it a gyre of chaos, cannibalism, and atrocity? In reality, both of these views are oversimplified. Whether in the Americas or on any other continents, the human experience in the past was as emotionally and socially complex as it is today. In some places and times, pre-Columbian Indian life was peaceful, while other places and times saw conflict. What is certain is that Indian peoples not only survived, but thrived, for millennia.

The story of American Indians, then, is a story that anyone can relate to but that carries its own specific events and subtleties. It is also a story for which there are many and sometimes contradictory versions. For archaeologists, historians, and others whose beliefs are shaped by physical or documentary evidence, it begins at least 15,000 to 20,000 years ago when intrepid families moved eastward from Asia, across or along the Bering land bridge, and into North America. For elders, traditionalists, and others whose beliefs are shaped by faith, it begins at the dawn of time when a Creator endowed humans with land and the means to make a living. Both sides believe tenaciously in their stories, which represent very different realms of explanation— one scientific and the other religious.

As readers with an interest in American Indians, we owe thanks to both groups of storytellers. The Americas have been home to vibrant and diverse peoples, and we can better understand those peoples, past and present, by opening ourselves to both realms of explanation. One provides insight on the events of the body, the other on the workings of the mind; they illuminate more together than either can alone.

Fortunately, there are an increasing number of people who work in these two realms simultaneously. These people are Indians who are also professors, lawyers, executives, politicians, or members of any of a number of other professions. By bringing their personal cultural sensibilities to their work, and their professional sensibilities to their cultures, they enrich both. Building on the Indian resistance that has continued unbroken from 1492 to the present, these individuals and their compatriots from other native groups have been able to bring their peoples' needs to the attention of the world. More than 500 years after the "discovery" of the Americas, their rights were recognized by the United Nations Declaration of the Rights of Indigenous Peoples (ratified Sept. 13, 2007). As someone who has worked with and for Indians for a large part of my career, this was an exciting event—and one whose time had definitely come.

Although gaining the support of the United Nations was a momentous occasion, it has not markedly changed life on the reservation, in the village, or in the city. Despite tremendous gains by many individuals and families, Indians as a whole continue to be among the most impoverished peoples in the Americas. Much of this poverty is the result of ill-informed and poorly executed public policy, the practice of which arose long before the first reserve lands were designated by the Proclamation of 1763. Poverty in turn creates an atmosphere in which inadequate health care, poor schools, substandard housing, and other dehumanizing conditions become the norm. Let us hope that as the 21st century continues, American Indian peoples make strides in economic development that are comparable to those they have made in human rights recognition.

NATIVE PEOPLES OF THE AMERICAS

The first people to live in the Americas were the Indians, or Native Americans. Their settlements ranged across the Western Hemisphere and were built on many of the sites where modern cities now rise. Native families and traders used paths now followed by roads and railroads. Indian words dot the maps of the United States, Canada, and the rest of the Americas. In the United States alone, 27 states bear names from the languages of the first Americans.

American Indian farmers were the first in the world to domesticate corn (maize), beans, squash, potatoes, tomatoes, and many other food plants that help feed the peoples of the world today. They found a variety of uses for such native American plants as rubber, tobacco, and the sugar maple. They also raised turkeys, llamas, and alpacas. These resources, along with others provided by hunting, gathering, and fishing, were used to support communities ranging from small villages to expansive cities with tens of thousands of residents.

Native peoples had lived in the Americas for thousands of years when the first European explorers set foot on their land. When Christopher Columbus landed in the New World, he called the native peoples *indios* (Spanish for Indians) because he thought he had reached a part of South Asia called the Indies.

Early explorers and settlers tended to think of the Indians as a single people, but the Indians themselves did not. An Indian considered himself a Delaware, a Dakota, a Navajo, or a member of one of the hundreds of other Indian nations in the Americas. The name of many peoples meant "the people" in their language.

The arrival of Europeans in the Americas proved devastating to the native peoples. Military conquest and epidemic diseases brought by the newcomers killed millions of Indians throughout North and South America. Many of the survivors lost their land and were forced into slavery. Under colonial authorities and later under national and state governments, native peoples were subject to discriminatory political and legal policies well into the 20th, and even the 21st, century. This history of injustice largely explains why Indians are among the most impoverished groups in the United States and other countries.

Nevertheless, American Indians have been among the world's most active and successful native peoples in bringing about political change. Since the late 20th century they have made gains in such areas as education, land ownership, religious freedom, and the law. They have worked for the revitalization of traditional culture by encouraging the use of native languages. They have also had some success in finding new sources of income to improve their economic standing.

The term American Indian is just one of many that have been used to refer to the native peoples of the Americas. In the 1960s many activists in the United States and Canada rejected the label because it is a misnomer applied by Europeans. In these countries Native American soon became the preferred term. Later, Native Americans in Canada began to refer to themselves as First Nations. The word nation has also been adopted by native peoples in other areas because it emphasizes their independent political status. Peoples of the American Arctic prefer the term Native Alaskan, Yupik, or Inuit. Nevertheless, many native people of North America continue to identify themselves as Indians.

KEY TO THE NATIVE PEOPLES

This book covers native peoples and cultures of prehistoric America as well as those that flourished at the time of European contact in the 1500s. The first four groups in the list below are notable prehistoric cultures covered in Part I. In the rest of the book, the native peoples are discussed largely in terms of the culture area to which they belonged. A culture area is a geographic region in which peoples share many cultural traits. Beginning with The Arctic, the 15 traditional culture areas of the Americas are listed below along with some of the peoples who lived in them.

The names used in this book are ones by which the native peoples are commonly known. Many ethnic groups have more than one name, however, and American Indians are no exception. Names can originate in a number of ways. The best-known names for many American Indian groups were given to them by their rivals and, when translated into English, can be considered quite insulting. For example, when the Ojibwa (Anishinaabe) and Fox (Meskwaki) were asked who lived to their west, French traders were told stories of the Winipig, or Winipyägohagi—a name that translates roughly to "Filthy (or Stinking) Waters." In 1993, after more than 300 years of using this name, the members of the Wisconsin Winnebago Tribe officially replaced it with Ho-Chunk, meaning "People of the Big Voice" in their language.

Other peoples have chosen to keep historical names even though they began as derogatory labels. The name Sioux, for example, comes from Nadouessioux—a name given to them by the Ojibwa that means "Adder" or "Snake." Many members of the dozens of bands and tribes within the Sioux nation prefer the names Lakota, Dakota, and Nakota, referring to the three dialects of their language. Yet Sioux is still widely used for several reasons: one is that it provides a convenient way to refer to the three dialect groups as a whole, and another is that it promotes ethnic unity among the many bands and tribes.

Paleo-Indians

Archaic Cultures

Prehistoric Farmers of Northern America

Adena culture
Ancestral Pueblo
Hohokam culture
Hopewell culture
Mississippian culture
Mogollon culture
Plains Village culture
Plains Woodland culture

Early Civilizations of Middle and South America

Chavín
Chimú
Maya
Olmec
Teotihuacán
Tiwanaku
Toltec

The Arctic

Aleut
Eskimo (Inuit)

The Subarctic

Beaver
Carrier
Chipewyan
Cree
Deg Xinag
Dogrib
Innu
Kaska
Ojibwa (Chippewa)
Slave
Tanaina

The Northeast

Abenaki
Algonquin
Delaware
Fox (Meskwaki)
Ho-Chunk (Winnebago)
Illinois

Iroquois (including the Cayuga, Huron, Mohawk, Oneida, Onondaga, Seneca, and Tuscarora)
Kickapoo
Massachuset
Menominee
Mi'kmaq (Micmac)
Mohegan
Mohican
Ojibwa
Penobscot
Pequot
Sauk
Wampanoag

The Southeast

Alabama
Apalachee
Caddo
Catawba
Cherokee
Chickasaw
Choctaw
Creek
Guale
Natchez
Seminole
Timucua

The Plains

Arapaho
Arikara
Assiniboin
Atsina
Blackfeet
Cheyenne
Comanche
Crow
Hidatsa
Iowa
Kansa
Kiowa
Mandan
Missouri
Omaha
Osage

Oto
Pawnee
Plains Cree
Plains Ojibwa
Ponca
Sarcee
Sioux (consisting of the Santee [Dakota], Teton [Lakota], and Yankton [Nakota] divisions)
Wichita
Wind River Shoshone

The Great Basin

Bannock
Gosiute
Mono
Paiute
Shoshone
Ute
Washoe

California

Chumash
Hupa
Maidu
Miwok
Pomo
Wintun
Yana
Yokuts
Yuki
Yurok

The Northwest Coast

Bella Coola
Chinook
Coast Salish
Haida
Kwakiutl
Nuu-chah-nulth (Nootka)
Tlingit
Tsimshian

The Plateau

Coeur d'Alene
Flathead
Kalispel

Klamath
Kutenai
Lillooet
Modoc
Nez Percé
Pend d'Oreille
Shuswap
Spokan
Umatilla
Wallawalla
Yakima

The Southwest

Apache
Cocopa
Havasupai
Hualapai
Maricopa
Mojave
Navajo
Pima
Pueblo
Tohono O'odham (Papago)
Yavapai
Yuma (Quechan)

Middle America

Aztec
Cora
Huastec
Huichol
Maya
Mixtec
Tarasco
Zapotec

Central America and the Northern Andes

Arawak
Caquetío
Carib
Cenú (Sinú)
Chibcha
Chocó
Guaymí
Jirajara
Kuna

Miskito
Páez
Quimbaya
Tairona

The Central Andes

Araucanian
Atacama
Aymara
Chanca
Chimú
Chincha
Diaguita
Huarpe
Inca

The Rainforest

Achagua
Arawak
Carib
Ge (including the Kaingang, Kayapó, Suyá, Timbira, Xavante, and Xerente)
Guahibo
Kawaíb
Makushí
Mundurukú
Palicur
Taulipang
Tupinambá

Marginal Regions

Abipón
Aché
Alacaluf
Botocudo
Charrúa
Chono
Guahibo
Makú
Mura
Nambikwara
Puelche
Querandí
Sirionó
Tehuelche
Vilela
Yámana

PART I
PREHISTORY

The first Americans arrived during the last Ice Age, when glaciers covered much of northern North America. It was the late stage of the period of Earth's history called the Pleistocene Epoch. As the glaciers absorbed water, sea levels dropped and a land bridge emerged along the present-day Bering Strait. From about 30,000 to 12,000 years ago the land bridge—known as Beringia—connected northeastern Asia to what is now Alaska. At its greatest extent Beringia may have spanned some 1,000 miles (1,600 kilometers) from north to south. Humans began to cross over from Asia at least 13,000 years ago and perhaps much earlier. As the glaciers melted, the land bridge disappeared under the rising seas and the migration ended.

Like most people at the time, those who moved into Beringia from Asia belonged to hunting and gathering cultures. Such cultures are characterized by small, family-based groups called bands that move from place to place. The earliest Americans ate wild foods, including plants, nuts, game, and fish. Beringia teemed with life and made a good home for people. In fact, it was probably inhabited for a long time before people moved into North America itself. Scholars believe this because of the long period during which the land bridge existed and because glaciers blocked passage at its eastern end until perhaps 13,000 BC. Beringia may have been inhabited for as long as 20,000 years.

Some people crossed the land bridge on foot and others traveled along its coast in boats. As the eastern glaciers began to melt, Beringians finally reached North America. Some followed the Pacific coast southward, perhaps combining walking with boat travel. Others found ice-free routes east of the Rocky Mountains that led into the heart of the continent. Such passages probably existed in the Mackenzie River basin and along the Yukon, Liard, and Peace river systems.

Continued melting of the ice gradually opened up the land, allowing people to spread out across North America and down through Central America into South America. No single person made any large part of the

long journey from Alaska down the continents. One group after another continued the march over many centuries.

Scholars have only limited knowledge of the peopling of the Americas. Most traces of this part of human prehistory have been erased by thousands of years of geological processes. The Pacific Ocean has covered or washed away most of the migration route along the coast. Sediment left behind by the melting glaciers has destroyed or deeply buried traces of the inland journey.

The earliest peoples of the Americas are known as Paleo-Indians. They lived by hunting and gathering. As people began to settle down and expand their diets, they developed what are called Archaic cultures. In addition to foraging, Archaic peoples began to experiment with agriculture.

By about 2300 BC peoples in the Andes Mountains of South America had adopted a fully agricultural way of life. They began to settle in villages. Farming villages appeared by 2000 BC in Middle America (present-day Mexico and Central America) and somewhat later in Northern America (present-day United States and Canada). Over time these prehistoric farmers developed new kinds of societies. Advanced cultures arose in Middle and South America that rivaled the great civilizations of ancient Egypt, Mesopotamia, and China.

PALEO-INDIANS

The very early people of the Americas are known as Paleo-Indians. They shared some cultural traits with peoples of Asia, such as the use of fire and domesticated dogs. However, they do not seem to have used other Old World technologies such as grazing animals, domesticated plants, and the wheel.

Paleo-Indians shared the land with such large mammals as mammoths, mastodons, and giant bison. Archaeological sites of Paleo-Indians often include bones from these animals. This has sometimes led to the mistaken idea that these peoples only ate big game. By the turn of the 21st century, however, excavations at sites such as Gault (Texas) and Jake Bluff (Oklahoma) had shown that Paleo-Indians also ate smaller animals and many wild plant foods, including fruit, tubers, nuts, and even seaweed.

Clovis and Folsom Cultures

The best-known Paleo-Indian cultures of North America are Clovis and Folsom. The Clovis culture is the older of the two. Its people left behind one of the most distinctive Paleo-Indian artifact types—the Clovis point. These spear points are thin, leaf-shaped, and made of stone. They are also fluted, meaning that they have grooves on each flat side. They were attached to spear handles and are most often found at sites where mammoths were killed and butchered, though they have also been found with fossils of extinct species of bison, horse, and camel. The culture was named for an archaeological site near Clovis, N.M., where the first such point was found among mammoth bones in 1929. Scrapers (used to clean the hide) and other artifacts used to process meat have also been found at Clovis sites. The Clovis culture was long believed to have lasted from about 9500 to 9000 BC. However, early 21st-century research suggested it may have lasted a shorter time, from about 9050 to 8800 BC.

Folsom culture seems to have developed from Clovis culture. It is also known for its own distinctive spear point. Like Clovis points, Folsom points are leaf-shaped, but they are more carefully made and have much larger flutes. The first Folsom point was discovered in 1908 at a site near Folsom, N.M., along with the remains of a now-extinct form of giant bison. The Lindenmeier site, a Folsom campsite in northeastern Colorado, has yielded a variety of scrapers, gravers (used to engrave bone or wood), and bone tools. The Folsom culture is thought to have lasted from about 9000 to 8000 BC. Related Paleo-Indian cultures, such as Plano, continued to between 6000 and 4000 BC.

Pre-Clovis Cultures

The Clovis and Folsom sites provided the first indisputable evidence that ancient Americans had coexisted with and hunted the Pleistocene mammals, a possibility that most scholars had previously doubted. Later research, in turn, challenged the belief that Clovis people were the first Americans. For decades scholars generally agreed that Clovis people first settled in the interior plains of North America and then colonized the Western Hemisphere. It was believed that as game became scarcer, they followed the remaining animals down through the plains of Central America and the Andes Mountains of South America. According to this theory, they avoided the coasts and tropical forests and reached the southern tip of South America by 10,000 years ago, the end of the Ice Age.

Caribou were among the game hunted by the Paleo-Indians of North America.

Early humans crossed from northeastern Asia to the Americas over a now-submerged land bridge across the Bering Strait. The locations of archaeological sites in the Americas suggest the migration routes followed by Paleo-Indians after the glaciers of the late Pleistocene Epoch melted.

The Clovis migration theory developed at a time when little was known of regions outside the Clovis heartland. However, discoveries of new sites in the late 20th century, along with new data from old sites, cast doubt on the theory. According to these findings, the Clovis culture did not exist early enough to be the ancestor of Central and South American Paleo-Indians. Several well-documented sites south of the U.S. border are as early as or earlier than those of Clovis peoples. Although many scholars initially doubted the evidence from the new sites, the late 1990s saw general agreement that humans had arrived in North and South America by at least 11,000 BC, some 1,500 years before the appearance of Clovis culture. In addition, the new evidence revealed that the first Americans settled in many different regions. Not only the plains but also the coasts and tropical

Clovis points are distinguished by the characteristic channels, or flutes, that extend from mid-blade to the base of the implement

Courtesy, Robert N. Converse,
The Archaeological Society of Ohio

The walls of Lapa do Boquete, a rock shelter in southeastern Brazil, feature rock art created by Paleo-Indians. The symbol that resembles a ladder was a sign of fertility among the Indians, and the yellow figure on the left appears to be an armadillo.

forests were occupied by the earliest-known people. Thus, Clovis was just one regional culture among many.

Pre-Clovis sites in North America include evidence for two cultures based in Alaska. The people of the Nenana culture, named for the Nenana Valley in central Alaska, used triangular and teardrop-shaped spear points and lived by hunting and gathering. Archaeologists have found plant remains and abundant bones of bison, other large and small mammals, birds, fish, and snails. The Nenana culture was closely related to hunting and gathering cultures in eastern Siberia. Evidence for another pre-Clovis group in Alaska was found at the Mesa site. Located on a ridge above the Arctic Circle, it was used as a lookout point for spotting game. Although they date from the same period as the Nenana culture, Mesa spear points differ from those found at the Nenana sites. Instead they closely resemble Clovis points, suggesting a close cultural relationship between Mesa peoples and the Clovis culture far to the south.

Other pre-Clovis sites are located throughout the continental United States. For years evidence of early migration was missing from the Pacific coast, which was flooded after the Ice Age. In the 1990s, however, archaeologists began to investigate Daisy Cave, a site on a hilly channel island near Santa Barbara, Calif. The Paleo-Indians of this culture adapted to their coastal environment, living on shellfish, fish, and marine mammals. Archaeologists have also found pre-Clovis artifacts at the Topper site in South Carolina, Cactus Hill in Virginia, Schaefer and Hebior in Wisconsin, and other sites.

Contrary to the Clovis-first theory, archaeologists now believe that Paleo-Indians reached South America by at least 12,500 years ago, and perhaps much earlier. They settled in what are now Tierra del Fuego, Argentina, southern Chile, the south-central plains of the Gran Chaco region, and portions of the central Andes. As with other very early Americans, these peoples organized themselves into small bands so it was easy to move to

areas with more plentiful food or a more favorable climate.

Many late Pleistocene sites have been discovered in South America. The oldest are as early as or earlier than Clovis and are distinct culturally. Triangular and/or stemmed points, similar to those found in Asia, have been found at most of the sites. The food remains indicate that these groups collected plants and caught small game. The habitats that these people lived in were diverse, ranging from the desert coast of the Pacific and the Atlantic tropical rain forests to the pampas and the icy shores of Patagonia in southern Argentina.

The oldest confirmed site of human habitation in the Americas is Monte Verde, a site in southern Chile. It dates to about 10,500 BC. First excavated in the 1970s, the site did not seem to agree with findings that placed the earliest humans in northeastern Asia no earlier than about 11,500 BC. It seemed very unlikely that people could have made their way from Siberia to Chile in just 1,000 years. However, excavations at the Yana Rhinoceros Horn site in Siberia later determined that humans were present on the western side of the Bering land bridge as early as 25,000 BC, providing ample time for such a migration.

Paleo-Indian sites in northern South America include Taima Taima, an oil field site in Venezuela, where fragmentary tools have been found with mastodon bones. Late Pleistocene people may have killed mastodons there, but exactly when is not certain. In nearby Colombia some sites contain triangular points, while others have ground-stone tools. Food remains are tropical forest fruits and nuts.

The first solid evidence of early Paleo-Indians on the Pacific coast of South America came from two sites in southern Peru. At Quebrada Tacahuay and Quebrada Jaguay, ancient hearths contained fragments of stone tools and remains of shellfish, small fish, and birds but no large game.

For more than 100 years researchers have claimed that there were very early human sites in the tropical forests of eastern South America. By the end of the 20th century a number of sites had produced evidence of human habitation at least 11,000 years ago. Unlike Clovis sites, which tend to be in open country, those in Brazil include caves and rock shelters where people decorated the walls by painting them. Food remains include nuts, legumes, fish, shellfish, and small game animals. Among the artifacts are triangular, sometimes stemmed points but no fluted points. The sites include Caverna da Pedra Pintada, Santana de Riacho, and Lapa do Boquete in Brazil.

Two early Paleo-Indian cultures have been found in far southern South America. The Fell's Cave site in Patagonia was first discovered in the 1930s. Fishtail spear points are distinctive Fell's Cave artifacts. They once were equated with Clovis points but now are known to have been made and shaped differently. Although some extinct horse and sloth remains were found, most animals hunted were smaller game, such as guanaco (a type of small, wild llama) and local birds. Farther north and west was the Los Toldos culture. Its sites contain rock paintings; stemmed, triangular points; and evidence of foraging for many kinds of food.

ARCHAIC CULTURES

The Archaic cultures developed from Paleo-Indian traditions. They arose in response to environmental changes. Beginning some 11,500 years ago temperatures rose dramatically worldwide. The glaciers melted, and sea levels rose. Very large animals such as mammoths and giant ground sloths could not cope with the changes and became extinct. Other animals, such as bison, survived by becoming smaller. At the same time new grasses, trees, and other plants developed.

As the environment changed, so did the Indians' lifestyles. The most visible change was in their diet. Archaic peoples used a wider range of plant and animal foods than the Paleo-Indians had. As very large game grew scarce, people relied more upon smaller animals such as deer, elk, antelope, and rabbits. They caught more fish and collected more shellfish from rivers and lakes. They also began to gather seeds, an addition to the larger plant foods used by the Paleo-Indians, such as fruit and roots. With these varied sources of food, people

A rock painting of a shaman in Panther Cave in the U.S. state of Texas dates from the Archaic period.

Bob Daemmrich/Corbis

no longer had to move constantly to feed themselves. They became somewhat more settled, tending to live in larger groups for at least part of the year. They often built seasonal camps along waterways. They also developed systems of trade between different geographical regions.

Archaic peoples adapted to their environments by inventing many new technologies. They introduced the spear-thrower, a short, hooked rod that enables a hunter to throw a dart accurately and with great force at a distant target. So-called bird stones may have been used as weights on the spear-thrower to increase the hunter's throwing power. Large fluted points became less popular, replaced by smaller side-notched points more appropriate for hunting with darts. Other new hunting tools included fishhooks as well as nets for catching fish, birds, and other small game. Woodworking tools created by Archaic peoples included grooved stone axes and gouges made from ground and polished stone. The development of basketry and netting aided the collection and storage of new foods, while grinding stones made it possible to turn hard seeds into more easily digested flour.

In the late Archaic period people began to farm. In Northern America, Archaic peoples east of the Mississippi River focused on growing pigweed and related plants. Groups in Middle America worked with wild varieties of corn (maize), and those in South America worked with wild potato species. However, Archaic peoples continued to rely upon hunting and gathering for the majority of their food. They are said to have shifted out of the Archaic and into the next cultural stage when they began to rely more heavily on food production and in most cases to make pottery.

By adopting an array of social, economic, and technological innovations, Archaic peoples enjoyed thousands of years of relative stability. The period lasted from approximately 8000 BC until at least 2000 BC in most of Northern America, from 7000 to 2000 BC in Middle America, and from 6000 to 2000 BC in South America. But in some places Archaic cultures persisted much longer. For instance, Indians in the Great Basin of what is now the western United States kept their foraging lifestyle well into the 1800s.

Northern America

The length of the Archaic Period varied considerably in Northern America. Though in some areas it began as early as 8000 BC, in others it began as recently as 4000 BC. Between 6000 and 4000 BC the wild squash seeds found at archaeological sites slowly increased in size, a sign of early domestication. Similar changes are apparent by about 5000 BC in the seeds of wild sunflowers and certain "weedy" plants such as sumpweed and lamb's-quarters. Northern Americans independently

The spear-thrower was an innovation of the Archaic period. It consisted of a rod with a hook or projection at the rear end to hold the weapon in place until its release. The device gave greater velocity and force to the spear.

domesticated several kinds of plants, including a variety of squash unrelated to those of Middle or South America, sunflowers, and goosefoot.

Archaic peoples living along the Pacific coast and in neighboring inland areas found a number of innovative ways to adapt to local conditions. Groups living in dry inland areas made rough flint tools, grinding stones, and, eventually arrowheads and subsisted upon plant seeds and small game. Where there was more precipitation, the food supply included elk, deer, acorns, fish, and birds. People on the coast itself depended on the sea for most of their food supply. Some groups subsisted mainly on shellfish, some on sea mammals, others on fish, and still others on a mixture of all three.

Archaic peoples in the present-day Plateau, Great Basin, and Southwest culture areas created distinctive adaptations to their dry, relatively impoverished environments. They lived in small nomadic bands and moved with the seasons. They ate a wide variety of animal and plant foods and developed techniques for harvesting and processing small seeds. Among their most important tools were milling stones, used for grinding seeds into meal or flour. These groups are known for having lived in caves and rock shelters. They

also made twined basketry, nets, mats, cordage, fur cloaks, sandals, wooden clubs, digging sticks, spear-throwers, and dart shafts tipped with pointed hardwood, flint, or obsidian. The best-known Archaic culture of these regions is the Cochise, which began by about 7000 BC in Arizona and New Mexico.

Plains Archaic culture began by about 6000 BC. It is marked by a shift from just a few kinds of fluted Paleo-Indian points to a great variety of styles, including stemmed and side-notched points. The main game animal of the Plains Archaic peoples was the bison, though they also hunted a variety of other game and foraged for many wild plant foods. As the climate became warmer, some groups followed grazing herds north into what are now the Canadian provinces of Saskatchewan and Alberta. By 3000 BC these people had reached the Arctic tundra zone in the Northwest Territories and shifted their attention from bison to the local caribou. Other groups moved east to the Mississippi valley and western Great Lakes area.

Archaic culture in the East began around 8000 BC and included much of the eastern Subarctic, the Northeast, and the Southeast culture areas. Because of this very wide geographical distribution, Eastern Archaic cultures show more diversity than Archaic cultures elsewhere in North America. Nonetheless, these cultures share a number of characteristics. The typical house was a small circular structure framed with wood and probably covered with bark. Cooking was done by placing hot rocks into wood, bark, or hide containers of food, which caused the contents to warm or even boil; by baking in pits; or by roasting. Eastern Archaic peoples used game-gathering devices such as nets and traps, as well as spears, darts, and dart or spear-throwers. They fished with hooks, and in some areas they built underwater pens called weirs to catch fish. They also collected roots, berries, fruits, and tubers.

Over time, Eastern Archaic peoples developed more sophisticated tools. They made a large variety of chipped-flint projectiles, knives, scrapers, drills, and

Bird stones are among the most striking artifacts left by the Archaic peoples who lived east of the Mississippi River in the United States and parts of eastern Canada. This typical example, found in Ohio, was carved from slate and measures approximately 3.5 inches (8.9 centimeters) long.

Archaic peoples were the first to use stones (left) called manos and metates in food preparation. The smaller mano, held in the hand, was used to grind corn against the larger metate. A palm-sized twig figurine from about 2000 BC (right) depicts a deer or a bighorn sheep. It was found in a cave at Grand Canyon National Park in the U.S. state of Arizona.

adzes (for shaping wood). They also gradually developed ground and polished tools such as grooved stone axes, pestles, gouges, adzes, and bird stones.

Eastern Archaic people in what are now the U.S. states of Michigan and Wisconsin produced the earliest examples of metalwork in the New World. They cold-hammered pure copper to make tools and weapons. Their Old Copper culture appeared in about 3000 BC and lasted some 2,000 years.

Middle America

In the early Archaic period, the peoples of Middle America were probably seasonal nomads who divided their time between small hunting camps and larger temporary villages. The villages were used as bases for collecting plants such as various grasses and maguey and cactus fruits. They began to experiment with plant domestication as early as 8000 BC, however, and improved their crops over thousands of years. The agricultural progress of this period would later make possible the rise of great Middle American civilizations.

Evidence of the origins of farming in Middle America has come from caves and rock shelters in the modern southern Mexican states of Puebla and Oaxaca. Remains of corn cobs from these sites show that Middle American peoples probably had domesticated corn by 5000 BC. Farmers gradually learned to produce hybrid varieties to increase the size of the corn kernels. Stones called manos and metates were used to grind the corn into meal or dough. Squash, beans, cassava (manioc), chili peppers, avocados, and cotton were other early crops. After about 3500 BC the use of cultivated plants increased at the expense of wild plants and, probably, at the expense of hunting.

As the amount of plant food grew, the settlement pattern shifted. In place of the temporary hunting camps and rock shelters, people built more-permanent villages of pit houses (houses of poles and earth built over pits).

As they became more settled, people also started to make pottery. Fired clay bowls and jars appeared in Puebla's Tehuacán Valley by 2300 BC. By the end of the Archaic period in about 2000 BC, the stage was set for the adoption of a fully settled lifestyle in Middle America.

South America

Archaic peoples of South America, like those in Middle America, began the process of plant cultivation early on. They domesticated squash, peanuts, lima beans, potatoes, and other crops. South American groups practiced shifting agriculture as early as 3000 BC. This means that they cleared a plot of land and grew crops there for a short period of time, usually a few seasons. When the soil was exhausted or the field was overrun by weeds, they abandoned it and moved on to another plot.

As in other places, however, the Archaic peoples of South America depended on sources other than farming for most of their food. People along the Pacific coast took advantage of the ocean, catching fish with cotton nets and shell hooks, collecting shellfish, and hunting sea mammals. Much of the coast is a desert, and in winter some people camped on the *lomas*, patches of vegetation that were watered in that season by fogs. In summer, when the *lomas* dried up, they built camps along the shore. The *lomas* provided wild seeds, tubers, and large snails. Guanaco (a wild member of the camel family), deer, owls, and foxes were hunted. Many spear points have been found in the southern part of this region, and stone tools have been found in the north. The El Estero site in northern Peru has yielded well-made polished stone axes and mortars.

In the Andes Mountains, Archaic peoples who originally hunted deer and guanaco gradually came to depend more on farming. The Andean peoples were the first to domesticate the potato. They also raised guinea pigs for their meat and llamas and alpacas for meat, wool, and transportation.

PREHISTORIC FARMERS OF NORTHERN AMERICA

In Northern America the transition from an Archaic way of life based mainly on hunting and gathering to one more dependent on agriculture took from a few hundred to thousands of years. Prehistoric farming peoples shared certain similarities. They lived more settled lives than Archaic groups, though most still did some hunting away from their settlements. They built more substantial houses than Archaic groups had, and they often protected their communities with walls or ditches. And many farming peoples developed hierarchical societies in which a class of priests or chiefs had authority over one or more classes of commoners.

The Southwest

In the first centuries AD three major farming cultures arose in the Southwest: the Ancestral Pueblo, the Mogollon, and the Hohokam. All had cultural connections to the earlier Cochise culture. Indians of the Southwest had begun to grow corn and squash by about 1200 BC. But they could not produce reliable harvests until they overcame the region's dryness using irrigation.

Each of these cultures reached its height between about AD 700 and 1300. At that time the population and cultures of central and western Mexico spread to the northwest. Materials entering the Southwest from Mexico during this era included cast copper bells, parrots, ball courts, shell trumpets, and pottery with innovative vessel shapes and designs. Another factor that encouraged population and cultural growth during this period was the climate. The Southwest received an unusually favorable amount of rainfall, which made farming easier and helped to support larger populations.

Ancestral Pueblo. The Ancestral Pueblo lived on the plateau where the U.S. states of Colorado, New Mexico, Arizona, and Utah now meet. Their descendants make up the modern Pueblo Indian tribes. As farmers, the Ancestral Pueblo and their nomadic neighbors were often hostile to each other. This is the source of the term Anasazi, a Navajo word meaning "ancestors of the enemy," which once served as the customary name for this group.

The Ancestral Pueblo culture began in about AD 100. At first these people combined hunting, gathering wild plant foods, and some corn cultivation. They typically lived in caves or in shallow pit houses constructed in the

The Ancestral Pueblo, prehistoric Indians of the Southwest, built multistory houses in the alcoves of canyon walls. Among the most impressive of these cliff dwellings is Cliff Palace at Mesa Verde National Park in Colorado, with 150 residential rooms and 23 underground religious rooms called kivas.

Cliff Dwellings

The cliff dwellings of the Ancestral Pueblo are among the most striking achievements of prehistoric Native Americans. The use of hand-cut stone building blocks and adobe mortar (a wet clay mixture) was unmatched even in later buildings. Ceilings were built by laying two or more large crossbeams and placing on them a solid base of smaller branches. The layers were then plastered over with the same adobe mixture used for the walls. Dwellings often consisted of two, three, or even four stories. They had a stepped appearance because each level or floor was set back from the one below it. The roofs of the lower rooms served as terraces for the rooms above.

Residential rooms measured about 10 by 20 feet (3 by 6 meters). Entrance to ground-floor rooms was by ladder through an opening in the ceiling. Rooms on upper floors could be entered both by doorways from adjoining rooms and by openings in the ceiling or roof. Each community had two or more kivas (ceremonial rooms).

Earlier Ancestral Pueblo villages were built in the open. Scholars believe that these people began to build cliff dwellings as a defense against invading groups that may have been the ancestors of the Navajo and Apache. In addition to the natural protection of the cliff, the absence of doors and windows to the rooms on the ground floor left a solid outer stone wall that could be surmounted only by climbing a ladder. The ladders could easily be removed if the town were attacked.

Many smaller communities joined together to form the large towns built beneath the cliffs. Two of the largest, the Cliff Palace at Mesa Verde National Park in Colorado and Pueblo Bonito at Chaco Culture National Historical Park in New Mexico, probably had about 150 and 800 residential rooms, respectively.

open. They also created pits in the ground that were used for food storage. As farming became more important, they built irrigation structures such as reservoirs and check dams—low stone walls used to catch runoff from the limited rains. Hunting and gathering became secondary to farming, and the Ancestral Pueblo adopted a more settled lifestyle. Originally they built partly underground houses in caves or on the tops of high, rocky plateaus called mesas. Later they built above-ground dwellings, both on mesas and in canyons. Using stone masonry they constructed a number of very large communities, some with more than 100 adjoining rooms. Kivas—underground circular chambers used mainly for ceremonial purposes—became important community features. Pottery came into widespread use.

The architecture of the Ancestral Pueblo culminated with the cliff dwellings. Built between 1150 and 1300, these massive houses were set along the sides or under the overhangs of cliffs. Large, apartment-like structures were also built along canyons or mesa walls. Cliff dwellings had 20 to as many as 1,000 rooms and could rise to four stories in height (*see* sidebar). The population became concentrated in these large communities, and many smaller villages and hamlets were abandoned. Agriculture continued to be the main economic activity,

and craftsmanship in pottery and weaving achieved its finest quality during this period.

The Ancestral Pueblo abandoned their communities by about 1300. A drought lasting from 1276 to 1299 probably caused massive crop failure. At the same time, conflicts increased between the Ancestral Pueblo and neighboring groups that may have been the predecessors of the modern Navajo and Apache peoples. The Ancestral Pueblo moved to the south and the east, near better water sources. The history of the modern Pueblo tribes is usually dated from about 1600 onward.

Mogollon culture. The Mogollon culture existed from about AD 200 to 1450. The homeland of the Mogollon was the mountainous region of what are now southeastern Arizona and southwestern New Mexico. Their territory also extended southward into what are now the Mexican states of Chihuahua and Sonora. Their name comes from the Mogollon Mountains in New Mexico.

The Mogollon obtained most of their food by hunting and by gathering wild seeds, roots, and nuts. At first they hunted mostly small prey, such as rabbits and

A bowl with a black-on-white design of a bat (left) dates from the Mimbres period of the Mogollon culture, which lasted from about 1050 to 1200. The Hohokam people made distinctive pottery of buff clay (right) painted with red designs.

lizards, that could be caught in nets or snares. Later they hunted deer and other larger game. Because the Mogollon lived in the mountains, much of their land was not good for growing crops. But they eventually began to grow corn, squash, and beans. They used small dams to pool rainfall and divert streams for watering crops.

At first the Mogollon lived in small villages of pit houses grouped near a large ceremonial structure. Early pit houses were circular with a ceiling made of wood covered with mud. The entrance was through a tunnel. Later pit houses were rectangular and made of stone. Between about 650 and 850 the Mogollon began to build larger pit structures to serve as ceremonial kivas. The appearance of these structures suggests the influence of the Ancestral Pueblo.

By about 1000 the Mogollon began to replace their pit houses with adobe and stone apartment-style houses like those of the Ancestral Pueblo. These houses were built at ground level and rose one to three stories high. These villages sometimes contained 40 to 50 rooms arranged around a plaza. Evidence from this period suggests that Ancestral Pueblo and Mogollon peoples lived peacefully in the same villages.

The Mogollon made the first pottery in the Southwest. At first the pottery was simple, made of red or brown clay and undecorated. Over time the Mogollon included designs on the pots and other vessels. They also learned to make and use paints. One group, known as the Mimbres, were especially well known for their pottery. It was decorated with imaginative black-on-white designs of insects, animals, and birds or with geometric lines.

The Mogollon culture ended for unknown reasons in the 15th century. The people abandoned their villages, perhaps spreading out over the landscape or joining other village groups.

Hohokam culture. The Hohokam people lived along the Salt and Gila rivers in what is now southern Arizona. Their culture dates from about AD 200 to 1400. The name Hohokam is said to mean "those who have vanished" in the language of the Pima people, who later lived in the area.

The Hohokam depended on farming for most of their food. They grew corn and eventually beans and squash. They supplemented their food supply by hunting and gathering wild beans and fruits. Cotton was another important crop, which they used to make cloth.

The Hohokam are famous for their complex network of irrigation canals, which was unsurpassed in prehistoric Northern America. The canals, some as long as 10 miles (16 kilometers), rerouted the Gila and Salt rivers to water the fields. They may have been built by cooperating villages. Some of the more than 150 miles (240 kilometers) of canals in the Salt River valley were renovated and put back into use in the 20th century.

The early Hohokam lived in villages of widely scattered pit houses made of wood, brush, and mud. After about 775 they built large ball courts, similar to those of the Maya of Mexico, and after 975 enclosed some of their villages with walls. After 1150 the Hohokam learned from their Ancestral Pueblo neighbors to construct multistoried community houses with massive walls of adobe. Some houses were built on top of platform mounds.

The Hohokam were active traders. From Mexican peoples they obtained such goods as rubber balls, copper bells, turquoise, obsidian, and macaws, which they kept as house pets. The Hohokam obtained shells from Indians living near the Gulf of California and the Pacific coast. They etched decorations into the surfaces of these shells with acid, becoming the first people in the world to use this artistic technique. Shell jewelry made by the Hohokam was a valuable trade item. They also made baskets and several kinds of pottery.

The Hohokam people abandoned most of their settlements between 1350 and 1450. It is thought that the drought of the late 1200s, combined with a subsequent period of sparse rainfall, contributed to this process. The

Pima and the Tohono O'odham (Papago) are modern descendants of the Hohokam.

The East

The prehistoric farmers east of the Mississippi River are known as Eastern Woodland, and later as Mississippian, peoples. Over the centuries Archaic Indians of the region had learned to cultivate such plants as sunflowers, squash, and sumpweed. Corn was introduced to the East in about 100 BC, but it did not cause immediate changes in local cultures. It was only a minor addition to the local crops.

Adena culture. One of the most spectacular Eastern Woodland cultures before the introduction of corn was that of the Adena. It occupied what is now southern Ohio and lasted from about 500 BC to AD 100, though in some areas it may have started as early as 1000 BC. These people are known chiefly for the earthen mounds they built. The name Adena comes from an Ohio estate where a large mound was discovered.

The Adena were mainly hunters and gatherers, but they also did some farming. They seem to have raised sunflowers, squash, and some other food plants, as well as tobacco for ceremonial purposes. The Adena usually lived in villages of cone-shaped houses. The houses were built by setting poles into the ground, connecting them with grass or branches, and covering the structure with mud. Some Adena lived in rock shelters. Artifacts from Adena sites include stone tools, simple pottery, and beads, bracelets, and other ornaments made from shells and copper obtained through trade.

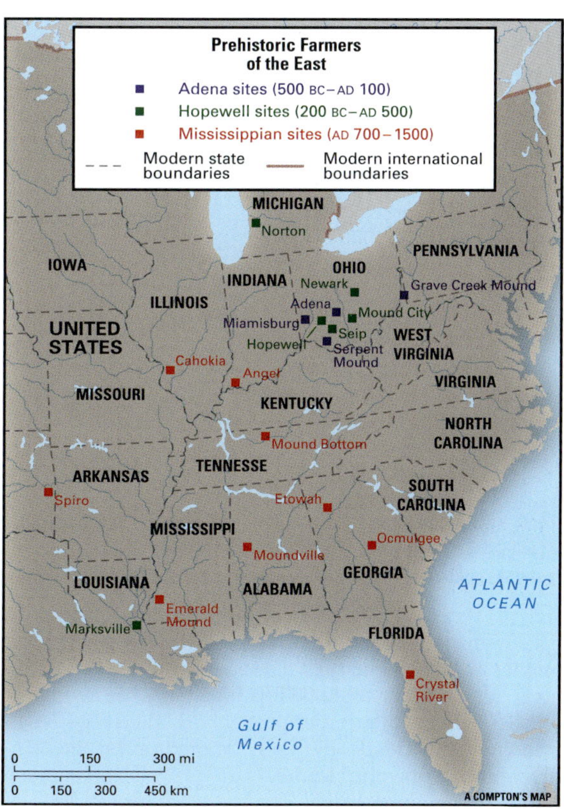

The most distinctive element of Adena culture was mound building. They buried their dead in large earthen mounds, some of which were hundreds of feet long. They also built great earthworks in the shape of animals. These are called effigy mounds. The mounds were built by heaping up basketful after basketful of earth. Some of these large mounds still exist.

Hopewell culture. The most advanced Eastern Woodland culture was that of the Hopewell people. It lasted from about 200 BC to AD 500, mainly in southern Ohio. Like the Adena, the Hopewell built elaborate earthworks for burial and other purposes. The Hopewell culture was named after the owner of a farm near Chillicothe, Ohio, where more than 30 mounds were discovered.

Hopewell villages lay along rivers and streams. Houses consisted of pole frames covered with bark, animal hides, or woven mats. The people raised corn and possibly beans and squash but still relied upon hunting and fishing and the gathering of wild nuts, fruits, seeds, and roots. Expert artists and craftsmen made carved stone pipes, a variety of pottery, and spear points, knives, axes, and other tools of flint and obsidian. They also made various ceremonial objects out of copper. The Hopewell traded widely. Material from as far away as the Rocky Mountains and the coasts of the Gulf of Mexico and the Atlantic Ocean has been found in Hopewell sites.

Some Hopewell mounds appear to have been used for defensive purposes, but more often they served as a

The Serpent Mound in southern Ohio is one of many animal-shaped effigy mounds built by the Adena people.

Richard A. Cooke/Corbis

A painting depicts the Mississippian town of Cahokia as it may have appeared in about 1150.

place to bury the dead. Some formed the bases of temples or other structures. The size of the mounds at many sites —up to about 30 feet high—has led scholars to believe that communities probably worked together to create them. The people likely labored under the direction of a powerful leader.

Mississippian culture. The last great prehistoric culture in Northern America was the Mississippian. Beginning in about AD 700 it spread throughout the Southeast and much of the Northeast. The Mississippian culture was based mainly on the production of corn. As in the Southwest, a favorable climate aided the expansion and cultural development during this period.

The people lived in large towns governed by priest-rulers. Each town had one or more huge, flat-topped mounds that supported temples or the houses of rulers. These mounds often rose to a height of several stories. They were generally set around a plaza that served as the community's ceremonial and social center. The largest Mississippian town was at Cahokia, near present-day St. Louis, Mo. At its peak, it housed 10,000 to 20,000 people. Monk's Mound, the largest mound at Cahokia, is about 1,000 feet (300 meters) long, 700 feet (200 meters) wide, and 100 feet (30 meters) high.

Mississippian peoples were united by a common religion focusing on worship of the sun and a variety of ancestral figures. An organized priesthood conducted elaborate religious rituals and probably also controlled the distribution of surplus food and other goods. Fine craftwork in copper, shell, stone, wood, and clay often displayed religious symbols. The elaborate designs included feathered serpents, winged warriors, spiders, human faces with weeping or falcon eyes, as well as human figures and many geometric motifs. These elements were delicately engraved, embossed, carved, and molded.

Mississippian people in the Southeast were among those who met the first European explorers. Many Mississippian practices continued among their descendants, the Northeast Indians and Southeast Indians. Some Mississippian groups, such as the Natchez, have maintained their ethnic identities into the 21st century.

The Plains

Prehistoric farmers of the Great Plains are known as Plains Woodland and then Plains Village peoples. In this region Archaic peoples dominated until about AD 1, when ideas and perhaps people from Eastern Woodland cultures arrived. Between that time and about AD 1000, Indians of Plains Woodland cultures settled in small villages along rivers and streams. They raised corn, beans, and eventually sunflowers, gourds, squash, and tobacco.

Around AD 1000 the Plains experienced a variation of the favorable farming conditions that supported the most elaborate forms of culture in the Southwest and the East. Plains peoples began to combine their small villages to form larger settlements. The riverbanks became more densely settled. Thus began the Plains Village period, which lasted until about 1450. Like the Mississippian peoples, these groups developed elaborate rituals and religious practices.

The period of increasing dryness that began in about 1275 caused hardship on the Plains. In some cases armed conflict broke out. For instance, at the early 14th-century Crow Creek site in South Dakota, nearly 500 people were killed violently and buried in a mass grave. Some village-dwelling peoples sustained their communities through this difficult period, while others retreated eastward and returned when the climate had improved. The descendants of the Plains Village groups include the Arikara, Mandan, Hidatsa, Crow, and Pawnee peoples. Their ancestors greeted European explorers in the 1500s, and they continue to live on the Plains in the 21st century.

EARLY CIVILIZATIONS OF MIDDLE AND SOUTH AMERICA

Some of the early peoples of Middle and South America developed technologies beyond those of the north. Farmers of these regions domesticated most of the plants the Americas have given the world. Corn, beans, squash, and other plants that later became so important in Northern America were originally grown to the south. After obtaining a dependable food supply from agriculture, peoples along the highland belt from Mexico to Chile were able to devote more time to activities such as the arts, architecture, and commerce. Eventually they developed sophisticated civilizations.

Olmec

The first great culture in Middle America was that of the Olmec. They lived on the hot, humid lowland coast of the Gulf of Mexico in what is now southern Mexico. San Lorenzo, the oldest known Olmec center, dates to about 1150 BC. At that time the rest of Middle America had only simple farming villages.

The Olmec built large towns where they came together to trade and hold religious ceremonies. The most important were San Lorenzo, La Venta, and Tres Zapotes. They were home to the upper classes of priests and other leaders, who lived in well-made stone houses. These leaders commanded the work of craftsmen and laborers. In the surrounding countryside lived farmers, whose work supported the upper classes. Corn was the most important crop.

San Lorenzo is famous for its extraordinary stone monuments. Most striking are the "colossal heads," which are human portraits on a massive scale. They measure up to 9 feet (nearly 3 meters) in height and have flat faces and helmetlike headgear. They may represent players in a sacred rubber-ball game. A later Olmec ceremonial center, La Venta, is marked by great mounds, a narrow plaza, and several other ceremonial enclosures. Between about 800 and 400 BC it was the most important settlement in Middle America.

The artifacts left by the Olmec range from the huge stone sculptures to small jade carvings and pottery. Much Olmec art depicted a god that is a cross between a jaguar and a human infant, often crying or snarling with open mouth.

The exotic materials used by Olmec artists and craftsmen suggest that the Olmec controlled a large trading network over much of Middle America. Obsidian, a form of volcanic glass used for blades, flakes, and dart points, was imported from highland Mexico and Guatemala. Most imported goods were used to make luxury items. Iron ore, for example, was used to make mirrors.

The Temple of the Sun, built in the 600s, was one of several sacred buildings in the ancient Mayan city of Palenque.

Ales Liska/Shutterstock.com

Robert Frerck/Odyssey Productions

The flat-faced, helmeted "colossal heads" carved by the Olmec people measured up to 9 feet (nearly 3 meters) in height.

The Olmec may have developed the first writing system in the Americas. In the late 20th century a stone slab engraved with symbols, or hieroglyphs, that appear to have been the Olmec writing system was discovered in the village of Cascajal, near San Lorenzo. The Cascajal stone dates to about 900 BC. In the 21st century inscribed carvings similar to later Mayan hieroglyphs were found at La Venta.

Olmec culture began to fade in about 400 BC. However, its influence spread north to central Mexico and south to Central America. Among those influenced by the Olmec were the Zapotec, Maya, and Teotihuacán civilizations.

Maya

Between AD 250 and 900 the Maya developed one of the Western Hemisphere's greatest civilizations. Their territory covered the Yucatán Peninsula and extended south into what is now Guatemala. The Maya built impressive cities and also reached great heights in astronomy and mathematics.

As early as 1500 BC the Maya were living in settled villages and growing much of their food. The main crops were beans, squash, and, most importantly, corn. They began to build ceremonial centers, and by AD 200 these had developed into cities with stone temples, pyramids, palaces, ball courts, and plazas. Temples and other buildings were richly decorated with carvings and murals depicting scenes of Mayan history and religious events. By 900 the Maya had more than 40 cities, each with a population between 5,000 and 50,000. The most important cities included Tikal, Palenque, Copán, and Bonampak. The peak Mayan population may have reached 2 million people, most of whom were settled in the lowlands of what is now Guatemala.

As was the case for most early civilizations, the Maya believed that religion and science were linked. The Mayan religion was based on a pantheon of nature gods, including those representing the sun, the moon, rain, and corn. Priests conducted an elaborate cycle of rituals and ceremonies, and they were also astronomers. On the

basis of their observations, they created an extremely accurate calendar. Using it, the Maya could predict eclipses and other astronomical events. Another great intellectual achievement was the invention of a numerical system that included the use of zero. The Maya were one of the first civilizations in the world to develop this important concept.

The Maya created a system of hieroglyphics, or picture writing. The hieroglyphs were carved into walls to celebrate great victories and to describe religious ceremonies. In addition, the Maya made paper from the inner bark of wild fig trees and wrote their hieroglyphs on books made from this paper; surviving books are called codices. Scholars spent many years trying to read Mayan writing, and by the end of the 20th century they had deciphered much of it. The hieroglyphs told them much about Mayan society and culture.

Many of the hieroglyphs depict the histories of the Mayan rulers and the wars they waged against rival Mayan cities. People captured in battle were tortured, mutilated, and sacrificed to the gods. The Maya believed that human sacrifices were the only way to ensure that the gods would keep the world in order. The drawing of human blood was thought to nourish the gods and was thus necessary to achieve contact with them. Therefore, in addition to sacrificing captives, Mayan rulers would also shed their own blood to please the gods.

After 900 the classical Mayan civilization declined rapidly. The great cities and ceremonial centers were left vacant and overgrown with vegetation until they were rediscovered in the 1800s. The causes of this decline are

A reconstructed Mayan fresco, or wall painting, shows people playing trumpets and percussion instruments. The original painting was made in about AD 800 in what is now the Mexican state of Chiapas.

Ygunza/FPG

The Temple of Quetzalcóatl at Teotihuacán was elaborately decorated with stone carvings of the god.

uncertain. Some scholars have said that warfare and the exhaustion of farmland were responsible. Discoveries in the 21st century, however, led scholars to suggest that the cause was probably the war-related disruption of river and land trade routes.

After the great lowland cities were abandoned, cities such as Chichén Itzá, Uxmal, and Mayapán in the highlands of the Yucatán Peninsula continued to flourish for several centuries. By the time the Spaniards conquered the area in the early 1500s, most of the Maya had become village-dwelling farmers who practiced the religious rites of their ancestors. In the early 21st century some 70 Mayan languages were spoken by more than 5 million people in Mexico, Guatemala, and Belize. Contemporary Maya are typically farmers, raising corn, beans, and squash. Although most are Roman Catholic, many also worship some Mayan gods, whom they associate with specific Catholic saints.

Teotihuacán

Located near present-day Mexico City, Teotihuacán was the greatest city of the Americas before the arrival of Europeans. At its height in about AD 500, it covered some 8 square miles (20 square kilometers) and may have housed more than 150,000 people. At the time it was one of the largest cities in the world. It was the region's major economic as well as religious center.

The origin and language of the residents of Teotihuacán (called Teotihuacanos) are unknown. Perhaps two thirds of them farmed the surrounding fields. Others made distinctive pottery or worked with obsidian, which was used to make weapons, tools, and ornamentation. The city also had large numbers of merchants, many of whom had emigrated there from great distances. Teotihuacán carried on trade with distant regions, and the products of its craftsmen were spread over much of Middle America. The priest-rulers who governed the city also staged grand religious pageants and ceremonies that often involved human sacrifices.

The city contained great plazas, temples, palaces of nobles and priests, and some 2,000 single-story apartment compounds. The main buildings were connected by a great street called the Avenue of the Dead, which stretched 1.5 miles (2.4 kilometers). The Avenue of the Dead was once thought to have been lined with tombs, but the low buildings that flanked it probably were palace residences.

The most prominent feature of Teotihuacán was the Pyramid of the Sun. It dominated the central city from the east side of the Avenue of the Dead. The pyramid is one of the largest structures of its type in the Western Hemisphere, reaching a height of 216 feet (66 meters).

An impressive stairway rises dramatically on its west side, facing the Avenue of the Dead. In the early 1970s exploration below the pyramid revealed a system of cave and tunnel chambers. In later years other tunnels were revealed throughout the city, and it was suggested that much of the building stone of Teotihuacán was mined there.

The northern end of the Avenue of the Dead was capped by the Pyramid of the Moon and flanked by platforms and lesser pyramids. The second largest structure in the city, the Pyramid of the Moon rose to 140 feet (43 meters). Its main stairway faced the Avenue of the Dead.

Near the exact center of the city and just east of the Avenue of the Dead was the Ciudadela ("Citadel"). It was a kind of sunken court surrounded on all four sides by platforms supporting temples. In the middle of the sunken plaza stood the Temple of Quetzalcóatl, the Feathered Serpent god. Numerous stone heads of the god projected from the walls of the temple.

In about AD 750 central Teotihuacán burned, possibly during a rebellion or a civil war. Although parts of the city were occupied after that event, much of it fell into ruin. Nevertheless, its cultural influence spread throughout Middle America.

Toltec

As Teotihuacán declined, numerous states competed to become the supreme power in Middle America. By about 900 the Toltec of central Mexico had prevailed. Between then and 1200 the Toltec built the most powerful and culturally advanced civilization in the region.

Under the ruler Topiltzin, the Toltec united a number of small states into an empire. Topiltzin introduced the cult of Quetzalcóatl, and he took the name of that god. This cult and others appeared in important Mayan cities to the south in Yucatán, such as Chichén Itzá and Mayapán, and to other Middle American peoples. The Toltec military orders of the Coyote, the Jaguar, and the Eagle also appeared among the Maya. The spread of these cultural traits shows the wide influence of the Toltec.

Toltec culture revolved around the urban center of Tula. Another name for the city is Tollan, which is the source of the name Toltec. Its exact location is unknown, but scholars believe it was located near the modern town of Tula, about 50 miles (80 kilometers) north of Mexico City. The town covered at least 3 square miles (some 8 square kilometers) and probably had a population in the tens of thousands. The heart of the town consisted of a large plaza bordered on one side by a five-stepped temple pyramid, which was probably dedicated to Quetzalcóatl. Other structures included a palace complex, two other temple pyramids, and two ball courts. Surrounding Tula were fields watered by irrigation ditches. There the Toltec grew corn, squash, and cotton.

Along with building great palaces and pyramids, the Toltec were known for their metalwork and sculpture. They made fine objects in gold, silver, and copper, which

A Chac Mool sits in front of the Mayan ruins of the Temple of the Warriors in Chichén Itzá. This type of sculpture originated among the Toltec and then spread to other Middle American cultures.

they obtained through an extensive trade network. Their sculptures included the Chac Mools—reclining male figures with a dish resting on the stomach. Thought to represent the rain god Chac, Chac Mools were probably used to hold the hearts of people sacrificed during religious ceremonies.

Beginning in the 1100s the nomadic Chichimec peoples invaded Toltec territory from the north. The invaders destroyed Tula in about 1150 and ended Toltec dominance of central Mexico. Among the Chichimec were the Aztec, or Mexica, who created the next great culture in the region (*see* "Middle America," page 65).

The Andes

Civilizations began to develop in the central Andes Mountains of South America by about 2300 BC. For several thousand years they became increasingly elaborate, both culturally and technologically. A thousand years before the Spanish conquest, the central Andes had the most developed agricultural and irrigational system in all of South America. The region also had the densest population south of Mexico and the most efficient system of overland transportation in the Western Hemisphere. The combination of these features enabled the growth of cities, intricate class systems, and eventually the development of empires.

A hammered gold crown (left) found at Chongoyape, Peru, was produced by the Chavín culture. Chavín goldwork was the earliest in the Americas, dating from 900 to 500 BC. An archaeologist (right) cleans a human skeleton at the Tiwanaku ruins in Bolivia.

The earliest advanced culture in pre-Columbian Peru was the Chavín. It dates from about 900 to 200 BC. During this time Chavín artistic influence spread throughout the northern and central parts of what is now Peru. Chavín artists made painted textiles, pottery, and stone carvings, many of them depicting animals or humans with animal features. Chavín culture marked the first time that many of the local or regional cultures of the area were unified under a common religion.

Beginning in about AD 1000 the peoples of the central Andes were organized into a number of kingdoms. Two of the most famous were Tiwanaku and Chimú. Tiwanaku spread its culture from what is today highland Bolivia northward to the area of Lima and beyond. The main Tiwanaku ruins are located near Bolivia's Lake Titicaca. Although archaeologists once thought it was mainly a ceremonial site, new finds in the late 20th century revealed that it was a bustling city. Still, relatively little is known about it.

The influence of Tiwanaku was largely a result of its remarkable agricultural system. This farming method, known as the raised-field system, consisted of raised planting surfaces separated by small irrigation ditches, or canals. This system was designed in such a way that the canals retained the heat of the intense sunlight during frosty nights and thus kept the crops from freezing. The Tiwanaku culture vanished by 1200.

The Chimú kingdom arose in the north of Peru. It expanded southward and overlapped the northern territory of the Tiwanaku culture, as the latter's influence began to decline. For two centuries the Chimú kingdom was the chief state in Peru. It was ruled from Chan Chan, on Peru's northern coast. Chan Chan is one of the world's most notable archaeological sites, with 14 square miles

A death mask from the Chimú culture of pre-Columbian Peru is made of a gold and silver alloy, with copper eyes and ears.

(36 square kilometers) of ruins. Among them are rectangular blocks and streets, great walls, reservoirs, and pyramid temples, all built of adobe mud. Chan Chan's population must have numbered many thousands.

Chimú culture was based on farming, which was aided by immense irrigation works. The Chimú seem to have had an elaborate system of social classes ranging from peasants to nobles. They produced fine textiles and gold, silver, and copper objects. They also made pottery in standardized types, which they produced in quantity using molds.

Between 1465 and 1470 the Chimú were conquered by the Inca. The Inca absorbed much from Chimú culture, including their political organization, irrigation systems, and road engineering, into the vast empire they created. The Inca civilization thrived until the Spanish invasion of the early 1500s (*see* "The Central Andes," page 73).

PART II

TRADITIONAL CULTURE

By the time European explorers reached the Americas in the late 1400s, the Indians had developed a remarkable cultural diversity. Northern America alone was home to more than 50 language families with between 300 and 500 languages. In contrast, western Europe at that time had only 2 language families and between 40 and 70 languages. Different tribes had different food, clothing, shelter, practices, and beliefs. But scholars have found that Indians who shared similar natural surroundings often lived in similar ways.

For purposes of organization, scholars who study the Indians have divided the Americas into culture areas. A culture area is a geographic region in which peoples share certain cultural traits. For instance, in North America between the 1500s and the 1800s, the Northwest Coast culture area was characterized by traits such as salmon fishing, woodworking, large villages or towns, and hierarchical social organization.

The number of culture areas in Native America has varied because regions are sometimes subdivided or joined together. According to most scholars, however, Northern America had 10 culture areas at the time of European contact: Arctic, Subarctic, Northeast, Southeast, Plains, Southwest, Great Basin, California, Northwest Coast, and Plateau. The Indians from Mexico southward belonged to five culture areas: Middle America, Central America and the Northern Andes, Central Andes, Rainforest, and the Marginal Regions. The map on page 21 shows these culture areas along with some of the peoples who lived in them. The articles that follow discuss the location, environment, languages, tribes, and common traits of the culture areas before they were heavily colonized by Europeans. Additional articles at the end of this section discuss the social and political organization, languages, religions, arts, and sports and games of traditional Native America as a whole.

The culture area approach is a useful way to organize the study of Indian cultures. However, it should be remembered that the culture area names and borders did not exist among the Indians themselves. They did not consider themselves Northeast or Great Basin Indians, for example, and peoples and cultural traits moved frequently from one region to another. Indians who lived along the border between two culture areas often reflected the two ways of living. In addition, peoples from widely separated geographical areas sometimes shared cultural traits.

ARCTIC OCEAN
POLAR INUIT
NORTH ALASKAN INUIT
MACKENZIE INUIT
CENTRAL ALASKAN YUPIK
DEG XINAG
GWICH'IN
NETSILIK INUIT
COPPER INUIT
IGLULIK INUIT
EAST GREENLAND INUIT
WEST GREENLAND INUIT
ALEUT
TANAINA
PACIFIC YUPIK
BAFFINLAND INUIT
TAHLTAN
TLINGIT
KASKA
SLAVE
DOGRIB
CARIBOU INUIT
TSIMSHIAN
SEKANI
CARRIER
CHIPEWYAN
LABRADOR INUIT
HAIDA
BEAVER
SHUSWAP
INNU
BELLA COOLA
KWAKIUTL
LILLOOET
CREE
INNU
NUU-CHAH-NULTH
KUTENAI
CREE
COAST SALISH
KALISPEL
BLACKFEET
SPOKAN
FLATHEAD
OJIBWA
ALGONQUIN
MI'KMAQ
CHINOOK
YAKIMA
WALLAWALLA
HIDATSA
OTTAWA
PENOBSCOT
MODOC
UMATILLA
NEZ PERCÉ
MANDAN
MENOMINEE
HURON
ABENAKI
SHASTAN
KLAMATH
CROW
ARIKARA
HO-CHUNK
IROQUOIS
MOHICAN
MASSACHUSET
YUROK
PAIUTE
BANNOCK
SIOUX
SAUK
KICKAPOO
SUSQUEHANNOCK
WAMPANOAG
HUPA
WINTUN
SHOSHONE
CHEYENNE
OMAHA
FOX
MIAMI
NARRAGANSET
YUKI
YANA
IOWA
PEQUOT, MOHEGAN
POMO
MIWOK
WASHOE
GOSIUTE
PAWNEE
MISSOURI
ILLINOIS
SHAWNEE
DELAWARE
MAIDU
MONO
UTE
ARAPAHO
KANSA
POWHATAN
SALINAN
YOKUTS
PAIUTE
KIOWA
OSAGE
YUCHI
TUSCARORA
CHUMASH
MOJAVE
NAVAJO
WICHITA
CHICKASAW
CHEROKEE
CATAWBA
GABRIELEÑO
YUMA
PUEBLO
APACHE
COMANCHE
CADDO
CREEK
GUALE
JUANEÑO
COCOPA
TOHONO O'ODHAM
TUNICA
CHOCTAW
LUISEÑO
PIMA
NATCHEZ
SEMINOLE
DIEGUEÑO
YAQUI
TARAHUMARA
CHITIMACHA
APALACHEE
TIMUCUA
MAYO
CALUSA
TEPEHUÁN
CORA
HUASTEC
CIBONEY
HUICHOL
OTOMÍ
TOTONAC
ARAWAK
TARASCO
AZTEC
MAYA
MIXTEC
ZAPOTEC
JICAQUE
CARIB
MISKITO
GUAYMI
TAIRONA
CAQUETÍO
JIRAJARA
KUNA
PALENQUE
MARAJOARA
CHOCÓ
CHIBCHA
GUAHIBO
ARAWAK
CARIB
PALICUR
PÁEZ
ACHAGUA
TAULIPANG
MAKUSHÍ
SHUAR (JÍVARO)
MAKÚ
CARIB
TUPINAMBÁ
OMAGUA
TAPAJÓ
INCA
MURA
MUNDURUKÚ
GE
CHIMÚ
NAMBIKWARA
TUPINAMBÁ
INCA
SIRIONÓ
AYMARA
BOTOCUDO
ATACAMA
ACHÉ
VILELA
DIAGUITA
GUARANÍ
ABIPÓN
TUPINAMBÁ
HUARPE
CHARRÚA
QUERANDÍ
PUELCHE
ARAUCANIAN
TEHUELCHE
CHONO
ALACALUF
YÁMANA
ARCTIC OCEAN
PACIFIC OCEAN
ATLANTIC OCEAN
PACIFIC OCEAN
ATLANTIC OCEAN
Gulf of Mexico
Caribbean Sea
A COMPTON'S MAP
Traditional Culture Areas of the Americas
Arctic
California
Central America and the Northern Andes
Central Andes
Great Basin
Marginal Regions
Middle America
Northeast
Northwest Coast
Plains
Plateau
Rainforest
Southeast
Southwest
Subarctic

THE ARCTIC

The northernmost lands of North America make up the Arctic culture area. This region lies near and above the Arctic Circle and includes parts of present-day Alaska and Canada. The land is relatively flat. Temperatures are very cold for most of the year, and winters are especially harsh. Trees and other vegetation are scarce. The region's extreme northerly location alters the daily cycle. On winter days the sun may peek above the horizon for only an hour or two. During the summer months, in turn, the sun sometimes never drops below the horizon. The cultures of the Arctic peoples were completely adapted to this extremely cold, snowy, and icy environment.

Peoples and Languages

The native peoples of the North American Arctic include the Eskimo and the Aleut. The Eskimo live not only in the North American Arctic but also in the Arctic regions of Greenland and far eastern Russia (Siberia). The Aleut are native to the Aleutian Islands and the western part of the Alaska Peninsula. These peoples are more closely related to Asians than to the American Indians to their south. A sizable percentage of Eskimo have type B blood, a characteristic that seems to be completely absent from the Indians. In addition, the languages of the American Arctic peoples are not related to those of the Indians. For these reasons scholars generally separate the Arctic peoples from the Indians. Many Alaskan groups prefer to be called Native Alaskans rather than Native Americans. Most of Canada's Arctic peoples prefer the name Inuit.

The traditional languages of these groups belong to the Eskimo-Aleut language family. Aleut is a single language with two surviving dialects, or regional variations. Eskimo consists of two divisions: Inuit, spoken in northern Alaska, Canada, and Greenland, and Yupik, spoken in southwestern Alaska and Siberia. In Greenland the Inuit language is called Greenlandic or Kalaallisut; in Canada, Inuktitut; and in Alaska, Inupiaq. Because of the wide geographic area in which the Eskimo live, both the Yupik and Inuit divisions include several dialects.

Food

The Arctic peoples of North America traditionally were hunters and gatherers. Some peoples moved with the seasons in search of food. Their migratory lifestyle followed that of their Thule ancestors and focused on

An Eskimo (Inuit) family sits inside an igloo lit by a kudlik, a soapstone lamp fueled by seal oil.
Wayne R. Bilenduke—Stone/Getty Images

The Granger Collection, New York

A photograph from the early 20th century shows an Eskimo ice fishing in Nome, Alaska.

the Brooks Range of northern Alaska, some people were year-round caribou hunters who also depended on traded sea-mammal oil as a condiment and for heat. In the Barren Grounds tundra region west of Hudson Bay, some groups used no sea products at all.

Other Arctic peoples were more settled, living year-round in villages along the coast. Among these groups the use of both land and sea resources (*see* sidebar, "Thule Culture"). In the summer these peoples followed migrating herds of caribou (reindeer). The ample summer sunlight supported an explosion of vegetation that drew caribou and other animals to the inland north. Fishing was another source of food in summer. In the other seasons these peoples hunted seals, sea otters, walrus, and whales on the coast. Food was also stored for use during the deepest part of winter.

There were exceptions to this pattern, however. People of the Bering Strait islands, for instance, depended almost entirely on sea mammals, especially walrus. In the Alaskan whaling villages between the Seward Peninsula and Point Barrow, caribou and seals were outweighed as food resources by bowhead whales. In

Thule Culture

Many aspects of traditional Eskimo culture originated with a group archaeologists call the Thule people. The prehistoric Thule culture developed along the Arctic coast in northern Alaska, possibly as far east as the Amundsen Gulf. Starting in about AD 900 it spread eastward rapidly, reaching Greenland by the 1100s. It continued to develop in the central areas of Arctic Canada, and cultural communication persisted between these Eastern Thule and the Western Thule of Alaska from about 1300 to 1700.

Thule was a maritime culture based on hunting whales and other large mammals in the open sea. The Thule people introduced the umiak—a large, open, skin-covered boat—for whale hunting. They also had kayaks for sealing. Another Thule innovation was the use of dogsleds for winter travel over land. These new forms of transportation enabled the Thule people to expand over a large geographic range. They lived in settlements of permanent houses built of whale bones and covered with walrus skin and sod. Some of these houses were built partly underground. While on hunting trips, the Thule people built igloos (snow houses) in winter and set up skin tents in summer. Stone lamps and cooking pots, ground-slate tools, and whalebone artifacts were characteristic of the culture. Thule art includes small carved ivory or wooden figures, possibly used for magic or religious purposes or as game pieces.

Thule culture disappeared from central Canada in the 1400s, probably because of climatic cooling. However, its influence among the Eskimo endures to the present.

were the southern Yupik and the Aleut. They got nearly all their food by fishing and hunting sea mammals. The Aleut also gathered shellfish and wild plant foods such as berries.

Settlements and Housing

Most Arctic peoples spent the winter in well-insulated houses built partly underground. The houses were made of stone or sod over a framework of timber or whalebone. In Alaska, except for the far north, they heated their homes with a central wood fire that burned beneath a smoke hole. In the north, heat was provided by a large lamp lit by oil taken from sea mammals.

The people nearest the Arctic Ocean relied on temporary houses called igloos in winter, when they moved onto fresh ice fields in search of seals. Caribou hunters and lake and river fishermen used igloos on land. An igloo was usually dome-shaped and made from blocks of snow. To build one, hard-packed snow was cut into blocks with a long knife made of bone, ivory, or metal. A clear piece of ice or seal intestine was used for a window. The family slept on a low snow platform covered with twigs and caribou furs. The igloo was heated and lighted by burning seal blubber in a shallow saucer.

The caribou hunters of northern Alaska often lived through the winter in dome-shaped tents made from a double layer of caribou hides. Heat and light were provided by burning caribou fat. In summer these people lived in lighter animal-skin tents.

Some peoples of the Arctic built a special large house called a *kashim*. It was used for public and ceremonial occasions and as a men's residence. The *kashim* was the place where men built their boats, repaired their equipment, took sweat baths, educated young boys, and hosted community dances. Women had their own homes in which they worked and cared for their children. Often the women's homes were connected to one another and to the *kashim* by a system of tunnels.

Clothing

Arctic peoples kept warm in clothing made from animal skins and furs. They wore pants, boots, mittens, and a hooded coat called a parka. In very cold weather they wore two of each garment. The inner one had the fur against the skin and the outer one had the fur facing out. Caribou skin was the preferred material because it was very warm but also lightweight. Sealskin was useful because it was waterproof; it was used to make boots called mukluks. Arctic peoples also used the skins of other animals, including polar bears, antelopes, dogs, and foxes.

Technology and Arts

Nearly all Arctic peoples used two types of boats: the kayak and the umiak. Both types were made of animal skins stretched over a driftwood or whalebone frame and were paddled. A kayak was covered except for a cockpit in which one or two paddlers sat. An umiak was larger and open on top. Men used kayaks for fishing and hunting, usually seals. They used umiaks for hunting

Arctic peoples traditionally depended on a team of large, powerful sled dogs to pull their sleds over snow and ice.

whales. Women used umiaks for transporting themselves, children, the elderly, and possessions. In winter people traveled on sleds that were pulled by dogs or by both dogs and people.

Arctic peoples hunted caribou and other land animals with bows and arrows. They used harpoons to kill seals and walrus, which they hunted either from shore or from kayaks. Kayak-based seal hunters often used a spear-thrower to increase the speed and force of the harpoon. An umiak used for whaling was manned by a professional crew. It was led by the boat's owner and a marksman who wielded a heavy harpoon.

Arctic peoples carved objects from stone, bone, and walrus ivory. Most of the items, such as containers, needles, and oil lamps, served an everyday purpose. They also carved small animal figures and masks to use in religious ceremonies. The women wove fine grass baskets.

Society

Eskimo societies were flexibly organized. In general, they did not form units such as clans or tribes, and they had no formal position of chief. The main form of social organization was small bands. This style of organization allowed people to move more easily with the seasons in search of food.

An Eskimo on the Bering Sea island of Nunivak wears a ceremonial mask.

Membership in a band was generally based on kinship (shared ancestry) and marriage. People depended on their kin for support and tended to avoid people who were not kin. However, the Eskimo had ways to create kinlike relationships with people outside their families. These relationships helped people to survive the harsh Arctic environment. For example, people bearing the same name as a relative might be treated as if they held the same relation. In addition, trading partners, song partners, meat-sharing partners, and partners created by the temporary exchange of spouses might also be treated as relatives.

Generally the Eskimo recognized kin on both the father's and mother's sides of the family to about the level of second cousin. Most Eskimo frowned upon marriage between cousins, but some groups allowed it. Certain groups also emphasized kin of the father's side over kin of the mother's side.

Outside of kin relationships, people also identified themselves with a larger group based on a shared place of residence. Among the largest such groups were those made up of people who lived in the same area and spoke the same dialect. The speakers of a particular dialect tended to seek spouses from within that group. Such groups might range in size from 200 to as many as 1,000 people.

Among the Eskimo there was a sharp division of labor between men and women. Men were the hunters and home builders, while women were the cooks, leather makers, and tailors. Men and women, therefore, were very dependent on each other. Some families included two or three wives married to one husband, especially if the first had not been able to have children. Women occasionally had two husbands. The Eskimo were fond of children, and orphans normally found homes with relatives and were well treated. In a land where there were no vegetable foods or roads, a mother nursed her children and carried them everywhere on her back until they were about three years old.

The Eskimo had no money economy and kept few possessions. Eskimo families had their dogs, their dwelling, and the few things they made for themselves: clothing, tools, sled, weapons, and kayak. There were also pieces of art, such as whalebone carvings and amulets (charms with protective powers). Even the dwelling ceased to belong to a family once it was deserted. Someone else might come along and take it over. The land was considered to belong to all, and food was shared in common. Fishing and hunting were such hazardous and uncertain pursuits that no one dared let others do without food, for fear that he might be the one to do without the next time.

Although the Aleut shared many cultural traits with the Eskimo to the north, they structured their societies quite differently. Their system of social organization was similar to that of the neighboring Northwest Coast Indians (*see* "The Northwest Coast," page 52). The Aleut had hierarchical societies made up of formal chiefs, other elites, commoners, and a class of slaves that was generally composed of war captives. The chief, typically a seasoned and talented hunter, might govern several villages or an entire island. His rule, however, was based on his wisdom, experience, and ability to build consensus rather than on raw power.

Religion

The traditional religion of the Arctic peoples was based on animism. They believed that all humans, animals, plants, and objects had souls or spirits. These spirits were neither friendly nor hostile, but they could become dangerous if they were not respected.

The souls of the dead joined the spirit world, and they could become hostile and interfere with the souls of the living. Soul loss—the departure of the soul from the body and its failure to return—meant illness or even death. Arctic peoples also had ideas of reincarnation, or the rebirth of the soul in another being. The name of a deceased person was given to a child who "became" that person by being addressed with kinship terms that had been used for the deceased.

Traditionally, all people were in contact with the spirit world. They carried objects called amulets, which were believed to have special powers to protect or bring good fortune. All people also experienced dreams and achieved special relationships with particular spirit-beings. Men and women who had an especially strong connection with the spirits became shamans. They were called on to cure the sick by recovering lost souls, to foretell the future, to determine the location of game, and so forth.

Arctic peoples took great care not to offend the spirits of game animals, since they could bring on sickness or famine. Therefore, there arose complicated systems of regulations concerning the preparation of food, all with the purpose of keeping harmony between people and the environment. In addition, courtesies given to freshly killed animals promoted their reincarnation as new animals of the same species.

THE SUBARCTIC

The culture area south of the Arctic is called the Subarctic. It includes most of what are now Alaska and Canada (excluding the Maritime Provinces—New Brunswick, Nova Scotia, and Prince Edward Island—which are part of the Northeast culture area). The climate is cool, and the land is fairly flat and covered mostly by swampy evergreen forest. This ecosystem is also called the taiga, or boreal forest. Wildlife is abundant.

Peoples and Languages

The Subarctic can be divided into two parts based on language families. The Eastern Subarctic is home to speakers of Algonquian languages, including the Innu, Cree, and Ojibwa (Chippewa). The Western Subarctic is largely inhabited by Athabaskan speakers, whose territories extend from Canada into Alaska. They include the Chipewyan, Beaver, Slave, Dogrib, Kaska, Carrier, Tanaina, and Deg Xinag.

Food

Subarctic Indians traditionally lived by hunting and gathering. Their diet included moose, caribou, bison (in the south), beaver, waterfowl, and fish. They gathered wild plant foods such as berries, roots, and sap. Subarctic peoples had great skill in hunting, but they also relied on magic and supernatural powers. To find game, for example, they heated a large animal's shoulder blade over fire until it cracked. Hunters then went in the direction of the crack. In general this method led them randomly to a fresh, relatively undisturbed piece of ground, which would improve hunting success.

Food resources were scarce in the harsh Subarctic landscape, and starvation was always a threat. One way people dealt with the scarcity was by preserving food. Across the region, people preserved meat by drying and pounding it together with melted fat and dried berries to make a food called pemmican. This was an excellent concentrated food and was often used when traveling or hunting. Near the Pacific coast, people preserved salmon by smoking it.

Settlements and Housing

Families and bands moved as the seasons changed. In northwest Canada groups scattered in early winter to hunt caribou in the mountains. Elsewhere, autumn drew people to the shorelines of lakes and bays where ducks and geese could be taken for winter storage. At other times people gathered around lakes to fish. In late winter the Deg Xinag left their villages and headed for spring camps, as much for a change of scenery as for the good fishing.

Subarctic peoples built well-insulated homes for protection from the cold. The Deg Xinag spent winters in houses dug into the soil and roofed with beams and poles. Other groups, such as the Cree and Ojibwa, built cone-shaped winter lodges durably roofed with branches, earth, and snow. On the trail during the summer, people put up portable, cone-shaped tents called tepees, which were covered with animal skins. They also used lean-tos—simple, open shelters made of brush and with a sloping roof. Sometimes they camped in the open facing a fire.

Clothing

Subarctic Indians made most of their clothing from moose and caribou skins. Women tanned the skins through a chemical process that used animal brains or human urine. Then they sewed the skins into garments with the help of bone needles and animal sinew. Subarctic Indian clothing included pants, shirts, robes, and soft, heel-less shoes called moccasins.

Technology and Arts

As hunters and fishers, all Subarctic groups relied on various weapons, traps, and tools for their livelihood. They used lances, spears and spear-throwers, and bows and arrows, which had stone or bone tips for different

Snowshoes—light wooden frames strung with thongs and attached to the foot—allowed Subarctic peoples to walk or run on soft snow without sinking.

Cornelius Krieghoff—Bridgeman Art Library/Getty Images

kinds of game. They captured game with pit traps and deadfalls—traps with logs or other weights that fall on animals and kill them. They also had snares for small game such as rabbits and decoys for birds. Fishing tools included basket traps, nets, and enclosures called weirs. Women braided rabbit skins into ropes and wove roots to form watertight baskets.

Vehicles were vital in the Subarctic. Survival depended on traveling long distances in search of new food sources. Subarctic peoples made bark canoes and wooden sleds called toboggans, which were used to haul heavy loads. Snowshoes enabled hunters to run down big game and made winter travel easier for everyone. Snowshoes consisted of a light wooden frame that was strung with animal tendons. When attached to the feet, they enabled a person to walk or run on soft snow without sinking. Another useful travel aid was snow goggles, which helped reduce the glare of the spring sun.

Society

Most Subarctic societies were organized around two- or three-generation families. The family consisted of married adults, their children—frequently including adopted children—and sometimes dependent elders. Households generally had one husband and wife pair, but in some marriages there were one husband and two wives. The intense importance of the family, especially during childhood, is revealed in folklore about the unhappy lives of cruelly treated orphans. Children with neither parents nor grandparents suffered the worst.

The next level of social organization was the band. It was made up of a few related couples, their dependent children, and their dependent elders. Bands generally included no more than 20 to 30 people who lived, hunted, and traveled together.

A cross-section drawing shows the interior of a traditional semi-subterranean dwelling of the Deg Xinag and other Subarctic peoples. Such homes were also common in the Arctic.

Members of a Chipewyan band of northern Canada rest in front of their tepee. Traditionally nomadic, the Chipewyan lived mainly in such portable tents.

Eastern Subarctic peoples traditionally identified themselves with a particular geographic territory. However, they generally chose not to organize politically beyond the level of the band. Instead, they identified themselves as members of the same tribe or nation based on language and kinship links to neighboring bands. Seasonal gatherings of several bands often occurred at good fishing lakes or near rich hunting grounds.

In the west near the Pacific, people organized themselves into villages. Each village had an associated territory for hunting and gathering. On the lower Yukon and upper Kuskokwim rivers, Deg Xinag village life centered on the *kashim*, or men's house. A council of male elders met in this building to hear disputes, and elaborate seasonal ceremonies were performed there.

Whether peoples were organized in bands or villages, individual leadership and authority were based on a combination of valued traits. Among them were eloquence, wisdom, experience, healing or magical power, generosity, and a capacity for hard work.

Subarctic peoples did not typically rank people by social class. The Deg Xinag, however, informally recognized three classes of families. Usually at least three quarters of a Deg Xinag village consisted of common people. Rich families, which accumulated surplus food thanks to members' hard work or superior hunting and fishing abilities, made up about 5 percent of the community. They led the community's ceremonial life. The rest of the people did little and lived off the others. As a result, they commanded so little respect that they had a hard time finding spouses.

The Indians of the Subarctic placed a high value on self-reliance. In teaching children, parents encouraged them to become independent and resourceful. These traits were vital for survival in such a difficult environment. At the same time, Subarctic peoples realized that an individual would sometimes have to rely on others—for example, during a time when food was lacking. In such circumstances they placed the well-being of the group ahead of personal gain.

In Subarctic cultures land and water, the sources of food, were not considered to be either individual or group property. Still, they would respect the privilege of another group that was using a berry patch, beaver creek, or hunting range ahead of them. Clothing, stored food, and other portable goods were recognized as having individual owners. When in need, a group could borrow from another's food supplies, as long as the food was replaced and the owners told of the act as soon as possible.

Religion

Subarctic peoples traditionally had a highly personal relationship with the spirit world. Most men and women undertook a vision quest in their youth. In a quest, a person tried to communicate with a guardian spirit. Often depicted in animal form, a guardian spirit was a supernatural teacher who guided an individual in every important activity through advice and songs. In the terms of the Kaska people, the vision occurred by "dreaming of animals in a lonely place" or hearing "somebody sing," perhaps a moose in the form of a person. Dreams also might tell a person how to behave to achieve success or avoid misfortune.

Many Subarctic peoples believed that hunting success depended on treating prey animals and their remains with reverence. Among other practices, they disposed of the animals' bones carefully so that dogs could not chew them. Bears inspired particular respect. Men took a purifying sweat bath before the hunt and made an offer of tobacco to a bear that had been killed. Afterward the people feasted and danced in its honor.

Two important concepts of the Innu and other Algonquian groups were *manitou* and the "big man." *Manitou* was a pervasive power in the world that people could learn to use on their own behalf. A person's big man was an intimate spirit-being who granted wisdom, competence, skill, and strength in the food quest as well as in other areas of life, including magic. Maintaining a relationship with this being required good conduct. Algonquian and certain Athabaskan groups also believed in animal-spirit "bosses" who controlled the supply of caribou, fish, and other creatures.

Like other indigenous peoples, Subarctic Indians respected shamans for their close connection to the world beyond. A shaman could be male or female. People believed that shamans cured the sick and foretold the future. It was thought that sometimes shamans became evil and could do harm. Shamanistic ability came to an individual from dreaming of animals who taught the dreamer to work with their aid. To be recognized as a shaman, however, the person's ability had to be proved through successful performance.

THE NORTHEAST

The Northeast culture area reaches from what is now southern Canada to the Ohio River valley. East to west, it extends from the Atlantic coast to the Mississippi River valley. The climate is mild, with plentiful rainfall. The land is generally rolling, though the Appalachian Mountains include some fairly steep slopes. Forests spread over the mountains and valleys. There is extensive coastline as well as many lakes and streams. The Northeast Indians largely depended on the trees, the animals that lived in the woods, and the fish and shellfish from the streams and the sea.

Peoples and Languages

Most tribes of the Northeast belonged to either the Algonquian or Iroquoian language family. Tribes that spoke Algonquian languages were more widely distributed. Their territories covered the entire region except the areas immediately surrounding Lakes Erie and Ontario, some parts of the present-day U.S. states of Wisconsin and Minnesota, and a portion of the interior of present-day Virginia and North Carolina. Among the Algonquian groups were the Algonquin, Wampanoag, Mohican, Mohegan, Mi'kmaq (Micmac), Abenaki, Penobscot, Massachuset, Pequot, Delaware, Menominee, Kickapoo, Ojibwa, Sauk, Fox (Meskwaki), and Illinois.

The territory around Lakes Erie and Ontario was controlled by Iroquoian-speaking tribes. They included the Mohawk, Oneida, Onondaga, Cayuga, Seneca, and Huron. The Tuscarora, who also spoke an Iroquoian language, lived in the coastal hills of present-day North Carolina and Virginia.

Although many Siouan-speaking tribes once lived in the Northeast culture area, only the Ho-Chunk (Winnebago) people continue to reside there in large numbers. Most of the Siouan speakers moved west in the 1500s and 1600s as a result of European colonialism. Most Siouan-speaking groups are usually considered to be part of the Plains culture area (*see* "The Plains," page 39).

Food

Most Northeast peoples relied on farming for food. Men and women cleared the ground for fields by burning off the trees and bushes. Trees were felled by girdling. A fire set at a tree's base charred the wood so it could be chipped with a stone ax until the tree fell. A ring of wet clay kept the flames from spreading up the trunk. Women then planted the fields with corn, squash, beans, pumpkins, and gourds. Corn-based soups and stews were staples of the diet. Some produce was dried and stored for winter meals. Northeast Indians also fed themselves by hunting and gathering. The diet included deer, elk, moose, waterfowl, turkeys, fish, leaves, seeds, tubers, berries, roots, and nuts.

Some parts of the culture area offered other things to eat. In the forests, people tapped the sugar maples and boiled the sap to make sugar. Rivers in the north and east had annual runs of fish such as salmon. In the north people tended to rely more on fish than on crops

A 16th-century sketch shows the Algonquin village of Pomeiock, near present-day Gibbs Creek, N.C., with huts and longhouses inside a protective palisade.

Photos.com/Jupiterimages

because the latter were often destroyed by frost.
Similarly, the Ojibwa and other tribes of the northern
Great Lakes area relied more on wild rice than on crops.
Peoples on the western fringes of the culture area relied
more on hunting the bison (buffalo) that roamed the
local prairies than on farming. On the Atlantic coast and
along major rivers, shellfish were plentiful and played
an important part in the diet. In contrast, residents of
the central and southern parts of the culture area
tended to rely quite heavily on crops, because wild
resources such as rice, fish, shellfish, and bison were
unavailable.

Settlements and Housing

The Northeast tribes that relied most heavily on farming
tended to form the largest settlements. Their villages
were usually clustered beside a lake, stream, or other
source of fresh water. Most villages had a few dozen to a

few hundred residents. The Indians drove
sharpened poles into the ground to make a high
fence, or palisade, around the village to protect it
from attack by other people or by large animals.
The farm fields lay beyond the fence. When the
ground lost its richness through years of
planting, the game in the area became scarce, or
the local supply of firewood was used up, the
villagers left their old homes and moved to a
new location.

Peoples living in areas with an abundance of
wild food sources such as wild rice or salmon
tended to live in smaller and less protected
villages. They spent more of their time in
scattered hunting and gathering camps. By the
first half of the 1600s, however, nearly every
village was ringed by a protective palisade.

The most widely used house in the Northeast
was the dome-shaped wickiup (or wigwam). The
Indians made a frame of small, flexible trees, or
saplings. They stuck them firmly in the ground in a
circle, then bent them overhead in an arch and tied them
together with tough bark fibers. Next, other branches
were wrapped in circles around the bent poles and tied
to them. Slabs of bark, reeds, or woven mats were tied to
this frame to form the roof and walls. A fire in the center
provided heat for cooking and for warmth.

The Iroquois and certain other tribes built a larger
kind of home, called a longhouse. Like wickiups,
longhouses were made of a framework of poles covered
with bark sheets. They were roughly rectangular in floor
plan, however, with a door at either end and an arched
roof. In terms of construction, a longhouse was rather
like a greatly elongated wickiup. A longhouse was
usually about 22 to 23 feet (6 to 7 meters) wide and
anywhere from 40 to 400 feet (12 to 122 meters) long
depending on the number of families living in it. A
typical longhouse probably was home to 10 families,

*Northeast Indians harvest wild rice by
threshing it into their canoe. A grain
that grows in shallow water, wild rice
was once a staple food of many Indians
of the northern Great Lakes.*

North Wind Picture Archives/Alamy

The interior of a reconstructed longhouse shows the typical living space shared by as many as 10 Iroquois families.

each with its own living space. A series of hearths was placed down the middle of the structure, with the families on either side of the central walkway sharing the fire in the middle.

Clothing

Although housing and the reliance on farming varied from tribe to tribe, clothing was fairly similar throughout the Northeast culture area. Northeast women made clothing from the skins of deer and other game. In summer, the women wore a wraparound skirt, the men a breechcloth. A breechcloth was a strip of soft

Moccasins worn by the Northeast Indians were sometimes decorated with quillwork and beads.

leather drawn between the legs and held in place by looping it over a belt at the waist. In winter, both men and women wore leggings—basically, two tubes of leather or fur also attached to the waist belt—and capes or robes made of leather or fur. Both men and women wore moccasins. Women decorated clothes with painting, porcupine-quill embroidery, shells, or shell beads. Glass beads, cloth, and ribbons were highly valued once they became available through trade.

For special occasions such as feasts and war expeditions, Northeast Indians sometimes decorated their bodies with paint and jewelry. Many people had tattoos, especially on the face. Long hair was admired and might be greased to add luster. A number of men plucked out some hair and cut the remainder to form roaches (a hairstyle now commonly referred to as a "Mohawk") or other distinctive hairstyles. Men's headdresses were of dyed deer hair or a few feathers.

Technology and Arts

Northeast Indians took advantage of the forests by making many items out of wood. Women of many tribes knew how to weave mats, baskets, and belts from shredded bark, wood splints, and other fibers. Dishes and spoons were fashioned from bark or carved wood. Mortars were made of hollowed logs, and small logs were used as pestles.

Northeast Indians skimmed over the many lakes and streams of their region in canoes of birch bark. Some canoes, called dugouts, were made from the hollowed trunks of whole trees. The forest also provided materials for the frames of snowshoes, which aided travel in winter and which were essential in the north. The shafts for bows, arrows, and spears were made of wood as well. Points for arrows and spears were chipped from stone, as were knives and other sharp-edged tools. A variety of bone tools were also made, mainly for processing animal hides into soft leather.

Cooking vessels included ceramic pots and birch-bark baskets (hot stones were placed in the latter). Brass pots and kettles were prized for cooking once they became available through trade.

Society

Peoples of the Northeast formed loosely organized bands and villages based on shared language and cultural traits. Bands tended to be smaller and to live in places where wild foods such as wild rice, salmon, or shellfish were plentiful. They moved often in pursuit of food sources. Peoples who depended more on farming formed larger villages. Several bands or villages made up a tribe, which was also loosely organized. In many parts of the Northeast a tribe was not so much a political or decision-making unit as a group of people who spoke a common language and had similar customs.

Chiefs, or sachems, led the tribes. Although chieftainships often were inherited, personal ability was the basis for a chief's influence. Leaders of various levels gathered frequently for councils, which might include 50 or more people. Such gatherings normally opened with prayers and an offering of tobacco to the divine,

The Ojibwa, like other Northeast Indians, made birch-bark canoes for water transportation. Birch bark made the best canoes in terms of the ratio between strength and weight.

The Granger Collection, New York

followed by the smoking of a sacred pipe, or calumet.

Groups of tribes sometimes joined to form powerful confederacies. These alliances were often very complex political organizations. They generally took their name from the most powerful member tribe. The most elaborate and powerful political organization in the Northeast was the Iroquois Confederacy. Its original members were the Mohawk, Oneida, Onondaga, Cayuga, and Seneca; the Tuscarora joined later.

Warfare was common among Indians of the Northeast. In many tribes, military honors were the most important measure of a man's status. Tribes raided other tribes to gain more territory as well as captive women and children. These captives were often adopted into the tribe to replace family members lost to death or capture. Captive men, however, generally fared less well than women and children. Among the Iroquois Confederacy and some other groups, men taken during raids might be either adopted into the tribe or tortured to death. If the captive had been taken to compensate for a murder, his fate was usually determined by the family of the deceased. Among the Iroquois it was not uncommon to close the event by cannibalizing the body, a practice that alienated surrounding tribes.

Family

Perhaps the most important and stable social group in the Northeast was the clan. A clan was essentially a large extended family whose members were descended from a common ancestor. Clan members considered themselves to be related whether or not a definitive genetic relationship could be traced. Members had certain obligations toward one another, such as providing hospitality to visitors of the same clan.

Clans divided the community into smaller cooperating units and created a means for uniting people from different villages or bands. Some tribes also grouped clans into larger units called moieties or phratries. (The term moiety is used when a tribe is divided into two complementary units; the term phratry when there are more than two units.) These larger groups had obligations to one another. Among many Iroquoians, for example, an important moiety responsibility was to bury the dead of the opposite group.

Membership in a clan was for life; it did not change upon marriage. Because clan affiliation was so important in structuring community life, those who were born outside the system and were later adopted into a tribe were also adopted into a clan of that tribe.

Clan membership was an important stabilizing device within native societies, as divorce and deaths from battle, childbirth, accident, and illness could change a person's fortunes quite quickly. A clan was responsible for the well-being of its members and ensured that those least able to provide for themselves—an orphaned child, an elder whose children had died or been killed, a widow or widower with several young children—were cared for.

Typically among Northeast peoples, labor was divided on the basis of gender and age. Grandparents, great-aunts and great-uncles, and older siblings and cousins helped parents care for children from toddlerhood on, teaching them the ways of the group. Women cared for infants, cooked, made clothing and basketry containers, gathered wild plants and shellfish, fished, and made the tools necessary for these tasks. They also planted, weeded, and harvested all crops. In total, women typically grew, gathered, or caught the majority of the food consumed by a group. Men held councils, warred, built houses, hunted, fished, and made the implements they needed for these activities.

Religion

Animism—the belief that everything has a soul or spirit—pervaded many aspects of life for the Northeast tribes. It was expressed in a wide variety of ways. Among many upper Great Lakes tribes, each clan owned a bundle of sacred objects. Together the objects in the bundle were seen as spirit-beings that were in some sense alive. The clan was responsible for performing the

A painting by Paul Kane depicts an encampment on the shores of Lake Huron in about 1845. While hunting and gathering away from their villages, bands of Northeast Indians lived in portable bark shelters.

The Granger Collection, New York

rituals that insured those beings' health and goodwill. The Iroquois had no comparable clan ceremonies. Instead, a significant part of their ritual life centered on ceremonies in recognition of foods as they matured. These rituals included festivals celebrating the maple, strawberry, bean, and green corn harvests, as well as a midwinter ceremony.

Medicine societies were also important. They were so named because one of their major functions was curing and because their membership consisted of people who had undergone such cures. Typically their practices combined the use of medicinal plants with what would now be considered psychiatric care or psychological support. The most famous medicine society among the upper Great Lakes Algonquians was the Midewiwin, or Grand Medicine Society. Its elaborate annual or semiannual meetings included the performance of various magical feats (*see* sidebar, "Grand Medicine Society"). Of the various Iroquois medicine societies, the False Face Society is perhaps best known. The wooden masks worn by members of this society during their rituals were carved from living trees. The masks were believed to be powerful living beings capable of curing the sick when properly cared for or of causing great harm when treated disrespectfully.

Not all curing was performed by members of medicine societies. Shamans had the power to cure, a power that was often indicated in a vision or dream. Dreams were especially important. They indicated not only the causes of illness and an individual's power to cure but also the means of maintaining good fortune in various aspects of life. They might indicate whether one had special ability in warfare, hunting, and other such activities. So much attention was paid to dreams that among some peoples a mother asked her children each morning if they had dreamed in order to teach them to pay attention to these experiences. Dreams could also influence the decisions of councils.

Boys in Northeast tribes sometimes undertook a vision quest, though this ritual was not as important in the

Grand Medicine Society

The Grand Medicine Society, or Midewiwin, was a secret religious organization open to men and women. It began among the Ojibwa Indians and then spread to other Great Lakes peoples, including the Miami, Sauk, and Fox, as well as the eastern Sioux, who lived near the Great Lakes before moving to the Plains in the 1800s. Its members were devoted to healing the sick and enlisting supernatural aid to ensure the welfare of the tribe.

According to Ojibwa religion, Grand Medicine Society rituals were first performed by supernatural beings to comfort Minabozho—a legendary hero and mediator between the Great Spirit and mortals—on the death of his brother. Minabozho, having pity on the suffering that humans must endure, passed along the ritual to the spirit-being Otter. Through Otter, it passed to the Ojibwa.

Traditionally, the Grand Medicine Society consisted at times of more than 1,000 members. Among them were shamans, prophets, and seers, as well as others who successfully undertook the initiation process. The four stages of initiation, held in a specially constructed ceremonial structure called a medicine lodge, involved the ritual death and rebirth of the initiate. Many Midewiwin ceremonies involved the use of medicine bundles, which were collections of sacred objects. The powers of an initiate included not only those of healing and causing death but also those of obtaining food for the tribe and victory in battle. Membership in the society was a source of social prestige.

Northeast as it was among the Plains Indians. The goal of a vision quest was to receive a sign from a supernatural being. A shaman then helped to interpret the vision. Girls typically went through a period of isolation and training when they experienced their first menstruation.

THE SOUTHEAST

The Southeast culture area extends from the southern edge of the Northeast culture area to the Gulf of Mexico. From east to west it stretches from the Atlantic Ocean to somewhat west of the Mississippi River valley. The climate is warm. The land includes coastal plains, rolling hills, and a portion of the Appalachian Mountains. As in the Northeast, deciduous forests once covered much of the region. Coastal scrub forest and wetlands were the other major ecosystems.

Peoples and Languages

The Southeast was one of the more densely populated areas of North America at the time of European contact. Among the Southeast Indians were the Cherokee, Choctaw, Chickasaw, Creek, and Seminole, which are sometimes called the Five Civilized Tribes. Other prominent tribes included the Natchez, Caddo, Apalachee, Timucua, and Guale. The Natchez were direct descendants of the prehistoric Mississippian peoples. Many other Southeast peoples also inherited cultural traits from the Mississippians, such as the use of ceremonial mounds and a heavy reliance on corn (*see* "Prehistoric Farmers of Northern America," page 10).

Traditionally, most Southeast tribes spoke languages of the Muskogean family. Among them were the Choctaw, Chickasaw, Apalachee, Creek, Seminole, and Alabama. There were also some Siouan language speakers, including the Catawba, and one Iroquoian-speaking group, the Cherokee. Some Caddoan speakers lived on the western boundary of the region.

Food

The economy of the Southeast was mostly agricultural. The leading crop was corn, followed by beans and squash. Southeast Indians grew several varieties of corn. Some varieties were baked or roasted on the cob, and some were boiled into succotash—a dish of stewed corn and beans. Other varieties were pounded into hominy or cornmeal. Some corn, beans, and squash were dried and stored for later use. Southeast Indians also raised sunflowers, which were processed for their oil, and tobacco. Wild plant foods, including greens, berries, nuts, acorns, and sap, were acquired through gathering.

Southeast peoples enhanced the fertility of their agricultural fields by burning off any stalks or vines that remained from the previous harvest. The length of the growing season in the region allowed many fields to be planted twice each year. The first planting was done in spring. Some produce was available by midsummer, when a second planting was undertaken. The major harvest time, in late summer and early fall, was a time of plenty during which most of the major ceremonies were celebrated. Most fields belonged to individual households, though some tribes also cultivated

The Caddo lived in villages of cone-shaped houses constructed of poles covered with a thatch of grass. These were grouped around ceremonial centers of temple mounds.

of fire. These activities created large areas of new growth, especially certain types of berry bushes and other useful plants. This vegetation was essential for supporting the large populations of deer, squirrels, rabbits, and wild turkeys on which people depended for food.

Settlements and Housing

Southeast Indians usually built their settlements in places with good soil for planting. There were two basic types of settlements. Most of the people lived in hamlets, or small villages, located in river valleys. Each hamlet typically contained storage buildings and summer kitchens in addition to a few houses. The other settlement type was the town, which was often surrounded with a protective timber palisade. Usually a number of hamlets were associated with each larger village or town where the whole community gathered occasionally for celebrations and ceremonies.

At the center of each town was typically a council house or temple. Often these structures were set atop large earthen mounds, as were the homes of the ruling classes or families. The heart of a town also included a central plaza or square and sometimes granaries or other structures for storing communal produce. Among the Muskogean-speaking peoples, the plaza was usually surrounded by benches or arbors pointed north, south, east, and west.

Housing styles varied in different parts of the Southeast. In much of the region people built circular winter houses with cone-shaped roofs. These houses were sealed tight except for an entryway and smoke hole. Summer dwellings were typically rectangular with a sloping roof made of thatch. The walls were built using the wattle and daub method—a framework of upright poles and woven branches was plastered with clay. In Florida the Seminole developed the chickee, a house with a raised floor, palmetto-thatched roof, and

communal fields. Communally grown produce was given to chiefs for distribution to the needy and for use in ceremonies and festivals.

Wild game was abundant in most of the Southeast. The Indians hunted deer, elk, black bears, beavers, squirrels, rabbits, otters, raccoons, and turkeys. In what is now the U.S. state of Florida, the diet included turtles and alligators. Many villages emptied somewhat during the winter months, when men took to the woods in search of game. In late spring and early summer, after the first crops had been planted, men went on a shorter hunt. Southeast tribes also fished in the rivers and the sea and gathered oysters, clams, mussels, and crabs. Along the coast, heaps of discarded shells mark the sites of many ancient camps.

The peoples of the Southeast altered the landscape significantly by girdling trees and by the controlled use

An engraving from 1591 depicts Timucua Indians tilling the soil and sowing seeds. It is one of a series of engravings based on paintings by the French artist Jacques Le Moyne, who was part of an expedition to Florida in 1564.

Library of Congress, Washington, D.C. (neg. no. LC-USZ62-31869)

The Seminole did not need a snug home in the warm climate of the Florida Everglades. They built stilt houses, called chickees, from palmetto trees. Palmetto leaves were used to thatch the roof, and the floor was raised off the wet ground. The painting Seminole Making Sofkey, *by Creek artist Fred Beaver, depicts Seminole preparing a sour corn drink or soup.*

Gilcrease Museum, Tulsa, Oklahoma, 0227.531

open sides. To the west, some groups lived in domed grass houses.

Clothing

Southeast Indian women were responsible for making clothing, most of which was made out of deerskin that had been tanned into soft leather or suede. Men typically wore a breechcloth and sometimes a shirt or cloak. Women usually wore a skirt with a tunic or cloak. Leggings and robes of bear fur or bison hide provided warmth in winter. The feathers of eagles, hawks, swans, and cranes were highly valued for ornamentation. Some people decorated their skin with tattoos or body paint.

Technology and Arts

Like the peoples of the Northeast, the Southeast Indians made the most of the abundant forests of their region. To make dugout canoes, they hollowed out a log by burning the inside and scraping away the charred wood. They used upright, partly hollowed logs as mortars. Other items made of wood included bows, arrow shafts, dishes, and spoons. The inner bark of the mulberry tree was used as thread and rope and in making textiles.

Other important raw materials in the Southeast included bone and stone, which were used to make arrowheads, clubs, axes, scrapers, and other tools. The Indians found many uses for cane, a tall, treelike grass once widespread in the Southeast. They used its hollow stems to make household goods such as baskets, mats, and containers as well as weapons such as knives, blowguns, and fishing spears. Southeast tribes obtained copper through trade with western Great Lakes peoples. They worked the metal to create beads, rings, and bracelets. Shells were used for beads and pendants and to decorate ritual objects.

Fishing equipment included weirs (underwater corrals or pens), traps, dip nets, dragnets, hooks and lines, bows and arrows, and spears. Poisons obtained from plants

Courtesy of the National Museum of the American Indian, New York City

A redware pottery bowl in the form of a cat was made by the Caddo people.

were released into ponds and sluggish or dammed streams, creating a rich harvest of stunned, but edible, fish.

Society

The village, with its associated hamlets, was the basic unit of social and political organization in the Southeast. Some Southeast communities housed more than 1,000 people, but they more often had fewer than 500 residents. A village might be linked to neighboring settlements by ties of kinship, language, and shared cultural traditions. Generally, however, each village was independent and governed its own affairs. In times of need, villages could unite into confederacies, such as those of the Creek and Choctaw.

Most Southeast cultures were chiefdoms, meaning that they had social classes with membership based on birth. Most cultures were structured around classes of elites and commoners, though some groups had additional status levels. The ruling class consisted of chiefs, who governed during peacetime, and war leaders. A chief inherited his power. The degree of a chief's authority varied among tribes. The Natchez were ruled by a supreme leader called the Great Sun, who was treated as a god. Other tribes, such as the Choctaw, Creek, and Cherokee, had chiefs with much more modest powers. In contrast to the chief's inherited power, war leaders usually achieved their position on the basis of personal accomplishment. They also tended to be active and assertive personalities and younger, by about a generation, than the "peace" chiefs. A war leader had authority in a village only when it was under the threat of attack.

Social ranking was highly developed in some parts of the Southeast and insignificant in others. The Chitimacha, who lived in what is now the U.S. state of Louisiana, appear to have been the only society to have had a true caste system. In such a system, the members of the ranked groups are allowed to marry only within the group. Social ranking was also very prominent among the peoples of Florida. Among the Timucua, for instance, the supreme leader enjoyed a greatly elevated status and was sometimes carried around by his followers. Natchez society included strict rules for marriage and social status. In other tribes, such as the Cherokee, social rank was relatively unimportant.

The practice of ranking could extend beyond individuals to include the organization of clans and towns. Member towns of the Creek Confederacy were sometimes ranked in terms of their tribal affiliations or on the basis of outcomes of ball games between towns. The Caddo were said to have ranked their clans on the basis of the strength of the clans' animal ancestors.

Southeast tribes had contact with other peoples both near and far. At a local level, neighboring groups took part in competitive activities, including ball games and hunting contests. Trade relations reached much farther. A lack of geographic barriers to the north and west allowed significant trade with Northeast and Plains peoples. There is also evidence of overseas cultural connections with the Antilles islands in the Caribbean Sea. Other cultural traits point to contact between the Southeast and Middle and South America.

Because each household in the Southeast was fairly self-sufficient, trade tended to center on nonessential and luxury items. For instance, because not everyone had access to salt deposits, salt became an important trade item. There was regular trade between the coast and inland areas. Coastal peoples exchanged shells— used for beads and pendants and to decorate ritual objects—for soapstone, flint, furs, and other inland resources. Pottery made with distinctive types of red clay and artifacts made of copper suggest that Southeast peoples had trade connections with Indians of the western Great Lakes.

Family

Among Southeast peoples, descent was almost always traced through the mother's side of the family. Many societies further organized kinship relations through clans—extended families in which all members could claim descent from a particular ancestor. Clans usually included members from different villages. This arrangement created helpful links between villages. For example, clan members were generally expected to offer hospitality to clan kin from other villages. In addition, certain ritual knowledge and ceremonial privileges were customarily passed down along clan lines.

The main division of labor in the Southeast was by gender. Women were responsible for most farming, gathering wild plant foods, and cooking and preserving food. They made baskets, pottery, clothing, and other goods. Women also took care of young children and

The Choctaw of Mississippi set up temporary camps while away from their villages on trading expeditions.
MPI—Hulton Archive/Getty Images

elders. Men were responsible for war, trade, and hunting; they were often away from the community for long periods of time. Men also assisted in the harvest, cleared the fields by girdling trees, and built houses and public buildings. Both women and men made ceremonial objects and took part in building earthen mounds.

Marriage was often marked by a symbolic exchange in which the groom presented the bride with game and the bride reciprocated with plant food. Among most groups multiple wives could share a husband, though usually new partners could not join the marriage unless all the existing partners agreed.

Children's early education was the task of the mother. As they grew older, girls were trained in duties such as the growing, preserving, and storing of food, receiving instruction from their mothers and other female relatives. Boys received instruction from their fathers and their mother's brothers. Boys enjoyed considerable permissiveness and spent much of their time with other boys. They wrestled, played games that imitated adult activities, and stalked rabbits, squirrels, and birds with blowguns or scaled-down bows and arrows. Girls, in contrast, were watched closely. They took on household responsibilities from an early age.

Religion

Traditional religion in the Southeast reflected the delicate relationship between humans and the natural world. The peoples of this region believed that not only humans but also animals, plants, and all other natural objects had spirits or souls. This belief system, called animism, was common among Indian peoples.

Southeast Indians believed that animal spirits were capable of harming human interests. Slain animals sought vengeance against humanity through their "species chief," a supernatural animal with great power. The Deer Chief, for instance, was able to take revenge on humans who dishonored his people—the deer—during the hunt. Hunting thus became a sacred act involving ritual, sacrifice, and taboo—strict regulations regarding what was and was not allowed. People thought that most disease was caused by failures in pleasing the souls of slain animals.

The plant world was considered friendly to humans. The Cherokee thought that every animal-sent disease could be cured by a plant antidote. Corn, the most important crop, was celebrated in the midsummer Green Corn Ceremony. Also called the Busk, this festival of renewal and thanksgiving was nearly universal throughout the Southeast. All fires in a village, including the central sacred fire, were allowed to die. Then the sacred fire was remade, and all the village hearths were rekindled from the sacred flames. Keeping with the theme of renewal, old clothing and stored food were discarded, and old debts and grudges were forgiven and forgotten.

Not only plants and animals were believed to have spiritual power. Shamans, or holy people, had stones, quartz crystals, and other items that were considered to be sacred. Other objects that were treated as sacred came to symbolize the unity of a group. The Tukabahchee Creek, for example, had sacred embossed copper plates.

A photograph from the 1920s shows a group of Seminole in traditional clothing.

Natural objects could be infused with sacred power in a variety of ways. One was contact with thunder, as in lightning-struck wood. Other ways were immersion in a rapidly flowing stream and exposure to the smoke of the sacred fire.

Most Southeast peoples had myths about the origin of their tribes. Often these stories told of legendary figures plunging into a great flood to secure a portion of mud that magically expanded to create the world. Beyond the creation stories, other myths told of an epic struggle between a heavenly hero who helped humankind and an underworld antihero who brought misfortune. Southeast myths and folktales were full of nature spirits, monsters, giants, and other supernatural figures.

Many tribes seem to have believed in a supreme being, sometimes depicted as the master of breath. This god was often linked to the sun and its earthly aspect, fire. For the average person, the supreme being was less important than the ever-present spirit-beings that intervened in their daily lives. Concern with the remote supreme being seems to have rested more with the priests.

In some of the wealthier societies, priests were given specialized training and became full-time religious practitioners. They were responsible for the spiritual health of the community and conducted the major religious rituals. In contrast, sorcerers, herbalists, healers, and other people with magical powers were generally part-time specialists. They addressed individual needs and crises, especially the treatment of illness.

THE PLAINS

The Plains culture area lies in the center of North America. It covers the Great Plains, a vast grassland that reaches from the Rocky Mountains to the Mississippi River and from what is now southern Canada to the Rio Grande in the U.S. state of Texas. Summers are warm and winters are cold. West of the Missouri River are dry, short-grass prairies. In the east are rolling tallgrass prairies that get more rain and snow. In some places the prairies are interrupted by tree-lined river valleys.

Peoples and Languages

The Plains tribes belonged to six different Indian language families: Siouan, Algonquian, Caddoan, Uto-Aztecan, Athabaskan, and Kiowa-Tanoan. The speakers of Siouan languages included the Sioux, Mandan, Hidatsa, Crow, Assiniboin, Omaha, Ponca, Osage, Kansa, Iowa, Oto, and Missouri. The Sioux consisted of three major divisions: the Santee, who spoke Dakota; the Yankton, who spoke Nakota; and the Teton, who spoke Lakota. Algonquian speakers included the Blackfeet, Arapaho, Atsina, Plains Cree, Plains Ojibwa, and Cheyenne. The Pawnee, Arikara, and Wichita were Caddoan speakers, whereas the Wind River Shoshone and the Comanche were of the Uto-Aztecan language family. The Sarcee spoke an Athabaskan language, while the Kiowa represented the Kiowa-Tanoan group.

Two other communication systems deserve mention. The Métis of the Canadian Plains spoke Michif, which combined Plains Cree, an Algonquian language, and French. Plains peoples also invented a sign language to represent common objects or ideas such as "buffalo" or "exchange."

The Plains culture area is unique in that the mobile culture it is best known for came about after contact with Europeans. Before contact, most Plains peoples lived in villages and, like their neighbors to the east, got their food from farming, hunting, and fishing. Among these tribes were the Mandan, Hidatsa, Pawnee, Arikara, Omaha, Osage, and Wichita. But after Spanish settlers brought horses to North America, many tribes on the Plains and in neighboring areas abandoned farming to spend their lives following herds of bison, or buffalo. Some of the new nomads, such as the Crow, were local villagers who changed their way of life. Others were agricultural tribes from the Northeast or Southeast who were drawn to the Plains by the opportunities offered by the new lifestyle. These groups included the Sioux, Blackfeet, Cheyenne, Arapaho, Comanche, and Kiowa. The mounted Plains hunter and warrior of this era remains the dominant image of the American Indian throughout the world.

Food

Plains villagers grew corn, beans, squash, and sunflowers. Women farmed these crops and also collected wild produce such as prairie turnips and chokecherries. Men grew tobacco and hunted elk, deer, and especially bison. Whole communities took part in driving herds of bison over cliffs. Fish, fowl, and small game were also eaten.

A painting by Andrew Standing Soldier, a Lakota Sioux artist, shows a typical scene at a Plains Indian camp. Tepee painting began with ceremonials and prayers. The color at the top represents the night sky. The horses show success in pony raids. Red on one tepee indicates that its owner has been killed in battle. One woman is painting a parfleche, and the other is embroidering with porcupine quills.

Andrew Standing Soldier

The Blackfeet were among the Plains peoples who became nomadic bison hunters after getting horses. They traditionally lived in what are now the Canadian province of Alberta and the U.S. state of Montana.

Stock Montage—Hulton Archive/Getty Images

The bison herds moved around constantly seeking pasture, and the Indians had a hard time catching them when they had to hunt on foot. Horses made the hunt much easier. Spanish settlers first brought horses to the Southwest. Between 1650 and 1750 they spread to the Plains. At first most hunters used bows and arrows while hunting on horseback. Later they used guns acquired through trade with Europeans (*see* sidebar, "The Bison Hunt").

Bison became the main food source for Plains tribes. After the hunt, the women skinned the carcasses and cut up the meat. Most of the meat was cut into thin strips and jerked. Jerking meant hanging the strips on a rack in the dry wind that swept the plains. This dried meat would keep for a long time. Sometimes it was pounded and mixed with fat and berries to make a preserved food called pemmican.

Settlements and Housing

Before 1700 most Plains tribes lived in villages along the Missouri and other rivers. Some villages had populations of up to a few thousand people. Typical village tribes planted crops in the spring, spent the summer as nomadic hunters, and returned to their villages in the autumn for the harvest. In the late autumn they hunted for a short time. Then they moved to hamlets of a few homes each in the wooded bottomlands, which provided shelter from winter storms. They returned to their villages in the spring to begin the cycle again.

Dwellings in the villages were mostly dome-shaped earth lodges. These were roofed and walled with earth and entered through a covered passage. Earth lodges averaged 40 to 60 feet (12 to 18 meters) in diameter and generally housed three-generation families. Earth lodge villages were usually protected by a defensive ditch and palisade, or fence.

Many Plains tribes gave up permanent villages after they got horses. As they became more reliant on bison hunting on horseback, they adjusted their way of life to match the habits of the animals. The largest bands or tribes came together in large camps only in late spring and summer, when the bison gathered for calving. During

---

The Bison Hunt

Before they gained the benefit of horses, Plains hunters had, over the centuries, worked out cunning methods by which they could kill enough bison to supply the tribe with meat and hides. If the herd was scattered, a few hunters might move softly among the animals and shoot several without scaring the others. In snowy weather, Indians would encircle a herd and kill many of the animals before they could get lost in a blizzard.

Another effective method was to drive the herd over a cliff. One Indian, draped in a buffalo robe, would move ahead of the herd toward the cliff. Then other Indians would jump behind the animals, shouting and waving robes. The bison would begin to trot, then gallop in terror, the animals in the rear pushing those in front. The decoy leader would dodge to safety at the last minute, and the crazed herd would pour over the precipice. Many were killed in the fall. The injured were disposed of with spears or clubs.

Once Plains tribes obtained horses, bison runs were wild, exciting affairs. First, scouts located a herd. Then the long line of mounted hunters rode forward. Sometimes fantastically dressed shamans trotted ahead, chanting and shaking rattles. At a signal the hunters charged among the buffalo at a gallop. Guiding his trained horse by knee pressure, the hunter pulled alongside his quarry and drove an arrow into its body. He gripped a pair of arrows in the left hand, which held the bow, and held another in his mouth. A skillful hunter might kill four or five animals during a run. The number increased after the Indians got guns from traders.

the rest of the year the bison roamed in smaller herds, and the Indians accordingly traveled in small bands.

The nomadic tribes lived in portable, cone-shaped tents called tepees. Village tribes also used tepees while on the hunt. A tepee was typically made by stretching a cover of sewn bison skins over a framework of wooden poles. The cover was usually decorated wth colorful paintings of animals and the hunt. A flap of the cover served as a door, and a flap at the top was left open to allow smoke from the central fire to escape. A tepee was usually 12 to 20 feet (3.5 to 6 meters) high and 15 to 30 feet (4.5 to 9 meters) in diameter, large enough to house a two- or three-generation family. Tepees could be easily disassembled and transported, making them an ideal dwelling for mounted nomads.

The Osage and the Wichita built houses that were similar to the wickiup of the Northeast culture area. The dwellings of the Osage were composed of upright poles arched over on top, interlaced with flexible branches, and covered with mats or skins. Wichita houses were more cone-shaped and thatched with grass.

Clothing

Plains women used bison hides and the softer, finer skins of deer and antelope to make garments. They decorated clothing with porcupine-quill embroidery, fringe, and, in later times, glass and ceramic beads. On the northern Plains, men wore a shirt, leggings, and moccasins. In cold weather they wore bison-skin robes, called buffalo robes, painted with scenes of battles they had fought. Among the villagers and some southern nomads, men left the upper part of the body bare and often tattooed the chest, shoulders, and arms. Billed caps and fur hats were used for protection from the bright sun and the cold. Some warriors wore warbonnets, or headdresses made with eagle feathers, on special occasions. Women's clothing typically consisted of a long dress, leggings, and moccasins.

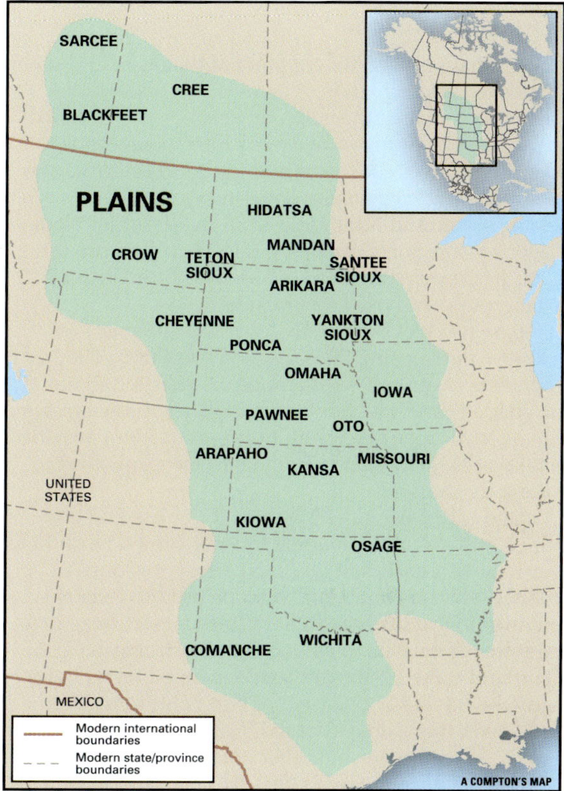

A bison hide painted by a Cheyenne artist in about 1878 depicts the battle of the Little Bighorn, in which northern Plains peoples fought U.S. forces led by Lieut. Col. George A. Custer.

Courtesy of the Museum of the American Indian, Heye Foundation, New York

Technology and Arts

Plains Indians used different parts of the bison and other animals to make all kinds of items. From bison hides they made bedding, utensils, and carrying cases, called parfleches. The horns were carved into spoons and ladles, the hooves cooked to make glue. Plains villagers cultivated their crops using antler rakes, wooden digging sticks, and hoes made from the shoulder blades of elk or bison. Some cooking pots also came from the bison. A stomach or a piece of hide was fitted into a hole in the ground and used for cooking.

One of the chief skills of the men was making weapons and keeping them in good condition. They whittled bows from Osage orange or other tough wood and shaped them in a double curve. They made arrows with a sharp stone head until European traders provided metal points. They lashed feathers to the arrow butt to make it fly straight.

Village tribes along the Missouri River used a bowl-shaped bullboat. They made it by stretching a bison hide over willow branches. It was too clumsy for long-distance water travel, but it could be used to ferry people and gear across a river or to transport large quantities of meat or trade goods downstream.

For land travel, Plains Indians depended on a device called the travois. It consisted of two poles in the shape of a V, with the open end of the V dragging on the ground. Tepee covers and other gear were placed on a platform between the two poles. At first the travois was pulled by dogs, which were the only domesticated animal before the horse. Later, horses did the pulling, allowing people to travel much farther.

Plains villagers made baskets and pottery. Nomadic tribes did not make these items because they were too bulky or too fragile to transport. However, the Cheyenne, Comanche, Arapaho, and some other nomadic groups made basket trays for gambling.

Society

Most Plains tribes were divided into bands. A band was made up of a few dozen to a few hundred people who lived, worked, and traveled together. Nomadic tribes generally included several large, independent bands that came together in summer for a group bison hunt. Village groups acted similarly. A group of related villages might gather for a band-level hunt, while smaller groups were more common for work and socializing.

Band organization relied on a combination of individual leaders and groups called military societies. In choosing their leaders, Plains peoples valued such qualities as wisdom, bravery, and success. Talent and skill were very important because many of the things that leaders had to do—for example, managing a large summer hunt or conducting a raid—were complex and often crucial to the group's survival. Military societies, which consisted of warriors, kept order and enforced the decisions of leaders. Each society had its own costumes, songs, dances, and symbols.

Each band centered its activities in a loosely defined area within the larger tribal lands. The bands within a

A member of the Hidatsa Dog Society performs the organization's traditional dance. This group was one of the military societies typical of the Plains Indians.

tribe did not fight one another, but the degree of unity among them varied. Among the nomadic Comanche, for instance, bands changed membership with ease and the people chose not to have a formal tribal council. The Skidi band of the Pawnee lived in 19 separate villages that were united in maintaining their independence from the other three bands within the Pawnee nation. The Cheyenne were the most politically organized Plains group. Their 10 bands sent representatives to a council of 44 peace chiefs, whose decrees had to be obeyed by the entire tribe.

Plains tribes did not have hereditary social classes, but they did rank individuals. The son of a wealthy family had an early advantage over a poor child because his family could pay for things such as craft apprenticeships and feasts. As time passed, however, such a man would have to prove himself independently. A poor man, in contrast, might spend his youth in modest circumstances but could win wealth and standing through bravery in war. Plains peoples also valued those who fulfilled their obligation to the community. For example, the status of an individual or family was elevated when they were generous to the poor, shared goods with relatives, and cooperated with others.

Most tribes ranked war exploits, but they did not all evaluate particular deeds alike. Fighting between tribes rarely involved large forces. Usually it was carried out by raiding parties of a few warriors to avenge a death, to steal horses, and especially to gain glory. Touching an enemy's body in battle was generally considered more honorable than killing him. This custom was called counting coup. (Coup is a French word meaning "stroke" or "blow.") Tribes rewarded courageous war deeds by giving warriors the right to wear eagle feathers in a headdress.

Trade between Plains tribes was common. It often involved an exchange of products between nomads and villagers, as in the trade of buffalo robes for corn. The Cheyenne were middlemen in the trade of horses between tribes of the southern Plains and those of the north-central Plains. The Assiniboin, Hidatsa, Mandan, Arikara, and Sioux controlled the trade of such items as guns, blankets, beads, and cloth from the British and French for skins and buffalo robes from tribes to the west. Tribes often fought to gain sole control of a trade route.

Family

Plains peoples organized themselves into extended family groups called clans. The members of a clan traced their descent back to a common ancestor. Some cultures traced descent through both the father's and mother's sides of the family. Other cultures traced descent only through the male or female line. In those cultures a child automatically became a member of either the father's or mother's clan. Because clan members came from different bands within a tribe, this system was a way to unify the tribe as a whole.

Plains tribes typically had a clear division of labor. Women were responsible for producing children, farming, gathering plant foods, building and maintaining the home, cooking, and making clothing. Men hunted for the household and provided defense for the community. Children were usually raised in extended families, with the grandparents playing an important role. Older children were also responsible for watching after the younger ones.

Training began early for Plains children, as part of their play. In preparation for her adult role, a young girl was given a doll to play with and care for. As she grew older her family might make her child-sized hide-scraping tools, which her female relatives would teach her to use. She would learn to sew by making clothes for her doll and to keep house in a child-sized tepee. Likewise, a young boy was given a bow and arrows with knobbed tips. As he grew stronger he would receive larger, heavier bows and be shown how to stalk small game and to hit moving targets. Groups of boys took part in shooting matches and play battles. The winners were acclaimed by their elders; the losers were praised if they had fought bravely. Children also engaged in horse races, foot races, swimming, and games of chance.

Children were encouraged to behave in desired ways by praise and reward. Many tribes gave special praise for the first successful completion of a task or skill. Thus an Oto father publicly gave away property to honor his son when the boy first walked, when he brought in his first small game, when he killed his first deer, and when he returned from his first war party. When a Crow boy killed his first big game animal, a song celebrating the achievement was sung at a public ceremony. Progress toward maturity was generally rewarded by removing restrictions and granting special privileges. Blackfeet boys who won shooting matches were allowed to wear feathers in their hair. As soon as he went on his first war party, a Cheyenne boy was relieved from the duty of herding horses. Girls were similarly recognized for their accomplishments in food production, cooking, quilling, beading, hide processing, and the like.

A Sioux family wears traditional dress.
Library of Congress, Washington, D.C.
(neg. no. LC-USZ62-47054)

Arapaho line up to take part in the Sun Dance. For nomadic Plains peoples, this annual ceremony provided an opportunity for otherwise independent bands to come together as a community.

Religion

Plains peoples generally believed in animism—the idea that animals, plants, the sun, moon, stars, and all other natural phenomena are inhabited by spirit-beings. Success in life was thought to depend on the intervention of these spirit-beings. The usual procedure for obtaining spirit help was to undertake a vision quest, in which a person would go to an isolated spot to fast and beg for aid. If the quest was successful, the spirit-being would give instructions for winning in battle, curing illness, or obtaining other skills or powers. The quest for supernatural power through a vision or dream was important among all of the tribes and among both girls and boys. Vision quests were often begun when a child was as young as six or seven years old.

All Plains tribes had people who communicated with the spirit world to perform acts of healing. In most groups ordinary illnesses such as headaches would be treated with common herbal remedies, while a shaman would be called in to treat more serious illnesses. Shamans could also locate enemies and game animals and find lost objects. Arapaho, Atsina, and Cheyenne shamans were said to walk on fire as a proof of their powers.

Some Plains peoples, including the Cheyenne, the Atsina, and the Pawnee, believed in a supreme spirit. The Cheyenne, for example, held that "the Wise One above" knew better than all other creatures; further, he had long ago left Earth and retired to the sky. In smoking ceremonies the first offering of the pipe was always made to him. Some other tribes, such as the Crow, believed instead in many gods, each of whom possessed about equal power.

Ceremonies and rituals were widespread on the Plains. They ranged from very simple rites to complicated events involving weeks of preparation and performances that lasted for several days. A number of common ritual elements were used alone or combined in various ways. Packages called medicine bundles figured prominently in rituals throughout the region. They held objects that were believed to have supernatural power, such as the sacred pipe. Some medicine bundles belonged to individuals; others belonged to the entire tribe and were kept by chiefs or shamans.

The most important religious ceremony on the Plains was the Sun Dance. It was practiced by both villagers and nomads. It was held once a year in summer, when the whole tribe could gather. Although the whole community took part, only one or a few individuals were pledged to undertake the ritual. Weeks or even months were needed for spiritual preparation and to gather the food, gifts, and other materials the pledges and their families were expected to provide. As the community gathered, a dance structure was built in the center of the camp circle or village. It had a central pole that symbolized a connection to the divine, as embodied by the sun. The pledges and other participants fasted and danced for several days, praying for power. In some tribes a ritual leader pinched some skin on the pledge's breast or back, pierced through it with a sharp instrument, and inserted a wooden skewer through the piercing. One end of a rope was tied to the skewer, and the other end was attached to the center pole. The dancer leaned back until the line was taut and strained until the line tore through his piercings. This act of self-sacrifice was supposed to bring good fortune to the tribe.

THE GREAT BASIN

A desert region, the Great Basin culture area reaches from the Rocky Mountains west to the Sierra Nevada. The Columbia Plateau lies to the north, and the Mojave Desert is to the south. The Great Basin encompasses almost all of the present-day U.S. states of Utah and Nevada as well as parts of Oregon, Idaho, Wyoming, Colorado, Arizona, and California. The region is so named because the surrounding mountains create a bowl-like landscape that prevents water from flowing out. The mountains tend to receive ample precipitation, but they form a rain shadow such that the interior averages as little as 2 inches (5 centimeters) of moisture per year. There are some pine forests in the mountains, but few plants grow on the desert floor. Game animals are scarce as well.

B. Anthony Stewart—NGS Image Collection/The Art Archive

A Shoshone woman makes beadwork as her baby sleeps in a traditional cradleboard hanging on the wall.

Peoples and Languages

Most of the Great Basin peoples traditionally spoke Numic languages. Numic is a division of the Uto-Aztecan language family, a group of languages common in the western United States and Mexico. The Numic speakers included the Mono, Paiute, Bannock, Shoshone, Ute, and Gosiute. The Washoe, whose territory centered on Lake Tahoe, spoke a Hokan language. It was related to languages spoken in parts of what are now California, Arizona, and Baja California, Mexico.

Food

The peoples of the Great Basin were hunters and gatherers. For most groups, wild plant foods and small game formed the bulk of the diet. Great Basin Indians used more than 200 species of plants, mainly seed and root plants. Each autumn they gathered nuts from piñon pine groves in the mountains of Nevada and central Utah, storing much of the supply for winter use. Early spring was a difficult time, as such resources were often exhausted, plants immature, and prey animals lean. Some Paiute groups did a little farming along the rivers. Game animals included antelope, rabbits, rodents, snakes, and lizards. Groups that lived near lakes fished and hunted waterfowl.

Many Indians in the northern and eastern Great Basin changed their way of life after horses became available. Horses brought to the Southwest by the Spanish may have spread to the Great Basin by the mid-1600s. The Great Basin peoples who used horses took on cultural traits similar to those of the nomadic Plains Indian people (*see* "The Plains," page 39). Bison (buffalo) became their major prey animal. They also hunted deer, elk, and mountain sheep on horseback. Shoshone-Bannock peoples caught salmon during the annual spawning run each spring. Fresh salmon was an important food source after the long winter, and some salmon was also dried or smoked for later use. All of the horse-owning tribes also collected seeds and roots when they were available.

Settlements and Housing

Great Basin peoples were nomadic, traveling the desert in search of food. The tribes that used horses were able to cover a much larger area than those on foot. Because of the limited food supply, Great Basin Indians traveled in small groups. In winter they typically lived in villages along the edge of valley floors near water and firewood. They moved their summer camps frequently so they would not exhaust the plants and animals in any given place.

Great Basin tribes traditionally built two types of shelters. In summer they used simple brush windbreaks. In winter they built domed wickiups, which consisted of a frame of saplings covered with brush, bark, grass, or reed mats. Tribes that used horses replaced these shelters with Plains-style tepees. Peoples in the west and south, however, used the traditional house forms well into the 1800s.

Clothing

Many Great Basin Indians wore little or no clothing, especially during the hot summer months. Among groups in the south and west, bark aprons and breechcloths were common. In winter rabbit-skin robes provided warmth. Peoples who lived near the Plains wore garments made from animal skins. Like the Plains Indians, these groups decorated their clothing with dyed porcupine quills and, later, glass beads. Many people went barefoot, but some wore leather moccasins or sandals made from yucca plants.

Technology and Arts

The tools of the Great Basin Indians were typical of hunting and gathering cultures: the bow and arrow, stone knife, basket, net, and grinding stone for processing seeds. They used sharp digging sticks to work the soil and to dig for edible roots. They caught rodents with snares and traps or pulled them from burrows with long hooked sticks. Rabbits were driven into nets and clubbed or were shot with bows and arrows. Antelope were driven into corrals and traps. Deer, elk, and mountain sheep were taken with bows and arrows or in traps. Waterfowl were netted, trapped, or shot with arrows that had rounded heads and were intended to stun the bird. Some groups made decoys of reeds covered with duck skins. Fishing equipment included lines and hooks, harpoons, nets, and weirs (underwater traps) made of willow.

Some Great Basin peoples wove baskets of branches and grasses. These were functional, but they were also works of art. Shoshone, Paiute, and Ute groups made coarse pottery. Some Shoshone made jars and cups from a soft stone called steatite. Rock art—drawings, paintings, and carvings on stone—was common among the tribes

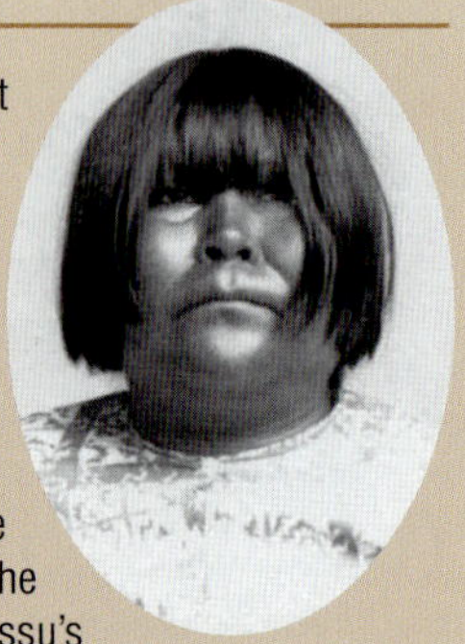

Of the many expert basket weavers among the Great Basin Indians, it is Datsolalee who is remembered above all. A member of the Washoe tribe, she was born in about 1835 near the California-Nevada border. She learned the fine art of basketry as a child. Datsolalee married Assu, a Washoe, and the pair had two children before Assu's death. In 1888 she married another Washoe named Charley Keyser. Thereafter she was also known by the name Louisa Keyser.

In the 1850s the Washoe fought over land with the neighboring Paiute. After winning the battle, the Paiute banned the Washoe from weaving baskets in order to remove competition for their own wares. The ban devastated the Washoe, who greatly depended on income from their basketry.

Defying the ban, Datsolalee brought several baskets to a clothing store in Carson City, Nev., in 1895. The proprietors, Abram and Amy Cohn, liked her work so much that they eventually bought more than 100 baskets, about one third of all the baskets she wove in her life. The Cohns treated Datsolalee's work as art, and the baskets came to be highly valued collector's items. Datsolalee became famous. She continued to weave even as blindness afflicted her, sometimes working on especially intricate pieces for more than a year. Datsolalee died in 1925. In the early 21st century her baskets sold for as much as $1 million each.

that did not use horses. The horse-using groups painted their tepees, rawhide shields, and bags and containers.

Society

The basic social unit among Great Basin peoples was usually a two- or three-generation family or the combined nuclear families (husband, wife, and children) of two brothers. Family ties were traced through both the mother and the father and were extended to distant relatives. These far-reaching family relationships allowed people to move from one group to another more easily when food was scarce.

The difficult environment also influenced marriage practices. Although divorce was easy and socially acceptable, having a partner to share in everyday labor was an advantage. Thus most people chose to be married (whether to one person or in a series of partnerships) during most of their adult lives. A newly married couple might live with the bride's family for the first few years until children were born. However, the availability of food was the key factor in determining where the family lived.

Children began to learn about and participate in the food quest while very young. Grandparents were

A Paiute family of the early 20th century rests outside of their wickiup.

Library of Congress, Washington, D.C.
(neg. no. LC-USZ62-51063)

responsible for most caregiving and for teaching children appropriate behavior and survival skills. The adults of childbearing age were busy providing food for the group.

Above the family level, Great Basin peoples organized themselves in bands. Among the tribes without horses, groups were typically small and moved frequently. These bands traveled through a given territory on an annual cycle, using the available food resources within a valley and its adjacent mountains. Food supplies were seldom adequate to allow groups of any size to remain together for more than a few days. People usually came together in larger groups only for certain brief periods— during rabbit drives in the spring or during the piñon nut season in the autumn. Where conditions allowed, as for the Washoe at Lake Tahoe, people would also gather when fish were spawning.

Social organization was also flexible among the tribes with horses. Because they had greater access to food resources, they could stay together in larger groups for much of the year. However, they still did create a formal system of leadership. Among all Great Basin peoples, a leader was followed as long as he was successful in leading people to food or in war. If he failed, people would simply join other bands or form new ones.

Traditionally, western Great Basin groups took part in trade involving shells, tanned hides, baskets, and food. Horse-using groups traded among themselves and with others, including fur traders. Shoshone clothing was particularly prized in trade for its beauty and durability. Between about 1800 and 1850 mounted Ute and Navajo bands preyed on Southern Paiute, Western Shoshone, and Gosiute bands for slaves. They captured and sometimes traded women and children to be sold in the Spanish settlements of New Mexico and southern California.

Religion

Like many other Indians, Great Basin peoples had a mythical explanation of the origins of the world. They believed that animal ancestors—notably Wolf, Coyote, Rabbit, Bear, and Mountain Lion—lived before the human age. During that period they were able to speak and act as humans do. They created the world and were responsible for the present-day landscape, ecology, food resources, seasons of the year, and distribution of tribes. They set the nature of social relations—that is, they defined how various classes of kin should behave toward each other. They also established the customs surrounding birth, marriage, puberty, and death. Their actions set moral guidelines and determined the physical and behavioral characteristics of modern animals.

Great Basin peoples also believed in powerful spirit-beings. These were animals, birds, or natural or supernatural phenomena, each thought to have a specific power. Some spirit-beings were thought to be helpful toward humans; others meant harm and were feared. Among the latter were the water babies—small, long-haired creatures that lured people to their death in springs or lakes and who ate children.

All Great Basin groups believed that certain people, called shamans, gained special powers through their connection to the spirit world. Both men and women could become shamans. A person was called to shamanism by a spirit-being. It was considered dangerous to resist this call, for those who did sometimes died. The spirit-being instructed an individual in curing disease, foretelling the future, or practicing magic. Curing ceremonies sometimes lasted several days. Shamans who lost too many patients were sometimes killed.

In the western Great Basin some men were thought to have powers to charm antelope and so led group antelope drives. Some groups believed that certain men were arrow-proof—and, after the introduction of guns, bulletproof. Among the Eastern Shoshone, young men sought contact with spirit-beings by undertaking a vision quest. The group probably learned this practice from their Plains neighbors.

CALIFORNIA

The California culture area includes most of what is now the U.S. state of California. It also extends down the Baja Peninsula, which is now part of Mexico. In the east the Sierra Nevada mountain range forms a natural barrier. The lower Coast Range runs parallel to the Pacific coast in the west. The area has an extraordinary range of natural features. Along with the coast and mountains, there are redwood forests, grasslands, wetlands, deserts, and valleys.

Peoples and Languages

The variety of environments provided ample natural resources throughout most of California. As a result, California was one of the most densely populated culture areas of native North America. California included peoples of some 20 language families, including Uto-Aztecan, Penutian, Yokutsan, and Athabaskan. Well-known tribes included the Hupa, Yurok, Pomo, Yuki, Wintun, Maidu, Miwok, Yana, Yokuts, and Chumash. Many spoke their own unique language.

Food

California Indians lived by hunting, fishing, and collecting wild plant foods. Typically, men hunted and fished while women and children collected plant foods and small game. The most important food was the acorn. The Indians cracked acorns, removed the kernels, and pounded them into flour. Then they treated the flour with hot water to remove the poisonous tannin. They used the flour to make soup, mush, or bread.

Other food resources were spread across the California landscape. Rabbits were common everywhere, and in some places deer, elk, and antelope also provided meat. Coastal peoples fished and collected oysters, clams, and other shellfish. Groups living in the foothills and valleys relied on waterfowl and the shoots and seeds of weedy plants and tule (a type of reed). Desert-dwellers collected piñon nuts and mesquite fruit. They also did some farming along the Colorado River.

Settlements and Housing

Most California Indians built permanent villages that they occupied year-round. Small groups routinely left the villages for a few days or weeks to hunt or collect food. In areas with few economic resources, people often lived in roaming groups of 20 to 30 individuals. They gathered together in large groups only temporarily for such activities as antelope drives and piñon-nut harvests. In general, peoples who lived along the coast or rivers enjoyed a more settled life than those living in the desert and foothills.

Traditional house types varied throughout California. The most typical houses were cone- or dome-shaped structures. They consisted of a pole frame covered with

California Indians gather acorns for winter storage. Acorns were a staple food for California peoples.

W. Langdon Kihn—NGS Image Collection/The Art Archive

Technology and Arts

Most of the items made by California Indians centered on their hunting and gathering lifestyle. Men made hunting and fishing equipment such as bows and arrows, spear-throwers, fishing gear, snares, and traps. Women produced nets and baskets for gathering as well as pots and other cooking utensils.

Native Californians had different kinds of boats for different bodies of water. The Chumash of southern coastal California made canoes out of cedar planks. These boats were sturdy enough for travel on the ocean. The Chumash used them for hunting seals, porpoises, and sea otters. Peoples living on the bays and lakes used tule balsas, or rafts. Groups along the rivers had flat-bottom dugouts made by hollowing out large logs.

The most notable art forms in native California were basketry and rock art. The baskets produced in California were among the finest in North America. They were woven so tightly that they would hold the finest seeds—and even water. Rock paintings and carvings

A Pomo uses a tool called a seed beater to knock seeds off plants and into a large-mouthed burden basket. The Pomo lived in central California.

grass, brush, bark, or mats of tule. In some places dwellings were covered with earth. In central California some Indians built their homes partly underground. Desert peoples made temporary brush homes as they traveled in search of food. In northern California some Indians built houses of redwood cedar planks, like the neighboring Northwest Coast Indians did. Houses ranged in size from 5 or 6 feet (almost 2 meters) in diameter to apartment-style buildings in which several families lived together in adjoining units.

Communal and ceremonial buildings were found throughout native California. They were often large enough to hold the several hundred people who could be expected to attend rituals or festivals. Sweat lodges were also common. These earth-covered structures were used by most California tribes for ritual purification through sweating.

Clothing

Because of the mild climate, California peoples wore little clothing. Women typically wore a short skirt made of animal skin or plant fibers, especially those of bark. Men wore a breechcloth or nothing at all. For protection from wind and rain, both men and women used skin robes. Indians of northern and central California wore moccasins. Peoples of southern California typically wore sandals. Ceremonial dress included elaborate headdresses, skirts, and feathered costumes. Body painting was also popular.

Photos.com/Jupiterimages

The Wappo were known for their fine baskets woven from sedge, redbush, and bulrush plants. One of four groups of Indians called Yuki, the Wappo lived in the Napa Valley of west-central California.

were widespread and served a range of functions, from recording rituals to marking trails. In southeastern California some peoples made pottery. This trait arose through contact with the nearby Southwest Indians.

Society

Most California peoples did not form tribes. Instead they organized themselves into tribelets—groups that recognized cultural ties with others but maintained their political independence. Tribelets generally ranged in size from about a hundred to a few thousand people, depending on the richness of locally available resources. Tribelet territories ranged in size from about 50 to 1,000 square miles (130 to 2,600 square kilometers). The relatively few groups that lived in areas with sparse natural resources preferred to live in small mobile bands.

Within some tribelets all the people lived in one main village. Some people left for short periods of time to collect food, hunt, or visit other tribelets for ritual or economic purposes. In other tribelets there was a main village to which people living in smaller settlements traveled for ritual, social, economic, and political occasions. A third variation involved two or more large villages, each linked with various smaller settlements. In such arrangements one village served as the "capital." It was the residence of the principal chief as well as the setting for major rituals and political and economic negotiations.

The role of chief, or tribelet leader, was generally an inherited position. In some groups, such as the Pomo, women were eligible to be chief. The chief was generally wealthier and more elaborately dressed than the average person. Typically the chief managed the resources of the group. He might give directions for particular tasks, such as indicating where food was available and how many people it would require to collect it. Such leaders redistributed resources of the community as needed and kept supplies for meeting emergency needs. Chiefs were the final authority within their communities, though they typically worked with the aid of a council of elders, heads of extended families, assistant chiefs, and shamans. In some areas the chief functioned as a priest, maintaining the ceremonial house and ritual objects.

Ishi

In 1911 a half-starved Indian wandered out of the wilderness near the city of Oroville, in northern California. He spoke no English, only his native language, Yahi. His appearance caused a sensation, with newspapers calling him "the last wild Indian." The anthropologist Alfred L. Kroeber called him Ishi, which means "man" in Yahi.

The Yahi were a band of the Yana people of northeastern California. Ishi was a child in the 1860s when nearby miners began a series of brutal attacks on the Yana. Over the course of several days the miners killed all but about 50 of the estimated 3,000 tribe members. The survivors retreated into the wilderness, living in isolated canyons for more than 30 years. Over the years Ishi's band dwindled, and by the time he emerged in 1911 he was alone.

After being jailed for a few days, Ishi was taken to the San Francisco Bay area. He lived there for the rest of his life while Kroeber and other University of California anthropologists studied him. Ishi told the anthropologists of Yahi stories and songs and demonstrated traditional toolmaking techniques for audiences at the university's anthropology museum. He died of tuberculosis in 1916. His fame grew with the 1961 publication of *Ishi in Two Worlds* by Theodora Kroeber, the wife of the anthropologist.

In native California larger groups such as villages and clans (groups of related families) generally owned and protected the land. Individuals and families usually did not own land; instead, they were given exclusive rights to use certain food-collecting, fishing, and hunting areas within the communal territory. Areas where valuable resources such as medicinal plants were spread unevenly over the landscape might be owned by either groups or individuals.

California peoples exchanged goods within their families and also through large trade fairs. The fairs were often ceremonial occasions. Both types of exchange allowed people to redistribute food that would otherwise spoil quickly and go to waste. A group with surplus food would exchange it for durable goods, such as shells. The durable goods could be used in the future to get fresh food in return.

Most California groups included professional traders who traveled long distances among the many tribelets. Goods from as far away as Arizona and New Mexico could be found among California's coastal peoples. Generally, shells from coastal areas were exchanged for products of inland areas, such as obsidian, a volcanic glass used to make very sharp tools. Medicines and baskets were also common trade items.

Religion

Spiritual life in native California centered on the Kuksu and Toloache religions. Both were religious societies that involved a long, formal instruction period for initiates and the chance for a series of promotions within the society. These processes could occupy initiates, members, and mentors throughout their lifetimes. Members of these religious societies had considerable economic, political, and social influence in the community.

The Kuksu religion was common among peoples of central California, including the Pomo, Yuki, Maidu, and Wintun. Kuksu ceremonies were held in special earth-roofed ceremonial chambers. Wearing colorful and dramatic costumes, the participants impersonated spirit-beings. The ceremonies were typically meant to ensure good crops or plentiful game or to ward off floods and other natural disasters such as disease.

The Toloache religion was prominent among groups in southern California, such as the Luiseño and Diegueño. Initiates in Toloache ceremonies drank a tea made from the toxic jimsonweed plant. The drug put them in a trance and provided them with supernatural knowledge about their future lives and roles as members of the sacred societies.

The religions of peoples living near the Colorado River differed slightly because they were not concerned with developing formal organizations or with recruitment procedures. Individuals received religious information through dreams. Members recited long narratives explaining the creation of the world, the travel of culture heroes, and the adventures of historic figures.

Peoples in the northwestern part of the California culture area held ceremonies of world renewal. At these rituals people recited myths that were privately owned; this meant that only a few individuals were allowed to recite them. Such ceremonies were an occasion for

A photograph from the 1920s shows a shaman of the Hupa people of northwestern California. She wears a shell necklace and headbands and holds two baskets.

displaying wealth through costumes and valuable possessions, such as white deerskins (from rare albino deer) or delicately formed obsidian blades. Such displays reaffirmed social rankings within the group.

A belief in the use of supernatural power to control events or transform reality was basic to every California group. Generally magic was used in attempts to control the weather, increase the harvest of crops, and foretell the future. Magic was thought to be the cause of sickness and death, but it was also considered to hold the cure for many diseases. In addition, magic could be used to protect oneself and to punish wrongdoers.

California peoples revered certain individuals who were believed to have supernatural power. These people, called shamans, enjoyed a status somewhat similar to that of chief. Most tribelets in California had one or more shamans, who could be men or women. They were active in political life, working with other leaders and using their powers for the benefit of the community. They served as physical and mental healers, diviners, advisers, artists, and poets.

California tribelets also included ritualists such as dancers, singers, and fire tenders. They were carefully trained in their crafts and earned considerable respect and often wealth because of their skills. When performing, ritualists were usually costumed in headdresses, dance skirts, wands, jewelry, and other regalia.

The colorful cave paintings made by the Chumash people of the California coast were probably made for religious purposes.

THE NORTHWEST COAST

The Northwest Coast culture area is a narrow belt of Pacific coastland and offshore islands. It stretches from what is now the southern border of Alaska to northwestern California. The Pacific Ocean is the western boundary. To the east are the mountains of the Coast Range and the Cascades. In many places the coastal hills or mountains fall steeply to a beach or riverbank. Abundant rains support dense, towering forests that are rich in animal life. This environment provided a wealth of resources for the Indians.

People and Languages

The Northwest Coast was densely populated when Europeans first made landfall in the 1700s. It was home to peoples speaking Athabaskan, Tshimshianic, Salishan, and other languages. Well-known tribes included the Tlingit, Haida, Tsimshian, Kwakiutl, Bella Coola, Nuu-chah-nulth (Nootka), Coast Salish, and Chinook.

Food

Northwest Coast tribes had no pressing food problems. They could get plenty of fish, shellfish, and even whales, seals, and porpoises from the sea and local rivers. The men built weirs (enclosures) and traps to catch huge hauls of salmon and candlefish as they swam upstream to spawn. The women preserved a year's supply of salmon by drying the fish over a smoky fire and pressed

the oil from candlefish. The Indians used large amounts of this oil, dipping dried foods into it at meals. Other important fish were herring, smelt, cod, and halibut. People also dug clams along the beach and smoked them just as they did salmon.

Northwest Coast peoples varied their fish-based diet through hunting and gathering. Families traveled to the mountains, where the men hunted deer, elk, mountain goat, and bear. The women collected bulbs, roots, berries, and seeds.

Settlements and Housing

Most groups built villages near waterways or the coast. Usually home sites and settlements were limited to narrow beaches or terraces because the land fell so steeply to the shore or riverbank.

Like other hunting and gathering peoples, Northwest Coast Indians had seasonal settlements. Summer was the time for catching and gathering food and processing it for winter storage. In this season a house usually had several bases of operation. The members divided themselves into small groups that moved between good fishing and berry-picking sites. In the winter most people lived in their kin group's main building, which was usually in a village on the coast. Most villages had several such buildings, each one the home base of a large extended family group. There was also at least

The Haida people raise a totem pole in honor of a deceased leader. These carved and painted logs were among the most impressive examples of woodworking by the Northwest Coast peoples.

one very large structure in which the highest-ranking group lived and where the village could hold a large potlatch, or celebration.

Northwest Coast Indians made their houses with wood from the forests, usually red cedar. The buildings were rectangular and up to 100 feet (30.5 meters) long. The Indians built a framework of cedar posts and attached planks to form the walls and roof. The planks could be taken down, loaded onto canoes, and moved from one site to another. Most homes had a central fire pit.

In northwestern California, at the southernmost limit of the culture area, people built smaller houses for single-family use. These peoples also built a combined clubhouse and sweat lodge, which was the focus of male activity. These structures were common in the California culture area to the south.

Clothing

Dress was fairly simple among Northwest Coast peoples. Although ceremonial garments and some hats could be highly decorated, most clothing was worn for protection from the environment rather than for show. Throughout the region women wore skirts or gowns of buckskin, soft leather, or woven wool or plant fibers. Men's dress varied from tribe to tribe but was in general quite minimal—most men wore nothing but ornaments on warm days. For protection from the rain, they had cedar-bark raincoats and a brimmed hat.

Winter garb included a robe or a blanket. People of high status wore robes made of or edged with strips of sea otter fur and yarn made of the wool of mountain goats. Salish groups near the Georgia Strait wove robes of mountain goat wool and also of wool from a special breed of shaggy dog. The blankets were made of cedar-bark fiber, mountain-goat wool, dogs' hair, and feathers.

Both women and men customarily wore some combination of necklaces, earrings, nose rings, bracelets, and anklets. These were made of various materials, mostly shells, copper, wood, and fur. Some people rubbed grease and ochre (an earthy iron ore) onto their skin to produce a red color, often accented with black. Tattooing was also practiced.

Technology and Arts

Woodworking was the outstanding skill of the Northwest Coast. Traditional carving tools included adzes, mauls, wedges, chisels, drills, and curved knives, all made of stone. Sharkskin was used for sanding or polishing wooden items. Boatbuilders hollowed logs

Totem Poles

The tall, carved logs called totem poles were erected by prominent people among certain Northwest Coast tribes. The carved and painted faces on a pole represented the owner's totem animal or bird. A totem was a person's mythical ancestor and might help in gaining power in war, hunting, whaling, or other activities. A totem was honored and respected but not necessarily worshipped. The animal was displayed as a type of family crest, much as an English noble family might have a lion on its crest.

Other, more elaborate poles had many animal images on them that were reminders of family legends. These poles were less common but are more widely known. Each figure carved on the pole had its own meaning. Combined in sequence with other figures, each one was an important element of the story. Usually the pole could be interpreted only by family members, who understood what the symbols meant and knew the history and customs of their clan.

The designs on a totem pole were carved to represent human and animal faces rather than to look exactly like them. Thus each figure bore a symbol of some sort to identify it. Erect ears distinguished an animal from a person. The killer whale had a protruding dorsal fin, and the eagle, a curved beak. These standard forms were familiar to all Indians of the Northwest Coast.

The totem pole was a sign of the owner's wealth because hiring an artist to make one was expensive. The finest poles were created in the early and mid-1800s, when village chiefs and other important people grew wealthy from the fur trade with whites. In addition, the introduction of steel knives around that time aided in carving. Few examples from the period remain, however, because the moist Pacific coast climate causes the cedar poles to rot and fall in about 60 to 70 years.

Two canoes carry a wedding party of the Qagyuhl people, a division of the Kwakiutl tribe. In the canoe in the foreground, the bride and groom stand on the "bride's seat" in the back while a relative of the bride dances on a platform in the front.

Edward S. Curtis Collection/Library of Congress, Washington, D.C. (neg. no. LC-USZ62-51435)

with fire to make the canoes they paddled in the streams as well as big seagoing whaling canoes. Other woodworkers steamed and bent planks to make boxes, tying the edges together with spruce roots. Some of these boxes were built to hold the huge winter stores of dried food. Others were used for cooking, which was done by adding hot rocks to the food in the boxes. Other everyday items made of wood included spoons and ladles, canoe bailers, trinket boxes, chamber pots, fishhooks, and even the triggers of animal traps.

Many items made by the woodworkers were artistic as well as functional. Dishes, for example, were sometimes in the form of animals or monsters. Faces of animals, birds, and people were carved on boxes, house fronts, house posts, boats, and grave posts. Woodworkers made wooden helmets and masks for ceremonial dances and dramatic performances. Most spectacular of the artworks was the totem or memorial pole (*see* sidebar, "Totem Poles," page 53).

Northwest craftsmen also had some native copper to work with. They made some of their arrowheads from it, as well as copper knives for weapons of war. They engraved designs on a plaque, called a "copper," that served in the place of a valuable bank note. One famous copper was valued at 7,500 blankets.

Another great skill of the Northwest Indians was weaving. The women wove long, ribbonlike strands of inner cedar bark into mats and beautiful baskets. Storage containers, receptacles for valuables large and small, and rain hats were also woven.

Society

The social organization of the Northwest Coast Indians was unusual among hunting and gathering cultures. Most such peoples formed only small bands in which everyone was considered to be social equals. This arrangement helped them to meet the food needs of the group as a whole. On the Northwest Coast, however, food was plentiful. Less work was required to meet the

needs of the population, and there were food surpluses. These circumstances were similar to those of some farming societies, such as those of the Southeast culture area. As in the Southeast, the Northwest Coast peoples developed a system of ranked social classes. Their class system of ruling elites, commoners, and slaves was unique among nonagricultural societies.

Tribes often organized themselves into groups called "houses." These were made up of a few dozen to 100 or more people who considered themselves to be related, though sometimes only distantly. They lived together for at least part of the year and shared the rights to particular resources, such as sites for fishing, berry picking, and hunting. House groups also held a variety of other privileges, including the exclusive use of particular names, songs, dances, and, especially in the north, totemic representations or crests.

Within a house group, each member had a social rank that was determined according to the individual's degree of relatedness to a founding ancestor. The highest in rank held a special title that in each language was translated into English as "chief." Usually a man or the widow of a past chief, this leader determined many of the patterns of daily life—when to move to the salmon-fishing site, when to build weirs and traps, when to make the first catch, which other groups should be invited to feasts, and so on.

In theory, people of high rank had vast powers. However, because a house group's property was held in common, all adults other than slaves could voice their opinions on group affairs. Most leaders avoided abusing other members of the house and community—not only were they kin, but the chief also needed their cooperation to accomplish even the most basic tasks. For example, many strong arms and sturdy backs were needed to acquire, assemble, and position the heavy materials required to build or repair a house.

Slaves, however, had few or no rights of participation in house group decisions. They usually had been captured in childhood and taken or traded so far from their original homes that they had little hope of finding their way back. They were property and could be traded away, married, killed, or freed at their owner's whim. A typical house group owned at least one slave but rarely more than a dozen.

The social status of each member of a house group was hereditary but was not automatically assumed at birth. Such things had to be formally and publicly announced at a potlatch, an event sponsored by each group north of the Columbia River. The term comes from the trade jargon used throughout the region and means "to give." A potlatch always involved the invitation of another house (or houses), whose members were received with great formality as guests and witnesses of the event. Potlatches were used to mark a wide variety of occasions, including marriages, the building of a house, and the funerals of chiefs.

Having witnessed the proceedings, the guests were given gifts and served a feast. The social statuses of the hosts and guests were affirmed through the potlatch. Such events were very expensive to sponsor, which reflected the rank of the hosts. Gifts were distributed according to the status of each guest, with the more splendid gifts given to the guests of highest status. Whether hosting or acting as guests at a potlatch, all members of a house usually participated in the proceedings. This served to strengthen everyone's identification with his or her group.

An interesting aspect of Northwest Coast culture was the emphasis on teaching children etiquette, moral standards, and other social traditions. Every society has processes by which children are taught the behavior proper to their future roles, but often such teaching is not a formal process. On the Northwest Coast, however, children were instructed formally. This instruction began at an age when children were still in their cradles or toddling, and all elder relatives, particularly grandparents, participated in it. Children born to high status were given formal instruction throughout childhood and adolescence. They had to learn not only routine etiquette but also the lengthy traditions that

went along with their rank, including special rituals, songs, and prayers.

Religion

The religions of the Northwest Coast had several concepts in common. One was that salmon were supernatural beings who voluntarily took the form of fish each year in order to sacrifice themselves for the benefit of humankind. On being caught, these spirit-beings returned to their home beneath the sea. There they were reincarnated if their bones or innards were returned to the water. If offended, however, they would refuse to return to the river. Thus the Indians prohibited acts that were believed to offend the spirit-beings and held a number of ceremonies to gain their goodwill. Chief among them was the first-salmon ceremony. This rite involved honoring the first salmon of the fishing season by sprinkling them with eagle down, red ochre, or some other sacred substance and welcoming them in a formal speech. Then the Indians cooked the salmon and distributed their flesh, or morsels of it, to all the members of the group and any guests.

Another religious concept on the Northwest Coast was the achievement of personal power by seeking contact with a spirit-being. Such contact usually came through a supernatural experience called a vision quest, which typically involved isolation and fasting. Among Coast Salish all success in life—whether in hunting, woodworking, accumulating wealth, military ventures, or magic—was granted by spirit-beings encountered in the vision quest. From these spirits each person acquired special symbols, songs, and dances. Taken together, the dances constituted the major ceremonies of the Northwest Coast peoples. Known as the spirit dances, they were performed during the winter months.

Shamans used supernatural power to heal the sick and to recover souls that strayed from their bodies. It was commonly believed that some shamans had the power to cause illnesses as well as to cure them. Witchcraft was used to kill others or to make them ill and was believed to be carried out by malicious persons with knowledge of secret rituals.

Three leaders of the Chilkat, a Tlingit group, wear ceremonial dress for a potlatch. They hold ceremonial rattles, and two wear Chilkat blankets, which were woven of cedar bark and decorated with clan crests.
MPI—Hulton Archive/Getty Images

THE PLATEAU

The Plateau culture area is named for the Columbia Plateau. This geographic region lies between the Rocky Mountains on the east and the Cascade Range on the west. It includes parts of the present-day U.S. states of Montana, Idaho, Oregon, and Washington and the Canadian province of British Columbia. The Plateau is drained by two great river systems, the Fraser and the Columbia. The landscape includes rolling hills, high flatlands, gorges, and mountains. Most precipitation falls in the mountains, leaving other areas rather dry. Some mountain slopes are forested, but grassland and desert are more common in the region.

Peoples and Languages

Most peoples of the Plateau traditionally spoke languages of the Salishan, Sahaptin, Kutenai, and Modoc and Klamath families. Tribes that spoke Salishan languages are collectively known as the Salish. They are commonly called the Interior Salish to distinguish them from their neighbors, the Coast Salish of the Northwest Coast culture area. Among the Salish tribes were the Flathead, Coeur d'Alene, Kalispel, Pend d'Oreille, Lillooet, Shuswap, and Spokan. Early European explorers incorrectly used the term Flathead to identify all Salishan-speaking peoples. Some of these groups flattened the foreheads of their babies with cradleboards. The people now called the Flathead did not do so, however. Speakers of Sahaptin languages included the Nez Percé, Yakima, Wallawalla, and Umatilla. The Kutenai and the Modoc and Klamath language families include the Kutenai and the Modoc and Klamath peoples.

Food

The Plateau Indians relied wholly on wild foods. Fishing was the most important food source. The rivers were abundant in salmon, trout, eels, and other fish. The Indians dried fish on wooden racks to preserve them for the winter food supply. They supplemented the fish catch by hunting deer, elk, bear, caribou, and small game. In the early 1700s some Plateau groups started to hunt bison (buffalo) after receiving horses from their neighbors in the Great Basin.

Wild plant foods were another important part of the diet. Especially important were roots and bulbs, including the starchy bulb of the camas flower. Plateau Indians also gathered bitterroot, onions, wild carrots, and parsnips and cooked them in earth ovens heated by hot stones. They harvested huckleberries, blueberries, and other berries as well.

Settlements and Housing

Plateau peoples lived in permanent villages in the winter. A village was home to between a few hundred and a thousand people, though the community could house more than that during major events. Villages were generally located on waterways, often at rapids or narrows where fish were plentiful during the winter. During the rest of the year the Indians divided their time between their villages and camps set up in good hunting

A Kutenai group wears traditional dress in a photograph from the early 20th century.

women wore leggings and dresses. Hair was typically braided. Fur caps and feathered headdresses also appeared because of the Plains influence.

Technology and Arts

The Plateau is notable for the wide variety of materials and technologies used by its peoples. Plateau Indians were continuously exposed to new items and ideas through trade with surrounding culture areas—the Plains, the Great Basin, the Northwest Coast, and California. They excelled at adapting others' technologies to their own purposes. For example, after adopting use of the horse, some tribes became well respected for their breeding programs and fine herds.

Plateau peoples navigated the rivers in dugout or bark canoes. Long-distance water travel was limited, however, by the many river rapids. Plateau fishermen used spears, traps, and nets. Communities also built and held in common large fish weirs (enclosures) made of stone or wood. Hunters used a bow and arrows and sometimes a short spear in their pursuit of deer, elk, bears, and other prey. In the winter they wore long and narrow snowshoes for tracking animals.

Society

In traditional Plateau societies the village was the basic unit of social organization. The method of governing each village varied from tribe to tribe. The Ntlakapamux peoples, for example, used a fairly informal consensus system, in which decisions were based on general agreement. The Sanpoil, on the other hand, had a more

and gathering spots. When horses became available, some groups became more nomadic. They stayed in camps as they crossed the Rocky Mountains to hunt bison on the Plains.

Village houses were of two main types, the pit house and the mat-covered surface house. Pit houses were usually circular and typically had a pit 3–6 feet (1–2 meters) deep. The roof was usually cone-shaped and supported by a wooden framework. The smoke hole in the top was also the entrance to the house. A person climbed onto the roof and then down through the smoke hole on a ladder or notched log.

In the southern Plateau the pit house was eventually replaced by the mat-covered surface house. These homes were formed by leaning together poles and covering them with grass or mats made of tule, a type of reed. Some of these houses were cone-shaped and lightly built, like tepees. They were used in the summer, when people moved often in search of food, and typically sheltered one family. Other mat-covered houses had an A-frame design. Much larger and more heavily built, these dwellings were used as winter residences for multiple families. As new goods became available through trade with whites, Plateau peoples often covered their houses with canvas instead of reed mats because the mats took a long time to make.

In their camps Plateau peoples used a variety of houses, ranging from small, cone-shaped lodges to simple windbreaks. Groups that traveled to the Plains to hunt bison typically used tepees.

Clothing

Plateau peoples traditionally wore a bark breechcloth or apron and a bark poncho. In winter men wrapped their legs with fur; women had leggings of hemp. They also used robes or blankets of rabbit or other fur. By the 1800s, through contact with the Plains Indians, all Plateau peoples used leather garments. Men wore deer- or elk-skin breechcloths, leggings, and shirts, and

Some Plateau Indians traditionally used cradleboards with a head-flattening panel. The pressure of the panel, gently and consistently applied over time, caused the child's forehead to elongate.

The Montreal Museum of Fine Arts, Purchase William Gilman Cheney Bequest

formal political structure. The village had a chief, a subchief, and a general assembly in which every adult had a vote—except for young men who were not married. The Flathead were perhaps the most hierarchical group, with a head chief of great power and band chiefs under him. The head chief decided on matters of peace and war and was not bound by the recommendations of his council.

In many Plateau societies chiefs and their families played a prominent role in promoting traditional values. Among the Sinkaietk, for instance, chiefly office obligated the chief and his family to exemplify virtuous behavior. For this group such behavior included the placement of a female relative among the chief's advisers. Similar positions for highly respected women also existed in other groups, such as the Coeur d'Alene.

Among some groups a sense of tribal and cultural unity reached beyond the village. These groups created representative governments, tribal chieftainships, and confederations of tribes. This was possible in part because the rivers provided enough salmon and other fish to support a relatively dense population. However, this region was never as heavily populated or as rigidly structured as the Northwest Coast.

Plateau culture emphasized the sharing of necessities. Food resources, for instance, were generally shared. Communities owned fishing sites in common. Each village also had an upland area away from the river for hunting, which usually was open to people from other villages. Items that were small or could be made by one or two people were typically the property of individuals. Peoples whose territory neighbored that of the Northwest Coast Indians held a variety of social events in which people exchanged property and gifts. These events were similar to the potlatches of the Northwest Coast.

The average Plateau kin group consisted of a nuclear family (husband, wife, and children) and its closest relatives. Most Plateau peoples traced their ancestry equally through the lines of the mother and the father. Family life, like other aspects of Plateau society, was marked by ritual acts. These rituals began before birth. Among the Sinkaietk, for example, a pregnant woman was supposed to give birth in a lodge that had been constructed for this purpose. A newborn spent the day strapped in a cradleboard. The training of the child was mostly left to the mother and grandmother. However, even as a small boy a Sinkaietk could join his father on fishing and hunting trips, while small girls helped their mothers around the house and in gathering wild foods. Children learned to be hardy through activities such as swimming in cold streams.

Religion

Plateau religions shared several features with native North American religions in general. One was animism, the belief that spirits inhabited every person, animal, plant, and object. Another was the idea that individuals could communicate personally with the spirit world. A third was the belief that people called shamans gained supernatural powers through their contact with the spirits.

A Klamath woman sits in front of a house thatched with tule mats.

The main rituals were the vision quest; the firstling, or first foods, rites; and the winter dance. The vision quest was required for boys and recommended for girls. This rite of passage usually involved spending some days fasting on a mountaintop in hopes of communicating with a guardian spirit. The spirit was thought to guide the individual to a particular calling, such as hunting, warfare, or healing. Both boys and girls could become shamans, though it was seen as a more suitable occupation for males. Shamans cured diseases by extracting a bad spirit or an object that had entered the patient's body. On the northern Plateau they also brought back souls that had been stolen by the dead. Because their work included healing the living and contacting the dead, shamans tended to be both wealthy and respected—and even feared.

Firstling rites celebrated and honored the first foods that were caught or gathered in the spring. The first-salmon ceremony celebrated the arrival of the salmon run. The first fish caught was ritually sliced, and small pieces of it were distributed among the people and eaten. Then the carcass was returned to the water while people prayed and gave thanks. This ritual was believed to ensure that the salmon would return and have a good run the next year. Some Salish had a "salmon chief" who organized the ritual. The Okanagan, Ntlakapamux, and Lillooet celebrated similar rites for the first berries rather than the first salmon.

The winter or spirit dance was a ceremonial meeting at which participants personified their respective guardian spirits. Among the Nez Percé the dramatic performances and the songs were thought to bring warm weather, plentiful game, and successful hunts.

THE SOUTHWEST

The Southwest culture area lies between the Rocky Mountains and the Sierra Madre of Mexico. It covers most of the U.S. states of Arizona and New Mexico as well as northern Mexico. It also includes small parts of the U.S. states of Utah, Colorado, and California. The north is dominated by the Colorado Plateau, a cool, high plain cut by canyons. Mesas, or flat-topped hills, rise up from the plain. South of the plateau, a series of isolated mountain ranges alternate with several broad, barren basins. The climate is very dry, with some areas averaging less than 4 inches (10 centimeters) of precipitation each year. Droughts are common, and the major ecosystem is desert. In most places, however, the soil is fertile.

Peoples and Languages

Southwest peoples spoke languages from several different families. The Hokan-speaking Yuman peoples were the westernmost residents of the region. The so-called River Yumans, including the Yuma (Quechan), Mojave, Cocopa, and Maricopa, lived on the Colorado and Gila rivers. Their cultures combined some traditions of the Southwest culture area with others of the California Indians. The Upland Yumans lived on smaller and seasonal streams in what is now western Arizona south of the Grand Canyon. They included the Havasupai, Hualapai, and Yavapai.

The Tohono O'odham (or Papago) and the closely related Pima spoke Uto-Aztecan languages. They lived in the southwestern part of the culture area, near the border between the present-day states of Arizona (U.S.) and Sonora (Mexico). Scholars believe that these peoples descended from the ancient Hohokam culture (*see* "Prehistoric Farmers of Northern America," page 10).

The Pueblo Indians lived in what are now northeastern Arizona and northwestern New Mexico. They spoke Tanoan, Keresan, Kiowa-Tanoan, and Penutian languages. They are thought to be descendants of the prehistoric Ancestral Pueblo culture. Among the best known Pueblo peoples are the Hopi and the Zuni.

The Navajo and the closely related Apache spoke Athabaskan languages. These peoples were relative latecomers to the region. They migrated from Canada to the Southwest, arriving before AD 1500. The Navajo lived on the Colorado Plateau near the Hopi villages. The Apache traditionally resided in the basin and range systems south of the plateau. The major Apache tribes included the Western Apache, Chiricahua, Mescalero, Jicarilla, Lipan, and Kiowa Apache.

A painting by Gerald Nailor, a Navajo artist, catches the flavor of the Southwest landscape. The man sits proudly on his spotted pony. The woman dyes yarn while the children play. Beyond stand the hogan and arbor. A corral for livestock lies at the foot of a distant mesa. Nailor's Navajo name is Toh-yah, meaning "walking by the river."

Gerald Nailor

Food

Most peoples of the Southwest combined farming with hunting and gathering. In the dry environment a tribe's nearness to water had a strong influence on how much it depended on one strategy or another. Groups who settled along the Colorado River or other major waterways could rely almost entirely on farming for food. For the River Yumans, the Colorado and Gila rivers provided plentiful water despite scant rainfall and the hot desert climate. Overflowing their banks each spring, the rivers left fresh silt for planting several varieties of corn as well as beans, pumpkins, melons, and grasses. Abundant harvests were supplemented with wild fruits and seeds, fish, and small game.

Many of the Upland Yumans, the Pima, and the Tohono O'odham did not have such a reliable water supply. Some farmed with the help of irrigation. Groups who lived near permanent waterways built stone channels to carry water from streams to their fields of corn, beans, and squash. Groups with no permanently flowing water planted crops in the sediment at the mouths of seasonal streams, which flowed only after summer storms. They built low walls called check dams to slow the torrents caused by the brief but intense rains. These groups relied more on wild foods than on agriculture. Some did no farming at all, instead living in a way similar to the Great Basin Indians (*see* "The Great Basin," page 45).

Pueblo peoples were mainly farmers, growing corn, squash, beans, and sunflower seeds in irrigated fields. They also raised turkeys. Later the Spanish brought them new crops, including wheat, onions, watermelons, peaches, and apricots. The Pueblo also hunted deer, antelope, and rabbits and gathered wild plant foods, including prickly pear cactus, pine nuts, and berries.

When they arrived in the Southwest, the Navajo and the Apache were nomadic hunters and gatherers. Gradually the Navajo and some Apache groups adopted some of the cultural traits of the Pueblo, settling into villages and learning to grow corn and other vegetables. After the Spanish introduced sheep, goats, and cattle, the

The multistoried adobe buildings of Taos Pueblo in New Mexico are typical of the architecture of the Pueblo Indians. Some of the buildings at Taos have been inhabited for more than 1,000 years.

Indians began tending flocks of these animals. The Chiricahua and Mescalero Apache continued to rely mostly on hunting and gathering. The chief food plant of the Mescalero was mescal, a desert plant that provided fruit, juice, and fibers. When food was scarce, both the Navajo and the Apache raided Pueblo villages and later Spanish and American settlements.

Settlements and Housing

The most remarkable dwellings in the Southwest were those of the Pueblo Indians. The Pueblo lived in compact, permanent villages of apartment houses modeled after the cliff dwellings of the Ancestral Pueblo. They were made from stone and adobe (sun-dried clay). When Spanish explorers saw these huge houses in the 1500s, they called them pueblos, from the Spanish word for village. Pueblo villages were located in river valleys and on high, rocky plateaus called mesas.

Pueblo homes had several stories and many rooms. Each family might have several rooms that they used as people do today, for food preparation, sleeping, or storage. To keep out enemies, the Indians made the ground story without doors or windows. The next story was set back the width of a room, and the roof of the lower story provided a "front yard" for the people of the second story. Higher stories were set back the same way, giving a terraced effect. The residents used ladders to reach their apartments. Special underground rooms called kivas were set aside for religious purposes.

The settlements of the Yumans, the Pima, and the Tohono O'odham differed depending on a tribe's access to water. Villages near rivers had dome-shaped houses made of log frameworks covered with wattle and daub (woven branches plastered with clay) or thatch. The Indians lived in these villages year-round. Tribes who lived along seasonal waterways divided their time between summer villages and dry-season camps. Summer settlements were near their crops. They consisted of dome-shaped houses built of thatch. During the rest of the year they lived at higher elevations where fresh water and game were more readily available. Their shelters then were lean-tos and windbreaks.

As the Navajo and some Apache groups gave up their nomadic lifestyle, they settled into villages and learned to farm. The Navajo made round houses, called hogans, of stone, logs, and earth. The Apache remained mostly nomadic. They built brush-covered wickiups and skin tepees for shelter.

Clothing

Rare among the North American Indians, the Pueblo wove most of their clothing from cotton they grew themselves. They began raising cotton and making cloth by the AD 700s. The woman's dress was a long strip of cloth that wrapped across the body and fastened on the right shoulder. A colorful, fringed belt held the garment at the waist. The man wore a breechcloth of white cotton cloth or a short woven kilt with a colorful border. Both men and women wore soft shoes or sandals.

A Tohono O'odham woman wears a basket tray headpiece.

The Navajo and the Apache traditionally wore clothing made of animal skins and plant fibers. After the Europeans came, the Navajo began to make clothes with cloth bought from traders.

Technology and Arts

During their centuries of living together in villages the Pueblo Indians developed ways to bring art to everyday life. Pueblo women made beautiful, strong pottery. Each village, and sometimes each family, had its own styles, colors, and designs. The women had been skilled at basketry since early times. They wove twigs, grass, and fibers from yucca and other tough desert plants into baskets, trays, mats, cradleboards, and sandals.

The men were the weavers among the Pueblo. They also did the work of tanning and making shoes and other leather goods. They made bows and arrows, stone knives, and tools. They drilled and polished turquoise and other stones to make beads. After the Mexicans taught them silverwork, they created silver jewelry set with these stones.

The Navajo were good at learning the skills of their neighbors and adding improvements and individual touches. They learned weaving from the Pueblo Indians, and their blankets and rugs became more valuable than the Pueblo products. The women did all the work—from shearing the sheep to the final weaving. Navajo men learned silverwork from Mexican artists. They adapted

A Navajo weaves a traditional rug outside her hogan. Navajo rugs and blankets are among the most colorful and best-made textiles produced by North American Indians. Traditional geometric designs remain the most common type of decoration used by Navajo weavers.

Don B. Stevenson/Alamy

designs from many sources, especially the patterns stamped on Spanish bridles and saddles.

Society

The Yumans, the Pima, and the Tohono O'odham were similar in their social organization. The most important social unit among these groups was the extended family, a group of related people who lived and worked together. Groups of families living in a given place formed bands. Typically the male head of each family participated in an informal band council that settled disputes (often over land ownership, among the farming groups) and made decisions regarding community problems. Band leaders were chosen based on skills in activities such as farming, hunting, and consensus-building. A number of bands made up the tribe. Tribes were usually organized quite loosely—the Pima were the only group with a formally elected tribal chief. Among the Yumans the tribe provided the people with a strong ethnic identity, though in other cases most people identified more strongly with the family or band.

The Pueblo were organized into 70 or more villages before the Spanish arrived. The villages, like the people themselves and their distinctive houses, are known as pueblos. Each pueblo was politically independent, governed by a council made up of the heads of religious societies. These societies were centered in the underground kivas, which also served as private clubs and lounging rooms for men. The Pueblo also established secret societies with specific themes, such as religion, war, policing, hunting, and healing.

Within the villages, kinship played a key role in Pueblo social life. Extended-family households of three generations were typical. Related families formed a lineage, a group that shared a common ancestor. Among the western Pueblo and the eastern Keresan-speaking peoples, several lineages were combined to form a clan. Many villages had dozens of clans. Other Pueblo Indians grouped lineages into two larger units called moieties. Many eastern Pueblo organized themselves into paired groups such as the "Squash People" and "Turquoise People" or the "Summer People" and "Winter People."

Clans and moieties were responsible for sponsoring certain rituals and for organizing many aspects of community life. They were also important in achieving harmony in other ways. Membership in these groups was symbolically extended to certain animals, plants, and other classes of natural and supernatural phenomena. This linked all aspects of the social, natural, and spiritual worlds together for a tribe. In addition, marriage between members of different clans or moieties smoothed social relations among the groups.

The Navajo and the Apache tended to live in scattered extended-family groups that acted independently of one another. Among the Apache, the most important social group in daily life was the band—a kin-based group of about 20–30 individuals who lived and worked together. Among the Navajo, similarly sized "outfits," or neighboring extended families, cooperated in resolving issues such as water use. Bands and outfits were organized under the direction of a leader chosen for his wisdom and previous success. They acted on the basis of consensus, or general agreement. People could, and often did, move to another group if they were uncomfortable with their current situation. A tribe was made up of a group of bands that shared bonds of tradition, language, and culture.

Family

Although Southwest peoples shared an emphasis on the extended family, they varied in their approach to tracing family ties. Among the Yumans, the Pima, and the Tohono O'odham, kin relations were usually traced through both the father's and mother's sides of the family. In the groups that raised crops, the male line was somewhat favored because fields were commonly passed from father to son. Kinship among the western Pueblo and the eastern Keresan-speaking groups was traced through the mother. The rest of the eastern Pueblo traced ancestry through the father or through both parents. The Navajo and the Western Apache had clans based on the female line, but the rest of the Apache traced kinship through both sides of the family and had little use for clans.

Like many other Indians, Southwest peoples divided household labor between women and men. Among the Yumans, the Pima, and the Tohono O'odham, women generally were responsible for most domestic tasks, such as food preparation and child-rearing. Men's tasks included the clearing of fields and hunting. Among the Pueblo, the women cared for young children, cultivated gardens, produced baskets and pottery, and preserved, stored, and cooked food. They also cared for certain clan fetishes—sacred objects carved of stone. The men wove cloth, herded sheep, and raised corn, squash, beans, and cotton. Navajo and Apache women were typically responsible for raising children; gathering and processing seeds and other wild plants; collecting firewood and water; producing buckskin clothing, baskets, and pottery; and building the home. The Navajo were an exception to the last rule, as they viewed home construction as men's work. Navajo and Apache men hunted, fought, and raided. Among the more settled groups, women tended gardens, men tended fields, and both took part in shepherding and weaving.

All Southwest tribes viewed the raising of children as a serious adult responsibility. Most felt that each child had to be "made into" a member of the tribe and that adults had to engage in frequent self-reflection and redirection to remain a tribe member. In other words, ethnic identity was something that had to be achieved rather than taken for granted.

Children were treated warmly and patiently. From birth, they were treated as an integral part of the family. Among the Navajo, for example, the cradleboard was hung on a wall or pillar so that the child would be at eye level with others seated in the family circle. From the beginning of childhood there was training in gender roles. Little girls began to learn food processing and childcare, and little boys were given chores such as collecting firewood or tending animals. Above all, however, they were taught that individuals must always pull their own weight according to their gender, strength, and talents.

When they were between five and seven years old, boys began to spend almost all their time with the men of their households. From then on the men directed their education into masculine tasks and lore. At about the same age, girls began to take on increasing responsibility for household tasks. As boys grew older, the Apache and other nomadic groups stressed the strength and skill needed for battle. Training in warfare intensified as a youth grew to young manhood. Even among the more peaceful Pueblo, however, boys learned agility, endurance, and speed in running. Racing was important to the Pueblo because it was considered to have magical power in helping plants, animals, and people to grow.

Religion

Like most Indian religions, those of the Southwest Indians were generally characterized by animism and shamanism. Animists believe that spirit-beings animate the sun, moon, rain, thunder, animals, plants, and many other natural phenomena. Shamans were men and women who achieved supernatural knowledge or power to treat physical and spiritual ailments. Shamans had to be very aware of the community's goings-on or risk the consequences. For example, a number of accounts from the 1800s report the execution of Pima shamans who were believed to have caused people to sicken and die.

The spectacular Pueblo ceremonies for rain and growth reflected a conception of the universe in which every person, animal, plant, and supernatural being was considered significant. Without the active participation of every individual in the group, it was believed that the life-giving sun would not return from his "winter house" after the solstice, the rain would not fall, and the crops would not grow. In fact, Pueblo groups generally believed that the cosmic order was always in danger of breaking down and that an annual cycle of ceremonies was crucial to the continued existence of the world.

The Mountain Spirit Dance, or Gahan, of the Apache celebrates a girl's coming of age. The dance is also sometimes performed to obtain cures from the spirits.

Kachina dolls are made by the Hopi people. Kachinas are viewed as the divine spirits of ancestors who serve as intermediaries between gods and people. The doll representations are hand-carved by Hopi men.
Tom Bean/Corbis

Kachinas

Central to the traditional religions of the Hopi and other Pueblo Indians were the kachinas—hundreds of spirit-beings who interacted with humans. They were the mythical ancestors of the Pueblo peoples. The number and form of the kachinas varied from one community to the next, but they typically reflected the concerns of life in a desert environment. Many of the more than 500 kachinas known to scholars were spirits of corn, squash, and rain. There were also kachinas of ogres, hunters, and many animals.

Kachinas were believed to live in the spirit world for half the year and with the tribe for the other half. They allowed themselves to be seen by a community if its men properly performed a ritual while wearing special masks and other regalia. The spirit-being depicted on the mask was thought to be present with or within the performer, temporarily transforming him.

Kachinas are also depicted in small, elaborately decorated dolls. These were carved from wood by the men of a tribe and presented to girls; boys received bows and arrows. They were beautiful objects as well as useful items for teaching the identities of the kachinas and the symbolism of their regalia. The identity of the spirit is depicted not by the form of the doll's body, which is usually simple and flat, but mainly by the color and ornamentation of its mask. Feathers, leather, and sometimes fabric were used in decoration.

According to the Pueblo, humans affected the world through their actions, emotions, and attitudes. Communities that encouraged harmony were visited by spirit-beings called kachinas each year. In ceremonies men in elaborate regalia impersonated the kachinas to call forth the spirits. The kachina religion was most common among the western Pueblos and was less important to the east (*see* sidebar, "Kachinas").

The Apache believed that the universe was inhabited by a great variety of powerful beings, including animals, plants, witches (evil shamans), superhuman beings, rocks, and mountains. All could affect the world for good or ill. The Apache talked to, sung to, scolded, or praised each one. Ceremonies appealed to these powerful beings for aid in curing disease and for success in hunting and warfare.

Navajo ceremonies were based on a similar view of the universe. The Navajo believed that power resided in a great many beings that were dangerous and unpredictable. These belonged to two classes: Earth Surface People (human beings, ghosts, and witches) and Holy People (supernaturals who could aid Earth Surface People or harm them by sending sickness). As they turned away from hunting and raiding in favor of farming and herding, the Navajo focused their attention on elaborate rituals or "sings." These aimed to cure sickness and bring an individual into harmony with his family group, nature, and the spirit world.

In contrast to the animistic religions of other Southwest tribes, the River Yumans believed in a supreme being that was the source of all supernatural power. Dreams were the only way to acquire the supernatural protection, guidance, and power that were considered necessary for success in life. Traditional myths seen in dreams were turned into songs and acted out in ceremonies. The spiritual quest sometimes caused an individual religious or war leader to abandon all other activities—farming, food collecting, and even hunting.

The religion of the Tohono O'odham shared features with those of both the River Yumans and the Pueblo. Like the River Yumans, they "sang for power" and went on individual vision quests. Like the Pueblo, they also held communal ceremonies to keep the world in order.

MIDDLE AMERICA

The Middle America culture area extends southward from what is now northern Mexico to Honduras. The heartland of Middle America is the central valley of Mexico. It is enclosed by mountains: the two Sierra Madre ranges on the east and west and a volcanic range that links them. In the southeastern part of Middle America lie the Chiapas–Guatemala highlands. Along the coasts are lowlands. There is tremendous variety in ecology, climate, and soil, all of which influenced the cultures of the peoples who lived there.

Peoples and Languages

Middle American peoples spoke hundreds of languages. Most of them belonged to one of three language groups: the Mayan (or Macro-Mayan), the Oto-Manguean, or the Uto-Aztecan. Each of these groups included a number of language families.

Mayan-speaking peoples lived in southeastern Middle America. They occupied a large territory in what are now southern Mexico, Guatemala, and northern Belize. One Mayan group, the Huastec, lived in the northeast. The people known as the Maya developed a great civilization that peaked in about 900 and then quickly declined (*see* "Early Civilizations of Middle and South America," page 15).

Speakers of Oto-Manguean languages occupied a wide area that centered on what is now the Mexican state of Oaxaca. They separated Uto-Aztecan peoples to the north and east from Mayan and other peoples to the south. Among the notable Oto-Manguean peoples were the Mixtec and the Zapotec. Both had large, powerful kingdoms at the time of the Spanish conquest in 1519.

The dominant group in Middle America when the Spanish arrived, however, was the Aztec. Through conquest, the Aztec had created an empire with a population of 5 to 6 million people. Their Uto-Aztecan language, Náhuatl, spread throughout Middle America as their empire expanded. Uto-Aztecan is the only Middle American family that also includes languages spoken north of Mexico, including those of such western U.S. Indians as the Hopi, Paiute, and Shoshone.

The Tarasco people lived in the mountains of what is now the state of Michoacán in western Mexico. They resisted Aztec attempts at conquest and built up their

A detail from Mexican artist Diego Rivera's mural Great City of Tenochtitlán *depicts market day in the Aztec capital. The city's great temple complex stands in the background. The mural adorns the National Palace in Mexico City.*

own empire. Their language, Tarascan, is not known to be related to any other.

Food

Agriculture was the base of Middle American cultures. The Indians planted a great many crops, of which corn, beans, and squash were the most important. Others included chili peppers, tomatoes, sweet potatoes, cassava, cotton, cacao, pineapples, papayas, peanuts, and avocados. Many crops could be raised only in certain environmental zones, which encouraged trade between regions.

Farming was most intensive in the highlands, where farmers used a variety of special techniques. In places with sloping land, farmers created terraces (stepped fields) to control erosion. The terraces were constructed of either earth and maguey (a hard fiber taken from the agave plant) or stone. In some places people built irrigation canals to water their fields. A unique feature of Middle American agriculture was the use of *chinampas*. These artificial islands were built up above the surface of a lake using mud and vegetation from the lake floor. After settling, the *chinampa* was a rich planting bed. Tenochtitlán, the Aztec capital, depended on *chinampas* for much of its food.

In the lowlands, people typically practiced slash-and-burn farming. First, toward the end of the dry season, a patch of forest was selected for planting. Next, a band of bark would be removed from the trunks of larger trees (the "slash"), which caused the tree to die and shed its leaves. Then the undergrowth and smaller trees were burned and cleared away. The new field was ready to be planted in time for the first rains. After a few years of planting, the fertility of the soil declined, weeds increased, and the field was abandoned to the forest. The slash-and-burn system was often supplemented by "raised-field" farming in the lowlands. The Indians built small earthen hills for planting in shallow lakes or marshy areas, similar to the *chinampas* of the highlands. In addition, farmers constructed terraces in some lowland regions.

The diet was similar throughout Middle America. The Indians boiled dried corn to soften the hull and then ground it into cornmeal. They used dough made of cornmeal and water to make thin, flat bread called

A 16th-century painting depicts the Aztec building a chinampa. These artificial agricultural islands began as branch and reed rafts, which were then covered with mud from the bottom of the lake. In time the rafts took root and became islands.

tortillas. The tortillas were eaten with sauces prepared from chili peppers and tomatoes, along with boiled beans. They also mixed ground corn with water to make a drink called posol. At higher altitudes they made pulque, an alcoholic drink, from the fermented sap of the agave plant. Luxury foods included cocoa drinks, meats, and fish. Meat came from small game or from the only two important domestic animals, the dog and the turkey.

Settlements and Housing

With their long history of farming, Middle American peoples established villages earlier than most other Indians. The basic requirement for settlement was water, and the main settlement sites were near major rivers and high valley lakes. Through the years, as their farming skills improved, their settlements grew larger. Some developed into great cities, such as Tenochtitlán, the Aztec capital. Tenochtitlán covered more than 5 square miles (13 square kilometers) and had about 140,000 to 200,000 residents at its height (*see* sidebar, "Tenochtitlán"). The great Mayan cities of the lowlands—including Tikal, Palenque, and Copán—declined after 900. In the highlands of the Yucatán Peninsula, however, Mayan cities such as Chichén Itzá, Uxmal, and Mayapán continued to flourish for hundreds more years.

When the Spanish arrived in the early 1500s, however, most Middle American Indians lived in fairly small rural villages. Houses in the villages were typically made of adobe bricks or a pole frame covered with plant material and mud. The roof was thatched.

Among the Aztec, the type of house in which a person lived was based on wealth and social class. The upper classes lived in two-story palaces of stone, plaster, and concrete. Merchants and the rest of the middle class typically had one-story adobe houses. Each house was built around a patio and raised on a platform for protection against lake floods. Commoners lived in small huts.

Clothing

Middle American Indians wore different kinds of clothing depending on their social status. Commoners had simple clothing woven from rough maguey fiber. Men wore a breechcloth covered by a cloak, while women wore a skirt and a blouse. The upper classes wore brightly colored cotton garments that were often lavishly dyed and decorated. Priests and nobles adorned themselves with jewelry and sometimes feather headdresses. Among the Aztec, turquoise jewelry and turquoise-colored clothing could be worn only by the emperor.

Technology and Arts

The advanced cultures of Middle America are especially remarkable considering that their technology was quite simple. Their tools were made mostly of chipped and ground stone, and with no large domesticated animals available, all power was based on human energy. In farming, the Indians used stone axes to clear vegetation and wooden digging tools to work the soil. They ground corn into dough on milling stones called manos and metates.

Stone and concrete architecture was a notable skill of the Middle American Indians. Another was woodworking. They made large dugout canoes, sculpture, drums, stools, and a great variety of household items. They worked metals—gold, copper, and sometimes silver—to produce jewelry and some tools. Their ceramics included pottery, figurines, and musical instruments. A variety of gourd vessels of many sizes and shapes were artistically painted using local materials and techniques. Among their other crafts were stone sculpture and basket making. Some groups were known for their skills in a particular craft—for example, sculpture among the Aztec, ceramics among the Mixtec, and architecture among the Zapotec.

Society

The basic social units among Middle American peoples were nuclear and extended families, with male members and elders dominating. Family ties were typically traced through both the father's and the mother's sides. On a larger scale, Middle American peoples tended to organize themselves into political units with a central

An Aztec calendar stone measuring about 12 feet in diameter and weighing some 25 tons was uncovered in Mexico City in 1790. The face of the Aztec sun god, Tonatiuh, appears at the center of the stone. Other symbols tell of the world's creation and foretell its destruction.

government. People were commonly ranked in social classes, with priests holding positions of great respect and authority.

Among the Aztec, an extended-family household usually consisted of a married couple, their married sons (or the husband's married brothers), and their families. A number of households, varying from dozens to several hundred, were organized into a group called a *calpulli*. *Calpulli* lands were owned communally but were distributed among various households. The household had the right to use the land, but only the *calpulli* as a

whole could sell or rent it. Some *calpulli* communities consisted of a cluster of houses surrounded by their farmland. Others had houses spread throughout the land holdings. The *calpulli* was ruled by a council of household heads led by a chief selected by the council.

Above the level of the *calpulli* was the state. Most states in Middle America were small; the Aztec Empire and other large states were exceptions. Just before the Aztec expansion there were 50 or 60 such states in Mexico's central valley. When the Spanish arrived, these states had an average population of 25,000 to 30,000 people. In less densely settled areas, the territories were larger and populations smaller. The range of size was from a few thousand up to 100,000.

The average small state included a central town with a population of several thousand. The rest of the people lived in rural calpullis. At the head of the state was a ruler called the *tlatoani*. The ruler lived in a large, multiroom masonry palace with a great number of wives, children, and other relations as well as servants and professional craftsmen. He was carried in a sedan chair in public and was treated with great respect. His many powers included promoting men to higher military status, organizing military campaigns, and collecting taxes from *calpulli* chiefs. He was assisted by a large staff, including priests, military leaders, judges, tax collectors, and accountants.

Aztec society was based on a complex hierarchy. At the top was the ruling class, consisting of priests and nobles. At the bottom were the serfs and slaves. Serfs worked on private and state-owned rural estates; slaves were used mostly for human sacrifice. A man could move up in class through promotions, usually as a reward for valor in war; women were similarly rewarded for braving the dangers of childbirth. Certain occupations—such as merchants, goldsmiths, and featherworkers—were given more prestige than others.

A scene from the pre-Columbian Mixtec manuscript called the Codex Zouche-Nuttall shows the 11th-century warrior-king Eight Deer Jaguar-Claw meeting with a tribal ruler. The Codex combines pictures, which depict historical events, with symbols called glyphs, which identify people and places and record dates. The glyph at bottom right—consisting of a deer's head and eight circles—identifies the king.

An Aztec priest performs a sacrificial offering of a living human heart to the war god Huitzilopochtli. The illustration comes from a reproduction of an Aztec manuscript called the Codex Magliabecchi.

Library of Congress, Washington, D.C.
(neg. no. LC-USZC4-743)

Middle American peoples traded extensively with one another. Agricultural products, luxury items, and other goods were exchanged at well-organized markets. Trade linked the far parts of the Aztec Empire with Tenochtitlán. Soldiers guarded the traders, and troops of porters carried the heavy loads. Canoes brought the crops from nearby farms through the canals to markets in Tenochtitlán. Trade was carried on by barter, since the Aztecs had not invented money. Change could be made in cacao beans.

The intellectual achievements of the Middle American peoples included the creation of an accurate calendar. It was based on observation of the heavens by the priests, who were also astronomers. The Aztec calendar was common in much of the region. It included a solar year of 365 days and a sacred year of 260 days. An almanac gave dates for fixed and movable religious festivals and listed the various gods who held sway over each day and hour.

Another great achievement of Middle American civilization was writing. Books were made from deerskin or bark paper. They recorded calendars, astronomical tables, taxes, court records, and the history of rulers.

Religion

Religion was a powerful force in Middle American life. The people worshiped a host of all-powerful gods. Some gods were male while others were female. Some personified the forces of nature, such as the sun and the rain. Others were associated with basic human activities, such as war, reproduction, and agriculture. There were also gods of craft groups, social classes, and governments.

Quetzalcóatl, the Feathered Serpent, was part god and part culture hero. With his companion Xolotl, a dog-headed god, he was said to have descended underground to gather the bones of the ancient dead. He sprinkled the bones with his own blood, giving birth to humanity. Quetzalcóatl was also revered as the patron of priests, the inventor of the calendar and of books, and the protector of goldsmiths and other craftsmen. As the morning and evening star, Quetzalcóatl was the symbol of both death and resurrection.

To obtain the gods' aid, worshippers performed penances and took part in innumerable elaborate rituals and ceremonies. Each god had one or more special ceremonies, in which offerings and sacrifices were made to gain the god's favor. Masked performers acted out myths in the form of dances, songs, and processionals. Human sacrifice played an important part in the rites, especially among the Aztec. Since life was humankind's most precious possession, the Aztec reasoned, it was the most acceptable gift for the gods. As the Aztec Empire grew powerful, more and more sacrifices were needed to keep the favor of the gods. The need for collecting captives led Aztec warriors to seek prisoners instead of killing their enemies in battle. At the dedication of the great pyramid temple in Tenochtitlán, records indicate 20,000 captives were killed. They were led up the steps of the high pyramid to the altar, where chiefs and priests took turns at slitting open their bodies and tearing out their hearts.

Ceremonies were led by professional priests. They acted as a link between the gods and human beings. Priests were required to live a simple life. They performed constant self-sacrifice by passing barbed cords through their tongue and ears. In this way they offered their own blood to the gods.

CENTRAL AMERICA AND THE NORTHERN ANDES

The culture area known as Central America and the Northern Andes covers the southern part of Central America, the northern coast of South America, and the islands of the Caribbean Sea. It includes parts of what are now the mainland countries of Honduras, El Salvador, Nicaragua, Costa Rica, Panama, Colombia, Venezuela, and Ecuador as well as Puerto Rico, the Dominican Republic, Haiti, Jamaica, Cuba, and other island countries.

The area lies entirely within the tropics. Lowlands tend to be hot, but elevation tempers the climate on some of the islands and in the mountains of Central America, Colombia, and Venezuela. Places with heavy rainfall have dense forests. Dry regions have little more than sparse grass.

A Tairona child stands in her village in northern Colombia.

brianlatino/Alamy

Peoples and Languages

Many different peoples lived in the lands surrounding the Caribbean Sea and in the northern Andes. When the Spanish came, the group with the highest degree of central political organization was the Chibcha of Colombia. Other peoples included the Tairona, Cenú (Sinú), Quimbaya, Chocó, Dabeiba, Páez, and Pijao of Colombia; the Manteño, Colorado, and Puruhá of Ecuador; and the Jirajara and Caquetío of northern Venezuela. On the largest of the Caribbean islands, the Greater Antilles, lived the Arawak, who had driven the Ciboney to a few isolated places on the western parts of the main islands. The Carib lived on the smaller islands known as the Lesser Antilles. The peoples of southern Central America included the Chorotega, Miskito, Guaymí, and Kuna. The languages of the area were many and varied, but most belonged to the Macro-Chibchan, Arawakan, and Cariban language groups.

Food

Farming was the main food source for most of these Indians, though some relied entirely on hunting, fishing, and gathering. Even among the peoples who farmed intensively, fishing and hunting were usually important. Many regions had abundant river or sea resources, and fish, shellfish, and marine animals such as sea turtles, manatee, and waterfowl provided a significant part of the diet. Some groups also hunted land animals such as deer and peccaries (similar to wild pigs).

Farming groups practiced slash-and-burn agriculture. They selected an area of forest, cut a ring of bark off large trees, causing them to weaken and die; and then set fires to burn away any other plants. After planting crops there for a few years the area would become less fertile, so they shifted to a new plot of land. About a decade later they might return to the old site and begin again. This type of farming produced abundant food without great effort and was environmentally sound. Staple crops included cassava, corn, sweet potatoes, potatoes, and beans. Some Indians also grew tropical fruits, chili peppers, tomatoes, and cacao for eating as well as the nonfood crops of cotton, tobacco, and coca.

Some peoples improved on the basic slash-and-burn pattern. Terracing was a method used in places with steep land. The Indians leveled off the slopes to make a series of stepped fields. In addition, groups such as the Arawak, Tairona, Chibcha, Jirajara, and Páez used irrigation.

Settlements and Housing

The size and form of communities among these Indians were linked to their lifestyles. For example, peoples who depended on fishing or gathering had the smallest houses and most widely spread settlements. Peoples who farmed intensively established the most densely populated villages with the largest and most permanent houses. Although houses varied in size and shape, virtually all had palm-thatched roofs and walls of thatch or adobe. To protect themselves from raids, some groups erected palisades or walls around their larger towns.

The Antillean Arawak were unusual in having communities with as many as 3,000 people. They were also the only group in the area to build ball courts and large ceremonial plazas. Their houses were constructed of logs and poles and had thatched roofs. The Tairona also had some large settlements with thousands of residents. They constructed their dwellings on stone terraces and built stone roads, bridges, and staircases.

In societies led by powerful chiefs, the chiefs and their families and attendants lived in separate areas. Within their compounds were often large courtyards, plazas, palaces, and temples. They often had storehouses filled with provisions such as produce and dried fish and meat as well as hordes of gold jewelry and other riches.

Clothing

Clothing was simple. It usually consisted of no more than a breechcloth for men and a short skirt for women.

Most of the Indians adorned their bodies richly, however, with painted designs and tattooing. The Colorado, for example, not only painted their faces and bodies red but also dyed their hair with a red pigment.

The Indians of the area wore a wide variety of jewelry and ornaments made of gold, shells, precious stones, pearls, feathers, and other materials. Among the gold ornaments were earrings, nose rings, armbands, pendants, breastplates, crowns, and helmets. In several cultures, gold pendants featured images of birds or other animals or humans with animal features, such as the head of a bat, crocodile, or jaguar.

Technology and Arts

Central America and the Northern Andes had many tribes, and crafts differed among them. A wide variety of baskets was made, usually by women. In most regions the Indians wove cotton or wool cloth on looms, and some groups, including the Chibcha, Tairona, and Cénu, were well known for their fine textiles. In some places the Indians made bark cloth. This nonwoven fabric was produced from the inner bark of certain trees and decorated by scratching or painting. The hammock apparently originated in this area and was widespread. Little other furniture was used.

Tools and weapons were varied and included digging sticks and hoes for farming, stone axes, wooden clubs, spears, bows and arrows, and blowguns that used poison darts or clay pellets. Nearly all of the peoples in the area made at least some pottery, and groups such as the Chibcha, Tairona, Cenú, Quimbaya, Chorotega, Guaymí, and Nicarao produced exceptionally fine and varied ceramics. Some peoples carved jade and other stones. The Indians in some places carved elaborate stone sculptures and metates, stone tables for grinding corn. Caribbean groups made ornately carved seats and other items out of a highly polished black wood.

Metalwork was the greatest art of many of the Indians. The Tairona, Cenú, Quimbaya, Calima, Chibcha, Manteño, and others worked metals with great artistry and skill. The Indians commonly used gold and a gold-copper alloy known as *tumbaga*, but a few groups also worked silver and platinum. The Indians made abundant ornaments of metal and of emeralds and other precious stones. Some of these were worn, and others were buried with distinguished men.

Land transportation was by foot. The Indians traded throughout much of the area without the benefit of either draft or pack animals. Dugout canoes, often large, provided transportation from island to island and along rivers. Chiefs of the Greater Antilles typically owned canoes that could hold 50 people or more.

Society

Throughout the area were numerous medium-sized societies of varying degrees of political and social complexity. They were typically led by chiefs. The cultures with highly developed agriculture generally had more extensive political organization. Among the most complex societies were those of the Chibcha, Tairona, Cenú, and Manteño. There were distinct social ranks, including elites, commoners, and slaves, in many of the chiefdoms. At the top of society were the chiefs. The chiefdoms with the greatest central organization were led by a paramount chief, whose authority extended over a region. Below this chief were local chiefs who in turn ruled over various lower-ranking leaders and officers.

The office of chief was inherited. Powerful in many spheres, the chiefs were social, political, economic, and religious leaders who were treated with great reverence. They generally organized and oversaw warfare, trade, festivals, and the production of some crafts. Regarded as godlike, the chiefs also controlled the important temples and the priests. The chief's subjects commonly gave him goods and food items and provided him with labor as tribute. The chief in turn hosted large feasts and religious ceremonies for the people and helped provide for them during hard times. Some chiefs also gave rare and valuable gifts to the elites that signified their high status.

The chiefs were treated with great reverence. Among the Chibcha, for instance, no one was allowed to look the chief in the face. The chiefs and other elites set themselves apart from commoners by displaying their great wealth and power. They adorned themselves with the most valuable ornaments of gold and precious stones, often of styles or materials that could be obtained only from distant regions. Chiefs and other elites often lived in large houses, married many women, and had many children, servants, and slaves. The most important men were buried with large quantities of luxury goods, and sometimes wives and attendants were killed and buried with them.

Warfare was a way of life among many chiefdoms in the area, especially in and around the Cauca Valley of Colombia. Such groups fought to expand or defend their territory as well as to bring political prestige to their chiefs and warriors. They also raided other groups to acquire goods and captives, who could be traded for other valuables or kept as slaves to provide labor. Female captives commonly became low-ranking wives within the conquerors' society, and their children were not considered slaves. Male captives, however, were often sacrificed to the gods in religious ceremonies. In some groups, the victorious warriors ritually killed and ate the male captives and kept their heads or other parts of their bodies as war trophies.

The Indians of the area also regularly traded peacefully with one another across extensive networks. A number of sites were established as markets. The Indians traded everyday goods and foods as well as valuable raw materials and luxury crafts such as gold and finished gold pieces, emeralds, seashells, pearls, and fine blankets and other textiles. Salt was another valuable commodity.

Some groups in the area, such as the Ciboney, Carib, Chocó, and Motilón, lived in simpler societies or tribes rather than chiefdoms. These groups did not have as much central organization. Many of them relied on hunting, fishing, and gathering more than farming.

A Chibcha gold figure known as a tunjo *was given as an offering to the gods.*

Religion

The Indians of the area worshipped a variety of deities. The most important gods of the Chibcha were those of the sun and the moon. Several groups worshipped idols of their gods. The Arawak of the Caribbean islands, for example, carved triangular stones called *zemis* to represent the guardian deities of each household. Making offerings to the gods played a prominent role in the religious observances of many groups, including the Chibcha. The Indians left offerings of valuable items such as gold, jewelry, textiles, or food and drinks at shrines, temples, or sacred natural sites. Some groups also sacrificed animals or humans to their gods.

In some of the larger villages, there were priests who maintained temples and shrines that were dedicated ceremonial centers. They also sometimes led public religious ceremonies. Peoples throughout the area had shamans, who were believed to communicate with supernatural powers, to cure the sick, and to ensure the prosperity and well-being of the entire community.

THE CENTRAL ANDES

The Central Andes culture area reaches from what is now southern Ecuador to southern Chile. It also encompasses parts of present-day Peru, Bolivia, and Argentina. The landscape is dominated by the peaks of the Andes Mountains, some more than 20,000 feet (6,100 meters) high. Between the eastern and western Andean ranges is a high plateau. The weather on the plateau differs less between seasons than it does between day and night. It has hot tropical sunshine during the day but freezing temperatures at night. On the west the Andes drop down to a desert that stretches for thousands of miles along the Pacific coast.

The Indians of the Central Andes learned how to make the most of this harsh environment. With their close familiarity with the land and its possibilities, they were able to support large cities. At the time of European contact, the Central Andes had the densest population south of Mexico. It also was home to the most advanced native civilization in South America—the Inca.

Peoples and Languages

Controlling a vast empire, the Inca ruled some 12 million people of more than 100 ethnic groups. When the Spanish conquered the empire in 1532, most peoples spoke variations of Quechua, at least as a second language. The Inca had made this widely spoken Andean tongue the language of their administration (though the Inca may have spoken a different language among themselves). Another major language spoken in the empire was Aymara. Before the Inca conquest, the Aymara Indians had several different states in the Lake Titicaca region of what are now Peru and Bolivia. From their homeland in south-central Peru, the Inca formed their empire by incorporating the many different states and societies, large and small, that had arisen in the area. The greatest of these was the kingdom of Chimú in northern Peru (*see* "Early Civilizations of Middle and South America," page 15). Other groups brought into the empire included the Chincha, Chanca, Atacama, and Diaguita.

In the southern part of the region were some peoples who remained outside the Inca Empire. Among them were the Huarpe, who lived in northwestern Argentina, and the Araucanians, a people of south-central Chile whose descendants are today known as the Mapuche.

Food

Andean civilizations flourished because intensive agriculture provided an ample food supply. The Indians achieved this despite harsh growing conditions such as frost on most nights of the year in the highlands. In areas with steeply sloping terrain, they built stone terraces to increase the amount of flat land for crops. Andean farmers raised corn, beans, squash, potatoes, quinoa, sweet potatoes, cassava, peanuts, cotton, peppers, tobacco, coca, and dozens of other plants. They developed thousands of varieties of their crops to suit different growing conditions. For example, they raised certain kinds of tubers and grains that thrived at high altitudes. Most of these specialized crops still grow only in the Andes. No other group on Earth has been as successful at growing crops at such high elevations as the Indians of the Central Andes.

The Indians also domesticated llamas and alpacas. They raised vast herds of these animals to carry loads

The ruins of Machu Picchu, one of the best-preserved ancient Incan sites, are found high in the Peruvian Andes, northwest of Cuzco. The settlement likely served as a retreat for the Inca emperor.

and to supply wool and sometimes meat. They also raised guinea pigs for meat.

Andean societies typically traded with other groups or controlled land in several separate locations with varying climates and terrains. The Indians thus had access to a wide array of resources: different types of crops grown in the lowlands and the highlands, fish and shellfish from the coastal deserts, and animals raised on the highland plains.

The Inca's massive state-controlled irrigation works made possible the production of huge agricultural surpluses. Andean peoples developed freeze-drying, a method for preserving meat, fish, and tubers so they kept indefinitely and weighed much less than the original food. They filled thousands of warehouses with these extra food supplies.

Settlements and Housing

Villages in the Central Andes first developed in coastal valleys where water was available for irrigation. Settlements then spread to the high Andean plateau, where some grew into cities. The largest city was Cuzco, the Inca political and religious capital. It had tens of thousands of inhabitants, perhaps as many as 200,000. (By comparison, London, England, had a population of more than 100,000 in 1550.) Most settlements in the Central Andes were small villages, however, home to a few hundred people.

A typical house in the Central Andes was small, rectangular, and built of stone or adobe. The most remarkable architecture was reserved for public

A 17th-century drawing by native Peruvian artist and writer Felipe Guamán Poma de Ayala shows Inca farmers using foot plows to sow a cornfield.

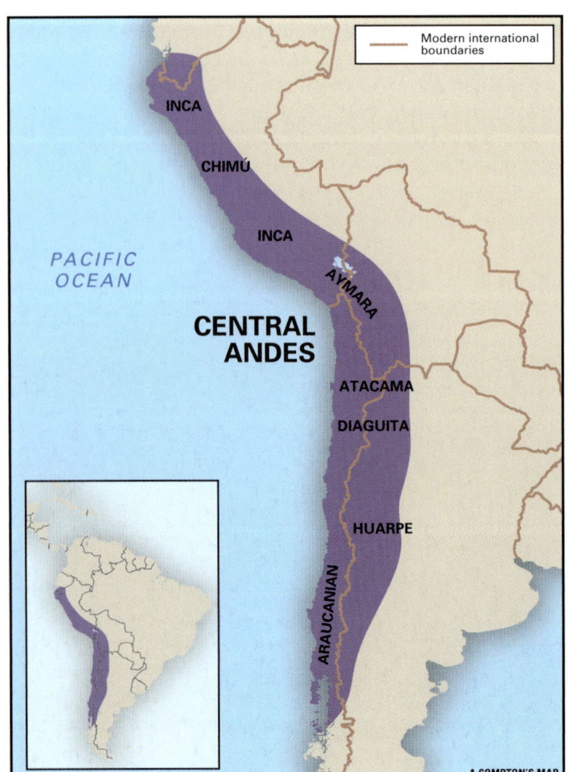

buildings. The Inca built massive stone palaces, temples, and fortresses without the use of mortar. Some of the walls still stand. They cut the stones precisely, fitting them so tightly that not even a knife blade can be inserted into most seams.

In Cuzco the religious building called the Koricancha had finely crafted walls sheathed in hundreds of silver and gold plates. Its roof was covered with a mixture of thatch and gold "straws" so that it glittered in the sunlight. The name Koricancha means "Golden Enclosure" in Quechua. The building is also known as the Temple of the Sun. It contained shrines to the sun god and other deities and was also the center of an astronomical observatory.

The most famous Inca ruins today lie to the northwest of Cuzco at Machu Picchu, perched on steeply sloping land between two sharp peaks. The settlement probably served as a royal retreat for the Inca ruler Pachacuti in the 1400s. Its numerous white granite structures include temples and other ceremonial sites, palaces, and small houses at various levels connected by stone staircases. Surrounding the residential area are hundreds of well-built stone terraces for farming that were once watered by an aqueduct system.

Clothing

Andean peoples wore garments made of woven cloth. The most common materials were llama and alpaca wool and cotton. Only the nobles could wear clothes made with the silky wool of the vicuña, a small wild relative of the llama. Men wore a breechcloth and a sleeveless tunic, while women wore long skirts that wrapped around the body. Both men and women wore cloaks. The designs on the cloth used to make garments were highly symbolic, with different patterns signifying the ethnic group or social status of the wearer. People also wore hats, crowns, headbands, and other headdresses that indicated their ethnicity or social rank. Nobles adorned themselves with gold and silver jewelry.

Technology and Arts

The Central Andean peoples placed a high value on craftsmanship. Their technology differed little from that of surrounding areas, but their products were exceptional for their quality and variety. The most outstanding items were made for the government and the nobility by highly skilled artisans.

Notable crafts of these Indians included metalworking, pottery making, and weaving. In addition to gold and silver ornaments, metalworkers made knives, axes, chisels, needles, and other tools from copper and bronze. Potters produced both everyday wares and fine ceremonial pieces for religious uses. Central Andean peoples also did some carving in stone, wood, and bone.

Weavers made not only clothing but also colorful textiles and tapestries, often with complicated patterns. Fine textiles were produced in great numbers. Weaving was the most important art in the Central Andes, and fancy cloth the most valuable commodity. Inca soldiers, for example, were rewarded for their service with cloth and *chicha*, a type of beer made from corn. Inca rulers gave gifts of fine cloth to nobles and local leaders, and textiles were commonly given as offerings to the gods.

Society

The Inca were just one small group among many others in the Central Andes until about the 1430s, when they began rapidly expanding their state. Within 100 years, the Inca had incorporated dozens of different ethnic

Aymara Indians from the Bolivian Andes dance while playing pan pipes and drums, in a 19th-century French artwork. The various peoples of the Central Andes traditionally wore distinctive clothing and headdresses that indicated their ethnic group and place in society. Under Inca rule, people were forbidden from wearing the dress of an ethnic group other than their own.

Inca Roads

A well-organized system of relay runners carried official messages quickly along an extensive road network that connected all parts of the Inca Empire. The system could carry messages at a rate of about 150 miles (240 kilometers) a day. The more than 15,000 miles (25,000 kilometers) of roads also allowed the state to efficiently move soldiers, settlers, officials, animal herds, food, and goods throughout the vast territory.

The two main royal highways ran north-south, one along the coast and the other across the mountains. Each was about 2,250 miles (3,600 kilometers) long. Many other roads linked the two main highways. The system also included short rock tunnels and suspension bridges supported by woven cables. Way stations with barracks and warehouses filled with provisions for official travelers were spaced along the highways at a day's walk apart or less. Only people on official state business were supposed to use the highways.

---

groups to control a vast empire. The Inca ruler took control of many societies by negotiating with the local leaders, giving them gifts or marrying their daughters to form alliances. Groups that refused to join the empire were conquered by military force.

Inca rule was based on a long-standing Andean tradition of reciprocity. Communities that joined the empire gave the state land and labor; in return the Inca ruler lavished gifts on the local leaders and provided feasts for the people when they worked for the state. The land and labor of the people throughout the empire produced the food, wool, clothing, and other goods that filled the state's numerous warehouses. These stores were controlled by the Inca ruler, who distributed them among the government, religious leaders, and the people according to a standard formula. The Inca redistributed goods and people and organized their labor on a vast scale, and this required a strong central government.

The Inca ruler had absolute authority. A large bureaucracy, composed of Inca nobles, oversaw the administration of the empire. The Inca state—which was named Tawantinsuyu, meaning "Realm of the Four Parts"—was divided into four territories, each governed by an Inca administrator. The four parts were in turn divided into many provinces, each with its own governor.

When a new community was added to the empire, the Inca usually allowed the local lords and chiefs to keep their positions. Now, however, their role was to administer the Inca system in the community. The Inca typically sent a group of loyal subjects who had lived under Inca rule for some time to settle in the new area. At the same time, the Inca made some members of the local ethnic group move to distant lands within the empire. This policy of forced resettlement weakened the ethnic group's ability to rebel.

The people of the empire did not pay taxes or give goods as tribute to the Inca. Instead, they provided the state with the land and labor that made it wealthy. Communities that joined the empire were allowed to keep some of their agricultural land but had to give some of it to the state and some to the state religion. The community had to farm these Inca lands or graze animals on them and give the harvested crops or wool to the state and the religion. Additionally, each community sent people to work for the state for a certain period each year. The state assigned people to work in the army; to build or maintain roads, buildings, or irrigation canals; to carry loads along the highways; to weave cloth or make other goods; or to farm land.

Inca society was highly stratified, with people occupying various social ranks by birth. At the top of society was the emperor and then all those who were ethnically Inca. These Inca nobles filled all the most important positions in government, the military, and the state religion. Some important posts were filled with people considered to be "Inca by privilege." People granted this status were generally from loyal non-Inca groups of the Cuzco valley. Below them were the various local chiefs and lords. Finally, the bulk of the people were commoners, most of whom made a living by farming or herding animals.

Considered a child of the sun, the Inca emperor ruled by divine right. When he died, his body was elaborately embalmed and mummified. The mummy continued to "live" in its palace and was revered as if it were still alive. The emperor's family tended the mummy and offered it food every day. The family also controlled the deceased emperor's vast estate, which remained his property after death. (The new ruler had to acquire his own land and wealth, which encouraged him to expand the empire.) The mummies of all the dead rulers were brought to important public festivals, along with idols of the gods. Other high-ranking people were also mummified. The mummies were thought to intercede in the spirit world on behalf of their descendants.

Religion

The Inca created a highly organized state religion based on the worship of their sun god, Inti. The Inca believed Inti was their divine ancestor. The Inca also worshiped the Andean god Viracocha, creator of the universe, the other gods, and people and animals. Other major Inca deities included Apu Illapu, the god of thunder and rain, and Mama Quilla, the goddess of the moon.

In the name of their gods, the Inca took control of new lands and spread their religion. As they expanded their territory, they incorporated some of the major local gods into the state religion. The Inca allowed the various

Inca Accounting

The Indians of the Central Andes had no written language, so they relied on official "memorizers" to preserve important cultural information. The Inca also used a type of textile called a *quipu* to keep detailed accounts of goods, services, and people throughout the empire. A *quipu* consisted of a long cord from which hung numerous secondary cords. Officials tied knots in the cords in patterns that tallied such things as the number of llamas in a particular herd or all the state herds; the population of a particular village; the number of people from each place who served the state as soldiers, road builders, farmers, or weavers; and the quantity of each commodity stored in each of the state's thousands of warehouses. Each commodity or service to be counted had its own cord, probably arranged in a conventional order. Cords were also differentiated by their color. Different types of knots and clusters of knots were tied. The position of the knots on each cord indicated the units they represented— ones, tens, hundreds, thousands, or more. Some researchers believe that the Inca also recorded historical narratives on *quipus*, but it is not known how the nonnumerical information would have been encoded.

groups within the empire to continue practicing their own religions, as long as they also worshiped Inti. They also had to farm the land and raise the herds that provided Inti and his priests with food and cloth.

Throughout the empire the Inca built temples and shrines dedicated to the gods. The temple complexes housed many priests and their attendants. They were also the home of the Chosen Women, temple maidens who wove cloth and made *chicha* for religious rituals and the state.

The Inca believed that life was controlled by numerous supernatural powers that pervaded all of creation. To communicate with these powers, the Inca consulted oracles—priests at certain shrines who interpreted messages from spirits or deities. Inca priests also practiced many forms of divination, the art of foretelling future events. They used divination to diagnose illnesses, to predict the outcomes of battles, and to determine who had committed crimes. Before the Inca decided on military and political actions, they consulted priests who studied the lungs of a sacrificed white llama. Other methods of divination included watching the paths of spiders and the patterns that coca leaves made in a shallow dish.

On every important occasion, the Inca made sacrifices to the gods of valued items such as food, *chicha*, fine cloth, coca leaves, guinea pigs, and llamas. Some sacrifices were made every day—for example when corn was thrown on the fire in a ritual for the sun's daily appearance in the sky. When a new emperor took office and in times of extreme need—such as great famine, disease, and defeats in battle—the Inca sacrificed humans. The victims were children who were considered physically perfect.

THE RAINFOREST

The Rainforest culture area is dominated by the vast basin of the Amazon River. It includes all of what are now the Guianas (Guyana, Suriname, and French Guiana), most of Brazil, and parts of Peru, Colombia, Ecuador, Bolivia, and Venezuela. The climate is generally hot, rainy, and humid. The dense tropical rainforests found in much of the area are home to an extraordinary variety of plants and animals. There are also swamps, dry forests, and savannas.

Peoples and Languages

A great variety of peoples with very diverse cultures lived in the Rainforest. They spoke hundreds of languages. Tribes belonging to the Arawakan and Cariban language families lived mainly north of the Amazon River. Arawakan-speaking peoples included the coastal Arawak as well as the Achagua and Palicur. Cariban speakers included the Barama River Carib, Taulipang, and Makushí. Tupian speakers were widespread south of the Amazon. Among them were the Tupinambá, Mundurukú, and Kawaíb. Speakers of Ge languages lived mainly in what is now central Brazil. They included the Timbira, Kayapó, Suyá, Xavante, Xerente, and Kaingang.

Food

Many Rainforest peoples combined farming with hunting, fishing, and gathering. Among their game animals were deer, tapirs, peccaries, monkeys, birds, large rodents, and turtles. Their crops included cassava and other tubers and roots, corn, beans, squash, tropical vegetables and fruits, and tobacco. The cassava they grew was mostly the bitter type, which contains a poison. The Indians developed a way to remove the poison and used cassava flour for baking bread.

Despite the rainforests' lush growth, the soil was generally not good for farming. Heavy rainfall leached nutrients out of the soil. Tribes who lived along the Amazon and other rivers, however, had good soil and farmed intensively. Along the riverbanks the land flooded seasonally, and the floodwaters enriched the soil with silt from the rivers. The Indians who lived along the floodplains stored harvested crops to eat during the flood season. They also fished and hunted, and some kept turtles in corrals. Fish and shellfish formed an important part of the diet of coastal communities. Away from the rivers and coasts, Indians probably relied more on hunting and on gathering and cultivating fruits, berries, and nuts. Many scholars believe that the rainforests today have a higher proportion of trees that are useful to humans because of the Indians.

Today, Indians of the Rainforest commonly prepare their fields by slashing and burning the thick forest growth. They choose an area, cut a band of bark off the larger trees to kill them (a process called girdling), and then burn the remaining forest plants. After some years of farming, the soil becomes unproductive, so they abandon their villages and fields and establish new ones. Some scholars believe that slash-and-burn agriculture was less common before the Indians received steel axes from Europeans. It would have required great expenditures of time and labor to girdle trees and clear an area of the dense forest with stone axes. For this reason, Indians in some areas may have farmed cleared land for longer periods of time by enriching the soil.

Settlements and Housing

Overall, the immense Rainforest area was sparsely populated. In most of the territory, the Indians were

In swampy areas, the Warao Indians of northern South America built their thatch houses on stilts. A 17th-century engraving shows a Warao house in Guyana.

Clothing

In the hot, humid climate, most Rainforest Indians wore little or no clothing. They preferred to paint their bodies and faces with geometric designs or pictures of animals. Besides being decorative, the markings often had religious meanings or indicated one's clan or age group. The Indians may also have applied these paints to repel insects. Some peoples, such as the Mundurukú and many Arawak tribes, tattooed their bodies. To create a tattoo, they pierced the skin in a pattern with animal teeth or thorns and rubbed in a dye.

Rainforest Indians also adorned themselves with jewelry made of shells, nuts, wood, stones, and feathers. They often pierced their ear lobes, noses, and lips. Many Ge peoples, for example, wore large wooden or stone disks or plugs that stretched their lips or ear lobes. Indians of the area also wore colorful headdresses and cloaks made from the feathers of tropical birds. Tribes that wore clothes made cotton tunics, skirts, and belts.

Technology and Arts

The Rainforest Indians made almost all of their utensils and tools from plant or animal material. In much of the area stones for making axes, arrowheads, and other objects were scarce. Tribes in the west made some metal items. Some peoples in the Rainforest imported some stone, gold, and silver items from Andean cultures.

Rainforest peoples were very inventive. They developed many types of harpoons, arrows, traps, snares, and blowguns. Some used poisons such as curare on their arrows and blowgun darts. In fishing the Indians released poisons into streams to stun or kill the fish without making them inedible. Throughout the region, tribes built rafts and dugout canoes for river travel, a key form of transport. Using palm leaves and shafts of bamboo, they made many kinds of baskets and hampers as well as sifters, traps, fans, mats, and other household items. They also used looms to weave hammocks, baby slings, and other textiles.

Nomadic peoples often used gourds and calabashes as storage containers and drinking cups, but more settled groups produced pottery. Indians made a variety of ceramic goods such as pots, plates, jars, bottles, baked-clay cooking stoves, griddles, smoking pipes, ocarinas (spherical flutes), rattles, and statues. In some societies, numerous ceramic items were included in elaborate burials.

The earliest known pottery in the Americas has been found in the Amazon River basin. Pottery from the Pedra Pintada cave near Monte Alegre, Brazil, dates back some 5,000 to 7,500 years. Similarly ancient pottery was found at Taperinha, a large mound made of shells near Santarém, Brazil. The pottery at these sites consists mainly of simple bowls. Peoples in the Rainforest first began making pottery that was ornately decorated with animal motifs and geometric patterns about 4,000 to 2,000 years ago.

From the 1st millennium AD, many cultures made complex pottery painted in several colors. On Marajó

dispersed in numerous small tribes. Clusters of villages existed mainly along the coast and the floodplains of the principal rivers, particularly the Amazon. Many scholars believe that these villages sustained fairly large populations for long periods of time. Many of the villages were probably home to several hundred people. Some settlements likely had several thousand residents, and a few may have had tens of thousands or more. Among the larger settlements were those on Marajó Island, a vast island in the mouth of the Amazon River, and at what is now the city of Santarém, Brazil. The latter was a settlement of the Tapajó chiefdom, which existed from about AD 1000 to 1550. The culture on Marajó Island lasted from about AD 400 to 1300.

Houses in the Rainforest were typically made of log frames covered with palm leaves or grass. Some peoples built large rectangular communal houses called *malocas*. Others built large roofed enclosures with an open side facing a central yard. Both these and the *malocas* could hold 200 or more individuals, even an entire tribe. Each family had its own living space. Other groups built one large communal house for adolescent boys and men, and either another large communal house or smaller houses for women and children. Regardless of the form of housing, hammocks were often the only furniture.

In several areas that flooded seasonally, including Marajó Island, Indians built settlements on top of man-made earthen mounds. Often earthen causeways (elevated roads) connected the mounds. Some villages also had fortifications such as moats or palisades, high fences made of sharpened poles.

Island, for instance, Indians created sophisticated pottery with red and black designs painted on a white background. They also engraved designs into the surface of the clay and carved them in low relief. Often animal and human figures modeled in clay were attached to the pottery. The pottery included bowls, plates, jars, statues, and stools. Like many other groups in the Rainforest, these Indians also made ceramic urns in which they buried the bones of their dead. Other peoples known for their fine pottery included the Omagua of the upper Amazon and the Tapajó.

In several places in the Rainforest, Indians built extensive public works made of earth. Thousands of mounds have been found in the area, and more were still being discovered in the 21st century. Mounds and clusters of mounds commonly served as platforms for houses and as cemeteries. Other mounds, including some shaped like people and animals at Sangay in eastern Ecuador, may have been monuments for ceremonial purposes. Many of the mounds are small, but the largest ones are tens of feet high and cover many acres. Inside, the earthen mounds often have fill layers of household refuse and large amounts of broken pottery. Along the coasts there are also numerous mounds made mainly of shells, not dirt.

The Indians also built earthen causeways and roads and maintained paths through the forest. People of the Moxos Plains of what is now eastern Bolivia built at least 1,000 miles (1,600 kilometers) of causeways. To create shortcuts for canoe travel across meandering rivers, Rainforest Indians built earthen canals. They also used canals for irrigation and drainage.

In swamps and seasonally flooded savannas, Indians built numerous raised fields—clusters of earthen platforms, ridges, or mounds on which they grew crops. Such fields kept the crops dry, so their roots did not rot. They also allowed farmers to improve the soil by aerating and enriching it. Drainage canals surrounding the fields collected nutrient-rich runoff, which the farmers reapplied to the soil.

Society

Many scholars believe that complex societies known today as chiefdoms developed in several places in the Rainforest. The earliest of these societies probably arose some 2,000 years ago. Many of the chiefdoms were clustered along the Amazon, Orinoco, and other main rivers. The villages were densely populated. Some chiefdoms had territories that stretched for thousands of square miles and included both main settlements and colonies. These societies were headed by "chiefs," but they varied greatly in their degrees of central organization. In those with the greatest central administration, a paramount chief had authority over many local chiefs to control an entire region. Those societies were warlike and fought to expand their territory. Some chiefdoms seem to have had ranked social classes, with nobles, commoners, servants, and slaves captured in warfare. Warriors, craftspeople, and others specialized in performing particular types of labor. In some societies, women as well as men were

To pick the fruit of a peach palm tree, a Yanomami man of the Amazon Rainforest ties poles to the thorny trunk as a climbing aid.

able to become high-ranking chiefs and leaders of religious rituals.

Many of the chiefdoms produced abundant corn and other crops and made tools, fine pottery, and other crafts on a large scale. The Indians produced some of these items for trade. Extensive trade networks along the rivers linked far-flung chiefdoms within the Rainforest area. Rainforest societies also traded with groups in the Andes.

In other areas and in earlier times, peoples probably lived more like Indians of the Rainforest do today, in numerous smaller seminomadic groups. Their societies would not have had much central organization, and tribe members would have been mostly social equals.

Household communities and kinship groups in the Rainforest were based mainly on relations through either the male or female line. Tribes that traced their lineage through the male line were more numerous. Chiefs and high-ranking men were often allowed to have more than one wife. In many Rainforest cultures, young men and young women underwent elaborate initiation rites, involving difficult ordeals and tests, when they reached puberty.

Religion

Like Rainforest tribes today, the Indians of the area probably believed that their well-being depended on being able to control countless supernatural powers that inhabited objects, plants, animals, and nature in general. The Indians of the Rainforest often used stimulants and narcotics as part of their religious rituals. Some practices were reserved for the shaman, who performed magic rites and led religious ceremonies. The shaman was also thought to communicate with the spirits and to cure the sick. The Indians worshipped a variety of gods and in some tribes also chiefly ancestors. The Tapajó, for example, mummified the bodies of important people and venerated them as gods. In the chiefdoms, burials were often elaborate.

MARGINAL REGIONS

The culture area known as the Marginal Regions encompasses parts of South America where the land is "marginal," or not good for farming. It includes much of the south and a few isolated places in the north. The Marginal Regions were remote from the centers of great cultural development. The inhabitants were nomadic hunters, gatherers, and fishers who took advantage of the scarce natural resources available to them.

Peoples and Languages

The Marginal Regions were home to a variety of peoples who spoke many different languages. These Indians lived in several different environments, many of them quite harsh. The area was sparsely populated.

The rugged terrain of what is now southern Chile is deeply cut by fjords (narrow arms of the sea) and includes numerous islands. This cold, rainy, and wind-battered region was home to the Chono, Alacaluf, and Yámana. The dense forests made land travel very difficult and farming impossible, so these Indians lived a marine life on the coasts and islands.

The Tehuelche, Puelche, Querandí, and Charrúa occupied the vast steppes and plains of southern South America, mostly in Argentina. This region includes the cold, dry, brush-covered plains known as Patagonia as well as the grasslands known as the Pampas.

To the north, in the plains region called the Gran Chaco, lived the Abipón, Caduveo (Mbayá), Mocoví, Toba, and other Indians who spoke Guaycuruan languages. The region was also home to peoples who spoke other languages, including the Wichí, Vilela, Lengua, and Zamuco (Ayoreo). The Gran Chaco was very dry in winter, especially in the west. In the summer rainy season, however, many areas flooded, and it sometimes got very hot.

Some peoples in the tropical rainforests of Brazil and surrounding countries followed a nomadic lifestyle rather than living in farming villages like many neighboring groups. Among them were the Makú, Guahibo, Aché, Sirionó, and Botocudo. Some rainforest groups that anthropologists have traditionally considered to be nomadic hunter-gatherers, however, such as the Nambikwara, grew some crops and were nomadic for only part of the year, like many peoples of the Rainforest cultural area. Also, some scholars believe that nomadic or seminomadic peoples of the rainforest such as the Sirionó, Aché, and others lived more settled agricultural lives in earlier times, perhaps before being forced to flee from their territory by Europeans or other Indian groups.

Within the tropical forests, the lives of some nomadic groups centered on the rivers. These tribes, sometimes known as aquatic nomads, spent most of their time in canoes. Among them were the Yaruro, Mura, and Guató.

Food

Food sources varied throughout the Marginal Regions. Southern Chile was poor in game animals and edible plants, and its waters had few fish. The Indians who lived there gathered shellfish, fished, and hunted seals, sea otters, and marine birds such as ducks, penguins, and cormorants. They also used whales that had been stranded on the beaches.

The Indians of the steppes and plains also were mainly hunters. They hunted guanaco (a wild relative of the llama and alpaca), rhea (an ostrich-like bird), and

An Indian in Argentina uses a bola to hunt the large flightless bird known as a rhea, in an engraving of 1818. After the horse was introduced by Europeans, hunting and raiding on horseback became a way of life for many Indians of the Gran Chaco and steppes and plains regions.

National Library—Gianni Dagli Orti/The Art Archive

The Indians used caves for shelter if they were available. The peoples of southern Chile and the Gran Chaco made domed huts of bent poles covered with bark, skins, or brush. When the people moved on, they left the frame for others to use, taking only the skin coverings with them. Some peoples of the southern plains made a skin-covered hut known as a *toldo*. In the dry season, when they lived as nomads, the Nambikwara used a lean-to or camped under trees, sleeping on fire-warmed ground.

Clothing

Peoples of the Marginal Regions had little clothing. Forest hunters such as the Sirionó and Nambikwara, who lived in tropical climates, wore nothing. The southern nomads wore robes and moccasins or sandals made from guanaco skin. In the Gran Chaco some groups wore lighter robes made of fiber from the *caraguatá* plant in hot weather and warmer skin robes in the cold. Featherwork, armbands and leg bands, necklaces, and body painting were common in the Marginal Regions, as were earplugs, nose plugs, and lip plugs.

Technology and Arts

Because they were nomads, the hunters and gatherers had few material goods and relatively simple technology. They made their tools largely from wood, bark, bone, and sometimes stone. They hunted with traps, nets, clubs, bows and arrows, spears, and bolas. Bolas were used in the steppes and plains and the Gran Chaco. A bola consisted of stone weights attached to long, slender ropes. The hunter threw the bola around legs of a guanaco or rhea. Entangled in the ropes of the bola, the animal would fall. After the Spanish brought horses, bolas became very important because the hunters could swing them easily on horseback. In southern Chile, hunters harpooned seals, sea lions, and porpoises from bark canoes. They relied on canoes for almost all of their travel.

Leatherworking and fiber crafts were important in many groups. Some Indians wove fabric by hand. They used yarn spun from native cotton and palm fibers. In the Gran Chaco, the leaves of the pineapple-like plant *caraguatá* were an important source of fiber for thread. The Chono of southern Chile wove clothing and mats out of the shaggy fur of their dogs, combined with bark and plant fibers. Later, some peoples learned to weave with looms. They wove long strips of fabric for making armbands and leg bands and other decorations. Netting was used for making fishnets and bags for carrying goods. Basketry was common, and hunters of the steppes and plains used containers made of skins.

In many groups, pottery was little used because pots were difficult to transport. Peoples of the Gran Chaco, however, made some coiled pottery bowls, jars, and pots. They also used gourds and calabashes as containers.

Society

The nomads of the Marginal Regions lived in bands of various sizes. Depending on the available food resources, the bands could be large or very small.

smaller animals. They also gathered some roots, herbs, and fruits.

The Indians of the Gran Chaco relied mainly on gathering plant foods, such as edible pods, fruits, berries, and tubers. Palm and algaroba (carob) trees were important sources of food. Many Indians of the Gran Chaco also grew corn, cassava, beans, pumpkins, tobacco, and cotton on a limited scale in gardens. Some groups fished and hunted and collected honey and insects as well. Common game animals included peccary (similar to wild pigs), tapir, armadillo, deer, turtle, and rhea and other birds.

Tropical forest nomads made their livelihood by hunting, fishing, and gathering fruit and other foods from wild plants, especially palms. Some groups also gathered honey and the eggs of birds and turtles. During part of the year, the Sirionó and Namibkwara grew some crops such as corn, cassava, tobacco, and cotton. The aquatic nomads fished and hunted the reptiles called caimans and other water animals.

The Indians of the Marginal Regions cooked meat and fish directly on coals or put them into earth ovens. The ovens were lined with heated stones and covered with earth and coals. The Chono boiled food by placing heated stones in tightly woven baskets.

Settlements and Housing

Because the nomads of the Marginal Regions moved constantly, they did not establish permanent villages. Instead, they lived and traveled in bands, setting up temporary camps.

A Yámana woman stands outside her hut in southern Chile, in the mid-20th century.
Interfoto/Alamay

In southern Chile, where food was scarce, the Chono, Alacaluf, and Yámana traveled in small family bands. These bands consisted of parents and their children and sometimes also an older relative or two. They had no chiefs or other tribal leaders. At times, several families would gather to feast on a stranded whale or to hunt seals or sea lions together. Other groups who lived in small family bands included the Guató and, during the dry season, the Nambikwara.

Other nomads lived in larger bands of extended families or multiple families. Indians of the steppes and plains who hunted guanaco and rhea could do so more productively when many families cooperated in the hunt. Their multiple-family bands typically included about 40 to 100 people. Chiefs, generally chosen for their ability to settle conflicts, led the bands.

The introduction of horses transformed the lives of the Tehuelche, Puelche, Querandí, and Charrúa of the steppes and plains and many peoples of the Gran Chaco. Among the so-called "mounted" groups of that region were the Abipón, Mocoví, Caduveo, Toba, and Lengua. Traveling on horseback allowed the Indians to adopt new hunting techniques, to roam larger territories, and to form much larger bands, ranging from 500 to 1,000 people. A strong, proven leader could attract numerous followers to his band. These Indians began to hunt wild cattle as well as guanaco, rhea, and other large game. They frequently raided Spanish settlements for cattle, horses, weapons, and tools. They also raided other Indian peoples for livestock, crops, and goods and took captives as slaves.

Warfare between bands of Indians increased as the mounted groups began traveling and raiding over larger areas. Even before, war was common among some peoples. Several groups in the Gran Chaco had long-standing enemies. They fought to avenge wrongs done to members of their band and over territorial rights to hunting and fishing grounds. Warriors often took the scalps or skulls of people they killed as war trophies.

Throughout the Marginal Regions, the warriors were men. The men also generally did most or all of the hunting, fishing, and collecting of honey. In southern Chile, however, it was mostly the women who dove for shellfish. In most parts of the Marginal Regions the women gathered plants for food, fibers, medicines, and dyes. They usually prepared and cooked the food. They also processed fibers, wove baskets and fabric, and made containers out of gourds or clay. The men usually made most of the other tools and weapons. In some groups, the women were responsible for building the huts. The women also spent much of their time caring for their children.

Children learned by imitating older children and adults and by listening to the stories and advice of elders. Some groups raised their children to be very independent at an early age. By the age of four, for example, the children of southern Chile were already catching and cooking their own meals of shellfish or sea urchins. Adults of the Marginal Regions were generally affectionate and permissive with young children and did not punish them. Instead, they sometimes lectured or ridiculed children for misbehaving.

Religion

The peoples of the Marginal Regions had a great variety of religious beliefs. In southern Chile the Indians prayed to a supreme being for success in hunting and fishing. The peoples of the steppes and plains believed in a supreme being who created the world but then was no longer involved in human affairs. They also believed in good and evil spirits. Indians of the Gran Chaco and forest nomads such as the Aché did not believe in a supreme being but did believe in various spirits and had many myths.

Shamans, who led religious ceremonies, cured the sick, and protected the tribe from harm, were important in most groups, especially in the Gran Chaco. The shamans were thought to receive their healing powers from the ghosts of dead shamans and special guardian spirits.

SOCIAL AND POLITICAL ORGANIZATION

Most Native Americans lived in small communities that were democratic in structure. They did not organize themselves into strict social classes or choose autocratic leaders. Members of the community worked together to make important decisions. But exceptions to these general rules could be found throughout the Americas—for example, in the Southeast, the Northwest Coast, Middle America, and the Andes. Taken as a whole, Indian societies ranged from groups of a dozen or so people led by the most able in a given situation, all the way to the vast Inca Empire in which 12 million people were ruled by one person. Regardless of a particular society's overall population, its method for appointing leaders, or the role it gave social class, it survived because it worked well for the people at a particular time and in a particular place.

Families

The most important social group for most Indian people was the family. The concept of family meant different things to different tribes. It could mean a nuclear family—just parents and children. Or it could mean an extended family, which could include relatives such as grandparents, aunts, uncles, or cousins. For Indians who lived in villages or towns, relatives usually lived nearby so that they saw extended family members daily whether they lived in the same home or not.

The clan was a larger family group. Members of a clan might live in different villages, but they claimed descent from a common ancestor. Inheritance and relationship could be traced through either the male or female line. Clan members had certain obligations toward one another, such as providing hospitality to kin from other villages. All members of a clan considered themselves to be related. Therefore, men and women were required to marry outside their clan.

Marriage customs differed from tribe to tribe. As a rule they were the result of mutual agreement by the husband-and wife-to-be. Often the bridegroom gave some sort of present to the bride's family to compensate for the loss of her help. Divorce usually was easy if a couple could not get along, but the children did not suffer from the breakup of their parents' marriage. They usually continued to live in the home in which they had been born, and as members of a clan they could rely on their grandparents, uncles, aunts, and many other relatives for attention.

Bands

Groups of Indian families joined to form bands. The families in a band lived, worked, and traveled together, cooperating in such activities as food acquisition, security, ritual, and care for children and elders. Membership was generally based on a combination of kinship, marriage, and friendship, and leadership was informal. The size of a band depended on the available food resources. In places where food was particularly scarce, a band could consist of as few as 10 or 12 people. In other places a band might have as many as several hundred people. Bands sometimes came together for ceremonies or a group hunt.

Leaders from the Mohawk, Seneca, Onondaga, Oneida, and Cayuga tribes gather around the Huron prophet Dekanawidah to recite the laws of the newly formed Iroquois Confederacy.

The Granger Collection, New York

An engraving from the early 1500s shows warriors carrying Atahuallpa, the last Inca emperor. The Inca treated the emperor as a god on Earth.

Tribes

Another form of social organization was the tribe. A tribe was made up of a number of bands or villages and typically had a population of several hundred to a few thousand people. Members of a tribe were usually linked by ties of kinship, language, and cultural traditions. They shared land and worked together in trade, agriculture, house construction, warfare, and ceremonies.

To organize such activities for a larger number of people, tribes needed more formal leadership than in bands. A tribe was led by one or more people, who were usually chosen because of their ability and wisdom. These leaders, sometimes called chiefs, advised the people and attempted to settle their disputes. War chiefs led raids or military campaigns. A group called the tribal council discussed and acted upon important matters. Like the concept of the family, the concept of the tribal council meant different things to different tribes. In many tribes it comprised the tribe's leaders and elders and might include men, women, or both. In other tribes it consisted of all of the adults or all of the adult women and married men.

Confederacies

Groups of tribes sometimes joined together to form confederacies. These alliances were often very complex political organizations. They generally took their name from the most powerful member tribe—for example, the Iroquois Confederacy and the Creek Confederacy. The usual reasons for forming a confederacy were to create peace in a region or to fight a common enemy.

The Iroquois Confederacy was the most elaborate political organization to be observed by Europeans among the Northern American Indians. In about 1570 the Mohawk, Seneca, Onondaga, Oneida, and Cayuga tribes (all of the Iroquoian language family) created this confederacy to promote peace among themselves. Tradition credits Dekanawidah, a Huron prophet, and Hiawatha, an Onondaga chief, with bringing the tribes together. The English called this league the Five Nations, and later the Six Nations, after the Tuscarora were admitted in 1722. The Iroquois called it the Brethren of the Longhouse.

The founders of the Iroquois Confederacy set up the framework of a code of laws that, though unwritten, had the force of a formal constitution. The Great Council, which met each year in the village of Onondaga, was its governing body. The council consisted of 50 sachems, or peace chiefs, who represented clans and villages. Each tribe had one vote, and everyone had to agree before a decision could be made.

Chiefdoms

Tribes were typically characterized by political and social equality among their members. Chiefdoms, while often the same size as tribes, were different because they had social classes with membership based on birth. The ruling class consisted of chiefs, who governed during peacetime, and war leaders. Though war leaders usually achieved their position on the basis of personal accomplishment, a chief inherited his power. Usually, though not always, a chief's responsibilities also included being a high priest. The chief had absolute power in all matters, including religion. Chiefdoms were common in the Southeast, Central America, and the Northern Andes. Northwest Coast Indians also lived in hierarchical societies with an elite class of hereditary chiefs. They affirmed social status through ceremonies called potlatches, in which the host distributed property and gifts to guests according to their social rank.

States and Empires

Some chiefdoms were so successful that they grew larger and more complex. These societies were known as states, and they often governed a very large territory and population. Power was concentrated in the hands of an absolute ruler. Everyone else was ranked in a hierarchy of social classes. States typically sponsored large public works that smaller societies could not organize, such as road systems that were hundreds of miles long, major irrigation systems, and the building of enormous monuments.

In the Americas, as in the Old World, early states were able to expand and conquer neighboring groups through a combination of military might and persuasion. The persuasive element was often in the guise of an official state religion. The Aztec built up an empire that covered much of Mexico. The emperor wielded both political and religious authority. Below him were the priests and nobles, who helped to administer the empire. There were also classes of warriors, merchants, and artisans. At the bottom of society were serfs, indentured servants, and slaves. In South America the Inca ruled an empire that extended from present-day Ecuador to central Chile. The Inca believed their emperor to be descended from the sun god and treated him as a god on Earth.

LANGUAGE

The languages spoken in pre-Columbian America were remarkably numerous and diverse. The peoples north of Mexico spoke between 300 and 500 languages from more than 50 language families. More than 20 language groups were represented in California alone. South American Indians spoke more than 500 languages, and the peoples of Middle America had at least an additional 80 languages. By comparison, at the same moment in history, western Europe had only 2 language families and between 40 and 70 languages.

Some scholars have proposed that all American Indian languages are related—that is, that they share a common origin in the remote past. Because the Indians originally came to the Americas from Asia, scholars have looked for relationships between Indian and Asian languages. This research has not proven the theory of a common origin, however. Rather, the great diversity of Indian languages suggests that the Americas were populated by waves of migrants from distinct language groups. Although some Indian languages share features of structure, there is no feature shared by all. At the same time, there is nothing primitive about these languages. They display the same complexity as do the languages of Europe.

Classification

Scholars have classified the American Indian languages, grouping them into language families based on similarities in vocabulary and grammar. Indian languages in the same language family show clear historical connections comparable to those between Spanish, Greek, and German. But the fact that two languages are in the same family does not mean that persons speaking one of these languages could understand another, any more than Germans and Greeks understand each other's language. For example, many North American tribes of the central Plains spoke related Siouan languages, but members of one tribe could seldom understand the speech of their neighbors.

Vocabulary, Grammar, and Sounds

American Indian languages are rich in words and intricate in structure. Their vocabularies differ in ways that reflect the relative importance of certain concepts in the culture of the speakers. For instance, while English has words for "airplane," "pilot," and "flying insect," the Hopi language of North America's desert Southwest generalizes with a single term *masa'ytaka*, which roughly translates to "flier." But while English uses a single general term, "water," Hopi differentiates *pahe* "water in nature" from *keyi* "water in a container." Similarly, the horsemen of the North American Plains used many words to describe horses. In the Arctic, the word that means "meat" in Inuit and some Yupik languages from Greenland to Siberia means "fish" in southern Alaska and also in Aleut. In South America, speakers of Quechua, Aymara, and Araucanian languages had detailed vocabularies for plants of medical or dietary importance.

Plains peoples recounted tribal history with records called winter counts, which they painted on bison hides. On this Sioux winter count, the pictographs represent events from 1800 to 1871.

Interfoto/Alamy

The grammar of American Indian languages is characterized by diversity rather than common traits. At the same time, however, some characteristics are common enough to be considered typical of certain regions. In North American languages, for example, it is common to combine several small word elements to form a complex word. The small elements serve as nouns, verbs, adjectives, and adverbs, but none can be used as a stand-alone word. The complex word may carry the meaning of a whole sentence in English. This practice is especially common in Eskimo and Algonquian languages, but it is also found elsewhere. An illustration from the Algonquian family is the Menominee word *nekees-pesteh-wenah-neewaaw*, meaning "but I did see him on the way."

American Indian languages vary as much in their systems of pronunciation as they do in other ways. The languages of the Northwest Coast of North America are notable for the unusual richness of their sounds. A language like Tlingit has about 50 distinctive consonant and vowel sounds, called phonemes; by comparison, English has 35. In South American languages the number of phonemes varies from 42 in Jaqaru (in the Quechumaran family) to 17 in Campa (Arawakan). Jaqaru has 36 consonants, while Makushí (Cariban) has 11. The large number of consonants in many Indian languages is based on pronunciation techniques that differ from those of European languages. For example, Indian languages often use more tongue positions than do European languages. Many Indian languages have two types of sounds made with the back of the tongue— a *k* much like an English *k*, and a *q* produced farther back in the mouth.

Language Contacts

American Indian languages, like all languages in the world, have always existed in contact with other tongues. Before the arrival of Europeans, interaction between tribes resulted in the sharing of words and grammar in their languages. In Middle America, for example, Mayan languages gave words to Xinca, Lencan, and Jicaque, and Zapotecan languages gave words to Huastec and Yucatec.

In some cases a language spread through conquest. Quechua, originally spoken in small areas around Cuzco and in central Peru, expanded greatly under Inca rule. In some places Quechua existed alongside local languages, while in others it took their place. It was the official language of the Inca Empire, and groups of Quechua speakers were settled among other language groups. Many Indian languages in the Andes and the eastern foothills borrowed from Quechua. Similarly, in Middle America the Aztec spread their language, Náhuatl, widely as their empire grew. Some peoples borrowed words from Náhuatl while others adopted it altogether. Another example comes from the Caribbean. In Island Carib (an Arawakan language), borrowings from Carib (a Cariban language) have formed a special part of the vocabulary, properly used only by men. These words were adopted after the Island Carib speakers were defeated by the Carib.

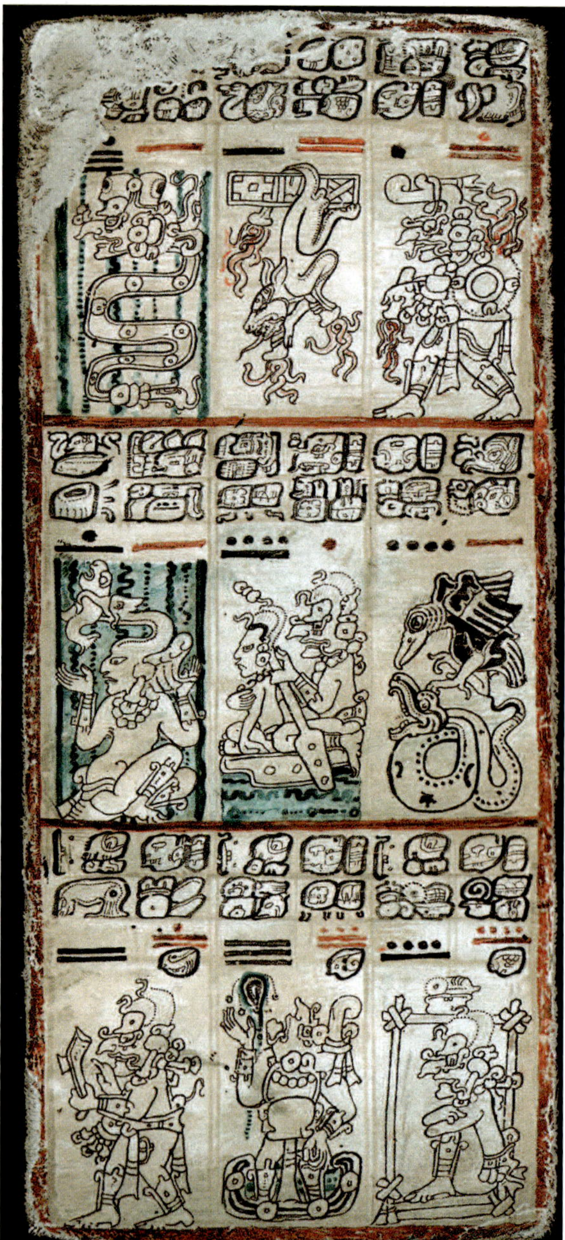

The Dresden Codex is one of the few collections of pre-Columbian Mayan hieroglyphic texts known to have survived the book burnings by the Spanish clergy during the 1500s. It contains astronomical calculations of exceptional accuracy.

After Europeans arrived, contact between Indian languages and the settlers' languages led to more borrowing. English, French, Spanish, Portuguese, and Russian all had an impact on Indian languages. In Middle America, for example, Indians have been taking words from Spanish since the Spanish conquest. Often the borrowed words are conjunctions and adverbs—for example, *ya*, meaning "already"; *pero*, "but"; *hasta*, "until"; *y*, "and"; and *o*, "or." In Aleut and in the Yupik of former Russian Alaska, there are many borrowings from Russian.

Among the Indians, the degree of adaptation to European culture varied greatly from tribe to tribe and even from one individual to the next. It typically depended on the tribe's (or person's) experience with Europeans. For example, the Karok of northwestern California suffered harsh treatment at the hands of whites. As a result, they borrowed only a few words from English—for example, *ápus* for "apples." However, they did create a large number of new terms in their language to describe new concepts—for example, a hotel is called *am-naam*, meaning "eating place."

South American Indian languages vary significantly in the number of loanwords from Spanish and Portuguese. Borrowing has been widespread in languages that have a long history of contact with the European languages, as is the case with Quechuan in the central Andes. Among Indians who strongly resisted the European conquest—for example, the Araucanians of Chile— loanwords are few.

While the Indians borrowed from European languages, the settlers, in turn, adopted many Indian words that are still used today. Many place-names, such as Massachusetts and Seattle, came from Indian languages. From Arawak, the first language encountered by the Spanish in the Caribbean, came the words canoe, maize, and tobacco, among many others. The Europeans commonly borrowed Indian names for native American plants and animals that lacked names in their own languages. The Spanish spoken in Middle America has taken many words from local languages, especially Náhuatl, the Aztec language. Many of the words borrowed into Spanish from Náhuatl have since passed into English. Among them are chili, chile, or chilli (Spanish *chile*), avocado (Spanish *aguacate*), chocolate, peyote, coyote, tomato (Spanish *tomate*), ocelot (Spanish *ocelote*), and guacamole. Notable Eskimo contributions to the vocabulary of English and other European languages are igloo and kayak.

In a few cases, language contact gave rise to a pidgin language. Combining elements of different languages, pidgin languages allowed peoples of different cultures to communicate with each other. They were used especially in trading. An example is the Chinook Jargon of the Northwest. Scholars believe that it originated among the Northwest Coast Indians, who traded widely among themselves and with communities to the east. A large proportion, if not most, of Chinook Jargon vocabulary was taken from the language of the Chinook people. The Indians probably developed the pidgin to communicate among themselves before contact with Europeans. After contact, Chinook Jargon came to be used by many whites in the fur trade. It absorbed many loanwords from French and English before dying out in the 20th century.

Indians of the Great Plains worked out a sign language so they could communicate with each other even if they spoke different languages. They could convey much information with hand gestures. Some of the gestures were so graphic they could be understood

Sequoyah invented a system for writing the Cherokee language.

by persons who did not know the signs.

Writing

The only true writing system in the Americas at the time of European contact was that of the Maya. Mayan writing was based on symbols called glyphs. Some glyphs were pictures that represented animals, people, and objects of daily life. Other glyphs represented parts of words or sounds. The Maya carved records on stone and also wrote them on a type of paper. The records noted events in the lives of Mayan rulers and their families. Other Middle American peoples, including the Aztec, also kept records. Unlike the Mayan system, however, Aztec writing could represent only numbers, dates, and names, not all speech.

North of Mexico, Indians used basic picture writing until Europeans arrived. Picture writing aided memory and helped to communicate ideas. It has been found in all parts of North America. Some examples were painted or carved on rock cliffs, on walls of caves, and on huge boulders. Picture writing was also done on portable materials. Many Plains Indians kept records of the past by drawing pictures or symbols of important events on bison hides. Such records are known as winter counts.

Written language arose in the north after European contact. Perhaps the most famous system is that invented in the 1800s by Sequoyah, a Cherokee. It is not an alphabet but a syllabary, in which the symbols stand for sounds in the Cherokee language. To create the symbols, he adapted letters from English, Greek, and Hebrew.

RELIGION

By necessity, American Indians devoted much of their time to day-to-day problems on which their survival depended, such as how to produce enough food, avoid illness, and avoid or win in war. Because the world can be unpredictable, religion was also a dominant force in their lives. Indian religious beliefs and practices influenced all aspects of their everyday existence, from educating children to building homes, farming, hunting, warfare, and medicine.

Indians often claim that their traditional ways of life do not include "religion." They find the term difficult, often impossible, to translate into their own languages. This fact points to differences between Indian and Western views of what religion is. Western cultures consider the spiritual world to be supernatural—that is, beyond, above, or outside both nature and the human realm. Indian cultures, however, consider the natural and the supernatural to be inseparable. The spiritual is ever-present in the world in which humans live.

Beliefs

Indian religions were as diverse as the rest of their cultures, with many unique traits arising in different areas and at different times. Some beliefs, however, were widespread and typical of Indian religion more generally. Most Indians believed in a supernatural force that was present in all things. Among the Algonquian peoples, this force was known as *manitou*. The Iroquois called it *orenda*, and the Dakota (Sioux), *wakanda*. This force, commonly called the Creator, was the source of the world and all of the other spirits therein. The other

spirits (or souls) inhabited humans as well as animals, plants, rocks, mountains, lakes, the sun, the winds, and other natural objects and phenomena. The Indians thought these spirits helped people that they liked and injured those who offended them. This belief system is called animism. The spirit world also included departed relatives as well as yet-to-be-born human beings. Religion was the way that the Indians related to all these spirits.

Many Indians believed that every individual could have a personal relationship with one or more spirits. When faced with a critical problem or decision, they generally sought help from the spirit world. The most common way to seek help was to undertake a vision quest. Many people tried their first vision quest as they entered adolescence, at about age 10 to 15. The quest typically involved fasting and praying for several days in an isolated location. In some cultures the participant would watch for an animal that behaved in a significant or unusual way. In others the participant discovered an object (often a stone) that resembled some animal. In the most common form, the person had a dream (the vision) in which a spirit-being appeared. Upon receiving a sign or vision, the person returned home and sought help in interpreting the experience. Among many peoples, the spirit that appeared in the vision quest became the participant's lifelong totem, guardian, or advisor. Such spirit-beings were usually animals. The Northwest Coast wood-carvers put the sacred animals on totem poles, while Plains Indians painted them on tepees.

For the Indians, participation was a more important

Hopi artist Fred Kabotie painted this picture of the best-known ceremony of his people—the Snake Dance. The Snake and Antelope societies perform it after days of secret rites in their kivas. The Antelope priests dance and shake rattles. Each Snake priest takes a snake from the leaf bower and dances with it in his mouth. The collector drops the snakes into a ring of sacred meal. Then the priests place them in the desert to carry prayers for rain to the gods.

Fred Kabotie

part of religion than belief. People did not typically argue about religious truths. Good-hearted participation in ceremonies and the everyday work of the community was the main requirement of a spiritual life. However, knowledgeable people with considerable life experience could informally discuss theology.

Generosity was a religious act as well as a social one in native cultures. People were taught to give in imitation of the generosity of the many spirits that provided for humans. The value of generosity was perhaps most dramatically shown in the potlatch of the Northwest Coast peoples, in which property and gifts were ceremonially distributed.

Shamans and Priests

People who had special powers to contact the spirits were known as shamans. They could be men or women of any age from childhood onward. Among many tribes they held a prominent place in society. Shamans acquired their supernatural power through a personal experience, such as a vision or a dream. They usually underwent initiation rituals as well.

Indians believed that shamans could control the weather, foretell the future, bring success in warfare and food gathering, and ease childbirth. In some cultures they were thought to guide the souls of the dead to their new home. South American shamans could perform sorcery, or witchcraft; they could, for example, become animals and drink the blood of their enemies.

The main task of shamans, however, was healing the sick. For this reason, they were sometimes called medicine men or medicine women. Some treatments included the use of roots and herbs as medicines. But Indians believed that some illnesses could be cured only by removing a foreign object from the body. In these cases the shaman often "removed" a symbolic object, such as a stone or arrowhead, through sleight of hand. Some groups, such as the Eskimo, believed that illness could result from the capture of the soul by a ghost. The shaman was said to undertake a journey to heaven or to the depths of the sea to retrieve the sick person's soul and restore it to its body. A shaman's performance was typically dramatic, and the cure was believed to be miraculous.

In some tribes shamans were organized into medicine societies. An example was the Iroquois False Face Society, whose members wore masks carved from living trees. In spring and fall they went from house to house shaking turtle-shell rattles and chanting to drive away evil spirits that caused disease. Another example was the Grand Medicine Society, or Midewiwin, of the Ojibwa and other Northeast Indians (*see* sidebar, "Grand Medicine Society," page 33).

Priests played an important role in the religious life of some peoples. Unlike shamans, who usually worked with individuals, priests performed public ceremonies. Among the Inca, Maya, Aztec, and some Southeast Indians, priests were political as well as spiritual leaders.

Ceremonies

Individuals, villages, and tribes used a great variety of ceremonies to seek help from the spirits. Many of these

A Tlingit shaman of the Northwest Coast waves a rattle over a sick patient. Shamans were believed to wield supernatural power obtained through contact with the spirit world.

ceremonies continue to be a feature of Indian life today. Ceremonies could be held on behalf of either an individual or the community as a whole. The Navajo and the Pueblo, neighboring peoples of the Southwest culture area, illustrate these contrasting approaches. Most traditional Navajo ceremonies were undertaken on behalf of individuals in response to specific needs, such as healing. Most Pueblo ceremonies, however, were held by the community for its shared benefit, and they were scheduled according to natural cycles.

Important ceremonies could last for many days and were usually preceded by periods of fasting and prayer. Preparation for a ceremony often included purification through sweating. Indians built a small, airtight structure, called a sweat lodge, for this purpose. Hot stones were placed in the building and sprinkled with water to make steam. People stayed inside until they were perspiring freely. Then they rushed out and plunged into a cold stream, washing away any impurities of body or mind. This treatment was also used as a cure for disease.

Indian ceremonies involved singing, dancing, and often the use of sacred objects. These objects, typically kept by shamans, were believed to have spiritual power. Among them were masks, drums, dolls, feathers, rocks, ears of corn, or parts of animals' bodies. Collections of sacred objects were sometimes held together in medicine

The Sacred Pipe, or calumet, was revered as a holy object among the Northeast Indians and the Plains Indians. The pipe was smoked in personal prayer and during communal ceremonies.

bundles. A central sacred object of the Northeast Indians and Plains Indians of North America was the Sacred Pipe, or calumet. Some tribes traced the origin of the pipe back to the time of creation. Smoking it was a sacrament that was believed to put humans in contact with the spirits. In South America the shaman's rattle was a most sacred instrument. The Warao of Venezuela believed that the first shaman ascended to heaven and then brought the original rattle back to Earth.

Usually men and women conducted different kinds of ceremonies. The right to have a particular ceremony typically belonged to a group called a society. Some societies were restricted not only by sex but also by age. Because women were usually in charge of farming and gathering plants, their ceremonies were often meant to ensure that harvests would be good. Growing and collecting plant food was usually a group activity, so women's societies would perform their rituals in front of the whole community. Men, on the other hand, tended to be involved in individualistic pursuits such as hunting and raiding. Therefore, men often had a building or location out of the public eye where their societies met, various sacred objects were kept, and the male ceremonies were taught to boys.

State-level societies generally made sacrifices to gain favor of the gods. The sacrifice could be an object, a plant, an animal, or a human. The Aztec sacrificed thousands of people each year by offering their hearts to the sun god. Some Inca rituals also included human sacrifice.

Rites of Passage

The array of Indian ceremonies included many that marked the passage of individuals from one life stage or status to another. These rites of passage generally took place at childbirth, puberty, marriage, initiation into a secret society, and death.

Pregnancy and childbirth were an especially dangerous time for expectant mothers. They typically refrained from eating foods or joining in activities that were thought to be dangerous to themselves or their pregnancies. Among other childbirth rituals was the couvade, which was especially common in South America. It brought the father into the birth process by having him imitate labor pains and the delivery of the child. The naming of a newborn child was a major event for many Indian peoples, though a child's initial name might later be changed. Reasons for doing so varied widely, including having received a name that did not fit one's personality or that had proven unlucky.

Ceremonial initiation into adulthood was widely practiced among the Indians, for both males and females. The transition was often marked by a vision quest. In some tribes nearly all young people underwent a quest, while in other groups only boys took part. For girls, the first menstruation was often accompanied by ritual. Many peoples believed that powerful spirits were acting on the girl to create the changes in her body. She was believed to be either especially empowered, and therefore potentially dangerous on a spiritual level, or in danger herself. To protect the girl and the community, she was isolated in living quarters some distance from the village for days, weeks, or even a year. The rituals during this time varied. Among the Gwich'in of the Subarctic, a girl wore a pointed hood that caused her to look down toward the ground. Other ceremonial precautions included a rattle of bone that was supposed to prevent her from hearing anything, a special stick to use if she wanted to scratch her head, and a special cup that should not touch her lips.

The Baniwa of Brazil covered the girl's body with heron feathers and red paint and hid her inside two baskets. The elders delivered dramatic speeches and whipped the girl to open her skin. Pepper was touched to her lips; then a small hole was made in the dirt floor, and she spat into it. She was introduced to various foods, over which chants were sung. After the baskets were opened, the girl stepped out and was decorated and presented anew to the group to the accompaniment of musical instruments and chants.

Death was an important life passage. Indians considered death to be a transition and not an ending. Many peoples thought of human beings as complex beings that bound together different kinds of essences, breaths, or spirits. After death, it was believed, some of these elements could be harmful for living people to encounter without the protection provided by ceremonies.

Methods of disposing of the dead varied among the tribes. Burial in the ground was most commonly practiced. In the North American Southwest, bodies were sometimes placed in caves where they dried, or mummified, in the dry air. On the northern Plains a common practice was to place the dead in trees or on scaffolds for a period of months, after which the remains would be buried. On the Northwest Coast they might be laid in canoes set high on posts. Cremation was practiced by numerous tribes. Usually the ashes were buried in pottery vessels. Almost always, domestic utensils, food, and the ornaments, implements, and other personal belongings of the departed were placed with the remains.

ARTS

Most Indians did not consider art to be a vocation in and of itself. Many Native American languages even lack a term meaning "art" or "artist." To describe a beautiful basket or a well-carved sculpture, the Indians usually used such terms as "well-done" or "effective." Similarly, music and dance largely served religious purposes, and storytelling preserved tribal history and traditions. Yet in all of these forms, the Indians displayed degrees of craftsmanship and creativity that raised their creations to the level of art.

Visual Arts

Many Indian art objects were meant to be functional—for example, to act as a container or a piece of clothing. As in all cultures, art often reflected the social organization or values of the people who produced it. For example, societies with a strong military found their major art forms in the world of weaponry and battle

A Navajo shaman creates a sand painting. Such paintings serve religious—especially healing—purposes. They feature traditional, symbolic designs made by trickling crushed, colored sandstone, charcoal, or pollen on a background of sand. A sand painting is destroyed after the ceremony for which it was created.

Ted Spiegel/Corbis

gear. The Plains, Aztec, and Inca civilizations all reflected the dominant warrior culture in their arts. Cultures in which priests were in charge of religion, such as the Maya, made more ceremonial art than those in which religion was the business of the individual.

Some items were reserved solely for religious uses, and some were only for secular needs. Many objects served a dual function: normally they were used for everyday household purposes, but under a different set of circumstances they could fulfill a religious function. In the right hands, an everyday article might release its supernatural power, calling upon unseen forces to aid its owner. A Crow warrior of the Plains, for example, might draw supernatural swiftness and strength from a symbolic drawing or sacred eagle feathers adorning his rawhide shield.

For the Indians, ritual was often vital to the process of creating art. Indian artists did not care only about their final product. Rather, they paid much attention to the creative process itself and interacted with their materials at all stages of creation. The Iroquois False Face mask, for example, had to be carved from the trunk of a living tree, and the mask was believed to be alive. The tree was ritually addressed before the carver began, and the mask and the tree were "fed" tobacco before the two were separated.

Although they often traded with others for materials from distant lands, Indians usually worked with the materials native to their homelands. Thus, they produced art that reflected their environment. Those peoples living in heavily forested regions, for example, became gifted sculptors in wood. In places where clay was plentiful, the Indians became skillful potters. Tribes living in the grasslands became fine basket weavers. Other natural materials mastered by the Indians include jade, turquoise, shell, metals, stone, birch bark, porcupine quills, deer hair, feathers, elk teeth, bear and cougar claws, llama dung, and sea lion whiskers. All were used by artists to lend color or texture to their work.

Some Indians took their decorative designs from natural forms. Others preferred geometric patterns. Some unique designs resulted from artists trying to re-create sights seen during dreams or visions. Certain symbols appeared in the art of various peoples, even over a wide area. In Middle America, for example, the deity Quetzalcóatl—the Feathered Serpent—can be found in some form in almost every culture.

Dance

Most Native American dances were held for ceremonial reasons. By honoring the holy, whether a spirit-being, a single Creator, or several gods, the Indians hoped to gain help and favor. Shamans danced to seek aid for the sick. Hunters danced the deer dance or the buffalo dance

Miguel Salgado

The deer dance performed by the Yaqui people of northwestern Mexico imitates the movements of the animal, which they consider sacred. On his legs the dancer wears rattles made from moth cocoons and filled with seeds or bits of broken seashells. Around his waist he wears deer-hoof rattles. In his hands he carries a pair of gourd rattles.

to honor and attract game. Farmers held dances to bring rain or to make the corn grow or ripen. Certain dances dramatized stories from the history or mythology of the tribe. Other ceremonies were held when children arrived at manhood or womanhood or to initiate them into the religious or secret societies of the tribe.

The roles of the participants in an Indian dance were often complex. Everyone who attended the performance participated in some way, either through active involvement in music and dance or by witnessing the event. In addition, unseen spirit-beings were usually thought to take part. Lead dancers and singers might be political as well as spiritual leaders of the community. Men or women alone began some dances, and the other sex might then join in. Men often symbolized aggressive supernatural beings and rain-bringing gods, whereas women symbolized fertility. In Iroquois ceremonies, women represented the Three Life-Giving Sisters—that is, the spirits of corn, beans, and squash. There were also separate roles for men and women in the animal realm. Ottawa and Ho-Chunk women imitated the flight of wild swans and geese, whereas Iroquois and Pueblo men represented eagles. Among the Yaqui of the Southwest, the solo deer dancer was always a man.

In many tribes there were clowns—representations of chaos—among the dancers. Their antics reinforced social values by demonstrating incorrect behavior and its consequences, which might range from embarrassment to the destruction of the world.

Music

Singing and music accompanied every public ceremony as well as the important events in an individual's life. For Native Americans, music, dance, and spirituality were tightly interwoven. They traced the origin of their traditional music to the time of creation, when songs were given to the first people by the Creator and by spirit-beings. Sacred narratives described the origins of certain musical instruments, songs, dances, and ceremonies. Songs were passed down by word of mouth from generation to generation. This is known as the oral tradition.

Indian music varied from group to group in vocal style, melody, rhythm, and instruments, among other elements. But some broad characteristics were typical of certain regions. Indians of Northern America emphasized singing, accompanied by percussion instruments such as rattles or drums, rather than purely instrumental music. Northern American musical genres included lullabies, songs given to individuals by their guardian spirits, curing songs, songs performed during stories, songs to accompany games, ceremonial and social dance songs, and songs to accompany work or daily activities. Mexican and Central American Indians emphasized instrumental music more than singing. Much of the traditional music from this region was performed by groups that used several different instruments. In South America, music was central to traditional healing practices. While each community had its own preferred vocal sound, many South American Indians used special

Two Dakota Sioux sing and play hand drums consisting of an animal-skin head stretched across a wooden frame. Plains peoples used such drums to accompany hand games, personal songs, or curing songs. The singer usually held the drum in his left hand and struck the head with a stick held in his right hand.

Library of Congress, Washington, D.C.;
Edward S. Curtis (neg. no. LC-USZ62-46980)

Without written languages, American Indians relied on storytellers to pass down myths, folktales, and tribal histories through the oral tradition.

techniques to mask the natural voice. This practice symbolized the presence of spirit-beings.

Some Native Americans considered songs to be property. They developed formal systems of musical ownership, inheritance, and performance rights. On the Northwest Coast of North America, certain songs were the exclusive property of clans and societies. Individuals in the clan, however, could sell or even give away songs that they created. Peoples of northwestern Mexico believed that certain songs belonged to the shaman who received them in a dream. After the shaman's death, however, those songs became available to the community as a whole.

A great variety of musical instruments accompanied dance and song. These included drums, rattles, whistles, flutes, and notched sticks rasped on bones. Bull-roarers, made of a wooden slab tied to a string or rawhide thong, were whirled in the air to create sound. The Indians made their instruments of materials at hand. In Northern America, Plains drums had heads of painted bison hide or horsehide. Northwest Coast tribes used wooden boxes, and their rattles were made from wood or native copper. The Pueblo and other farming tribes made gourd rattles. The Mixtec and Maya of Middle America struck turtle shells with a stick or antler. The Warao of the South American rainforest used calabashes to make an unusually large rattle that required the use of both hands.

Many instruments carried symbolic significance. Among certain groups of eastern North America, for example, the sound of a gourd rattle symbolized the sound of Creation. The sound of the drum had symbolic meaning for many peoples. A rapid drumbeat in certain songs from the Northwest Coast signified the transformation of a Thunderbird spirit into a human state. Wind instruments were strongly linked with shamanism and sacred ceremonies because many Indians associated wind with the spirits as well as with breath, the essence of life. North American Indian flutes might be carved with symbolic designs or decorated with feathers and sacred objects.

Storytelling

Folktales were always an important part of the social and cultural life of the Native Americans. As they gathered around a fire at night, people could be transported to another world through the talent of a good storyteller.

Every tribe had its legends of the origins and history of the tribe. There were also many stories of animals and mythical beings that could assume human form and yet retain some of their own particular traits. These stories both entertained children and taught them what kinds of behavior and actions were appropriate and inappropriate. Many stories were told about Coyote, Raven, Rabbit, and Fox, who were all thought of as tricksters. A trickster is a crafty character that usually gets caught in his own schemes. Coyote, for instance, was often said to be hungry and greedy, and no matter how hard he tries to trick the other animals into giving him food, he usually ends up still hungry—or with terrible indigestion. Like songs, Indian stories and myths were passed down through the centuries as part of the oral tradition.

The effect of a story came not only from the tale itself but also from the imaginative skill of the narrator. The storyteller often added gestures and songs and occasionally adapted a particular tale to suit a certain culture. One frequent adaptation was the repetition of incidents. The description of an incident would be repeated a specific number of times. The number of repetitions usually corresponded to the number associated with the sacred by the culture. In American Indian traditions the sacred was most often associated with groups of four (representing the cardinal directions and the gods associated with each) or seven (the cardinal directions and gods plus those of skyward, earthward, and center). The hero would kill that number of monsters, or that many brothers would go out on the same adventure. This type of repetition was very effective in oral communication, for it firmly set the incident in the minds of the listeners.

(Top row, left to right) Werner Forman/Corbis; By courtesy of the Linden-Museum für Volkerkunde, Stuttgart, Germany; Collection of the Newark Museum, New Jersey; (middle row, left) Courtesy of the trustees of the British Museum; (middle row, center) Courtesy of the Museum of the American Indian, Heye Foundation, New York; (middle row, right, clockwise) Courtesy of the Denver Art Museum, Colorado; Courtesy of the University Museum of Archaeology and Ethnology, Cambridge; Courtesy of the Denver Art Museum, Colorado; (bottom) Adolf Spohr Collection, Gift of Larry Sheerin—Buffalo Bill Historical Center, Cody, Wyoming/The Art Archive

American Indian artists produced a great variety of objects using diverse styles and materials. Examples include: (top row, left to right) an Inca textile depicting a god, from the Central Andes; an Iroquois buckskin bag decorated with porcupine quills and deer hair, from the Northeast; a Navajo blanket, from the Southwest; (middle row, left) a wooden Haida thunderbird, from the Northwest Coast; (middle row, center) a wooden Eskimo mask, from the Arctic; (middle row, right, clockwise) Pueblo pottery, from the Southwest; a Diaguita copper plaque depicting a man between two cats, from the Central Andes; a Karok twined basket, from California; (bottom row) a Hidatsa rawhide shield decorated with a grizzly bear figure and eagle feathers, from the Plains.

SPORTS AND GAMES

American Indians took part in many sports and games. Both men and women participated in physical contests as well as games of chance. Children had their own games and toys.

Physical Contests

The "ball play" popular throughout eastern North America has become the modern sport lacrosse. People trained extensively for this game because tribes often played it against one another. The ceremonial dancing and feasting before the games may be compared to modern American football pep rallies. Intervillage footraces were held by the Pueblo, and both foot- and horse racing were popular among the Plains tribes.

Ring-and-pole and hoop-and-pole games were popular in many areas. The players shot poles or spears through stone rings or into a netting on a rolling hoop. Snow snake was popular among northern tribes. The players hurled a long stick, sometimes painted to resemble a snake, to see who could send it farthest over the ice or frozen ground.

Shinny was a hockeylike game among women in many North American tribes. It was played with a curved stick and a ball. Plains women used a small buckskin-covered ball of bison hair. Women of the Southwest played a kind of football. They kicked a small ball around a long course. In early times the game was thought to have magical powers, such as protecting the fields against sandstorms. Women in the Plains and the Plateau enjoyed a game like Hacky Sack, in which a small ball was kept aloft without using the hands.

Games of Chance

Indians of all tribes liked guessing games. The most common was called the hand game. A player held two bone or wooden cylinders, one plain and the other marked. His opponents attempted to guess which hand held the unmarked piece. One camp might compete against another. Backers lined up beside the players, shouting and singing to distract them. A person might lose his horses, buffalo robes, or everything he owned in the excitement.

Numerous games used markers resembling dice. The markers typically had two faces that were distinguished by colors or markings. Common among northern tribes was the bowl game. Players tossed marked peach or plum pits in a bowl and bet on the outcome.

Children's Play

Indian children in the past played much as children play today. Girls played with dolls dressed in the costumes of their people, and their mothers, aunts, and grandmothers often made them child-sized homes to play in. Boys shot small arrows from toy bows and crept through the woods pretending to be hunters or warriors. Children also had tops, stilts, slings, and other toys and made cat's cradles with string.

Children learned from games then as they do now. Archery, target practice, and footraces taught skills needed by hunters. Pueblo children learned about their people's ancestral spirits from their kachina dolls (*see* sidebar, "Kachinas," page 64).

George Catlin's painting Ball Play of the Choctaw *shows the tribe playing a game that later became known as lacrosse.*

The Granger Collection, New York

PART III

LIFE AFTER EUROPEAN CONTACT

Although native peoples had already lived on the land for thousands of years, Europeans knew nothing of the Americas until 1492. In that year Christopher Columbus landed in what became known as the New World. Sailing under the flag of Spain, he had been searching for a sea route from Europe to Asia. His chance discovery was one of the great events in the history of the world—with far-reaching implications for both the Europeans and the native peoples.

King Ferdinand and Queen Isabella of Spain sponsored Columbus' voyage in the hope of spurring trade with South Asia, with its markets of spices and other valuable goods. Although Columbus did not find a new route to Asia, his journey nonetheless opened the way to overseas wealth. Spain would go on to conquer the Aztec and Inca empires, seizing great riches, and then to colonize the Southeast, the Southwest, and California in Northern America.

Other European countries sought their own opportunities in the New World. France focused mainly on creating income through trade and shipping. Beginning with Jacques Cartier's voyage of 1534, the French claimed dominion over parts of the Northeast, the Southeast, and the Subarctic. England was interested mainly in territorial expansion. In the early 1600s the English began establishing colonies along the Atlantic coast of North America from New England to Virginia. Later, in the 1700s, Russia occupied the northern Pacific coast to obtain rich sea-otter furs for trade with China.

The native peoples met the first Europeans with curiosity. The intentions of the newcomers were not always clear. Some Indian communities were approached with respect, and in turn they greeted the odd-looking visitors as guests. For many native peoples, however, the first impressions of Europeans were characterized by violent acts including raiding, murder, rape, and kidnapping. Traders often got the Indians drunk to take

advantage of them, and European diseases such as smallpox and tuberculosis wiped out whole tribes. Many Indian skills and much of Indian tribal identity were lost through the gradual adoption of European ways and increasing dependence on European goods.

A difference of attitudes over ownership of land was a major cause of conflict between the Indians and the Europeans. Unlike the Europeans, none of the native peoples had developed a system of private landownership. Instead, they practiced communal landownership. Within the boundaries of each tribe's territory, the land was used by all members of the tribe. No individual owned any of the land, and no one person, not even the tribal leader, could dispose of it. While European settlers thought they were obtaining permanent title to Indian lands by purchase, the Indians thought they were agreeing only to share or rent the land. This basic conflict between Indians and Europeans was only sharpened by differences in language, religion, and lifestyle.

Another source of conflict was that the Europeans did not consider themselves to be under the sovereignty of the Indian tribes on whose land they had settled. Instead, they claimed the land in the names of their mother countries. The European settlers began to mark off boundaries and to assert their land claims by the force of superior weapons and, eventually, by their far-greater numbers.

UNITED STATES

At the time of Columbus' arrival, there were probably about 1.5 million Native Americans in what is now the continental United States, though estimates vary greatly. The subsequent history of the American colonies and then the United States cannot be discussed without considering the role of the Indians. As a whole, the Indians were an important influence on the European cultures that took root in the New World. Native foods and herbs, methods of raising crops, war techniques, and words were among the many contributions of the Indians to their European conquerors. The lengthy and brutal conflict between Indians and whites caused by the westward expansion of the United States is one of the most tragic chapters in the country's history.

EARLY COLONIZATION

The level and the nature of interaction that different Native American peoples had with European explorers and settlers varied for several reasons. First, areas that were good for farming or ranching were generally most attractive to the Europeans. Thus, Indians who lived on rich agricultural land typically had more contact with Europeans than those who lived by hunting and gathering in more remote areas. In addition, the cultural backgrounds of the Indians influenced how they interacted with the Europeans. For example, Indian farmers living in stratified societies, such as the Natchez, engaged with Europeans differently than did those who lived in bands and relied on hunting and gathering, such as the Apache. Finally, the Indian experience of European contact was affected by the differing goals and methods of the various colonial powers.

The Southwest

After conquering the Aztec and Inca in Mexico and Peru, respectively, Spain turned its attention northward. In 1540 Francisco Vázquez de Coronado, the governor of Nueva Galicia province in western Mexico, began exploring the Southwest. Settlement efforts began in 1598, when Juan de Oñate led 400 settlers to a location near what is now El Paso, Texas.

The native peoples of the Southwest had never before experienced occupation by a conquering army. The Spanish troops were often brutal. They typically camped outside a town and then extracted heavy tribute in the form of food, labor, and women. Native communities that resisted these demands were often destroyed.

Missionaries came with the troops to convert the Indians to Roman Catholicism. They were often harsh in their methods as well. They were known to beat, dismember, torture, and execute Indians who tried to maintain their traditional religious practices. In response, the Indians staged a number of small rebellions from about 1640 onward. These culminated in the Pueblo Rebellion of 1680—a carefully organized revolt of Pueblo peoples against the Spanish missions and military posts. The Spanish fled to Mexico, leaving some 400 dead, including nearly all the priests.

The Spanish retook the region beginning in 1692, killing an estimated 600 native people in the initial battle. In later years the Southwest tribes engaged in a

The Choctaw, led by their chief Tuscaloosa, battle the Spanish explorer Hernando de Soto and his army in 1540 in what is now the U.S. state of Alabama. The battle resulted in the slaughter of several thousand Native Americans, one of the bloodiest single encounters between Europeans and native peoples in North America.

The Granger Collection, New York

variety of nonviolent forms of resistance to Spanish rule. Some Pueblo families fled their homes and joined Navajo and Apache foragers. Other Pueblo remained in their towns. They maintained their traditional cultural and religious practices by hiding some activities and combining others with Christian rites.

The Southeast

In 1540, the same year that Coronado entered the Southwest, Hernando de Soto was sent to establish Spanish control of the Southeast. At first the Indians treated de Soto and his troops as they would any large group of visitors, providing gifts to the leaders and food to the rest. In return, however, the Spanish often forced the Indians into slavery.

News of such treatment traveled quickly, and the de Soto expedition soon met with military resistance. Native warriors harassed the Spanish almost constantly and engaged them in many battles. Native leaders made a number of attempts to capture de Soto and the other leaders of his party, often by welcoming them into a walled town and closing the gates behind them. The Spanish troops responded to these situations with violence, typically storming the town and killing or capturing its residents.

The first permanent European settlement in the Southeast was St. Augustine, founded in 1565 in what is now Florida. As colonization continued, losses of people to capture, slaughter, and European diseases devastated the region's Native American population. The survivors were subjected to the missionaries and their brutal tactics. In addition, many Indians were kidnapped and transported to the Caribbean to be sold as slaves. Some Indians moved to the few benevolent Catholic missions to take advantage of the protection offered by resident priests. Others banded together for defense or fled to remote areas.

The Northeast

Beginning with Jamestown in 1607, the English established colonies along the Eastern seaboard of what became the United States. At first the Indians helped the English colonists establish settlements, raise crops, and adjust to living in an environment that was quite different from England's. Powhatan (Wahunsonacock), leader of an Algonquian-speaking confederacy in Virginia, and Massasoit (Wasamegin), leader of the Wampanoag Indians in New England, established generally peaceful trade relations with the English. But the spirit of friendship deteriorated as the expanding colonies pressed further into Indian territory, routinely breaking their boundary agreements.

By 1609 the region was experiencing a third year of severe drought. In response to English thievery (mostly of food), Powhatan prohibited the trading of food to the colonists. He also began to attack any colonists who left the Jamestown fort. These actions contributed to a period of starvation for the colony (1609–11) that nearly caused its abandonment.

After Powhatan's death in 1618, his brother and successor, Opechancanough, tried to force the colonists

Pocahontas

A familiar story about colonial times in North America recounts how Pocahontas, daughter of the powerful Indian leader Powhatan, saved the life of the English colonial leader John Smith. According to Smith's account, Powhatan's warriors had captured him and were about to put him to death. When Pocahontas pleaded with her father to spare him, Powhatan relented, and Smith was allowed to go free. Many historians doubt that the incident took place. But whether or not Pocahontas saved Smith's life, she was instrumental in maintaining peace between her people and the early Virginia settlers.

Pocahontas was a girl of age 10 or 11 when she first met the Jamestown colonists. She often brought food to the near-starving settlement. She also warned the colonists of proposed Indian attacks. In 1613, while visiting a tribe on the Potomac River, Pocahontas was abducted by Samuel Argall. He took her to Jamestown as a hostage. Relations between Powhatan and the Virginians had become strained, and Argall hoped to use Pocahontas to negotiate a peace between them.

In Jamestown the settlers treated Pocahontas kindly. She converted to Christianity and was given the name Rebecca. In 1614 she married the colonist John Rolfe. Both the Virginia governor, Sir Thomas Dale, and Powhatan agreed to the marriage. Afterward, peace prevailed between the English and the Indians as long as Powhatan lived.

In 1615 the Rolfes' only child, Thomas, was born. The next year the family, with several Native American attendants, sailed to England for a visit. The English were delighted with Pocahontas. The king and queen received her at the palace, and the bishop of London entertained her. In 1617 the Rolfes prepared to return to Virginia, but before they sailed Pocahontas fell ill, probably with lung disease. She died in March 1617 in Gravesend, England.

out of the region. In 1622 his men launched attacks against Jamestown that killed some 350 of the 1,200 colonists. The so-called Powhatan War continued off and on until 1644, eventually resulting in a new boundary agreement between the Indians and the colonists. The fighting ended only after a series of epidemics had devastated the region's native population, which shrank even as the English population grew. Within five years, colonists were once again trespassing in Powhatan territory.

Another early clash between Indians and whites took place in Connecticut in 1636, when colonists attacked the principal village of the Pequot. About 600 Indians were killed, and the Pequot tribe was virtually destroyed. In

Native Americans attack a Massachusetts village during King Philip's War of 1675–76. The bloody conflict temporarily devastated the colonial communities but eventually ended native military resistance to European colonization of the region.

1675 various Indian tribes in New England formed an alliance to resist white settlement. It was led by Massasoit's son Metacomet (or Metacom), who was called King Philip by the colonists. Metacomet's forces were at first victorious, but after a year of savage fighting they were defeated. Some 600 Europeans and 3,000 Indians had been killed.

In the eastern Great Lakes region, the Iroquois and the Huron competed bitterly with each other in the fur trade. The Iroquois formed an alliance with the English and the Dutch, and the Huron joined with the French. From the French the Huron acquired iron axes, which for a time gave them an advantage over the Iroquois. After 1620, however, the Iroquois obtained guns from the Dutch and the English, giving them the upper hand.

In the mid-1600s it became increasingly clear that beavers, the region's most valuable fur-bearing animals, had been overhunted to the point of extinction in the home territories of both the Iroquois and the Huron. The Iroquois blockaded several major rivers in 1642–49, essentially halting canoe traffic between the Huron and their trading partners in the Subarctic. In 1648–49 the Iroquois gained a decisive victory against the Huron and burned many of their settlements. In 1649 the Huron chose to burn their remaining villages themselves before retreating to the interior.

Having defeated the Huron to their north and west, the Iroquois took the so-called Beaver Wars to the large Algonquin population to their north and east, to the Algonquian territory to their west and south, and to the French settlements of the Huron lands. The Iroquois fought the alliances of these groups for the rest of the 1600s, finally accepting a peace agreement in 1701.

COLONIAL RIVALRIES AND NATIVE ALLIANCES

By the end of the 1600s the Indians' struggles for their land became caught up in a series of wars between England and France for dominance in North America. These conflicts began in Europe and then spread to eastern North America. Some Indians aided the English, while others helped the French. In Queen Anne's War of 1702–13, the English allied with some Southeast Indian nations, notably the Creek and the eastern Choctaw. The French joined with the Spanish and other Southeast Indians, notably the western Choctaw. The French lost and had to give up a vast territory in what is now Canada. In the Southeast the war left territorial borders in dispute, and the Indians fought the Europeans in a number of wars. One of the better known of these conflicts was the Yamasee War of 1715–16, in which an alliance of Yamasee, Creek, and other tribes fought unsuccessfully against English expansion.

From 1754 to 1763 England and France battled in the French and Indian War. The English, allied with the Iroquois Confederacy once again, faced a much-larger coalition made up of many Algonquian-speaking tribes, the French, and the Spanish. Surprisingly, given their

The Ottawa leader Pontiac displays his war hatchet to some of his Indian allies during the conflict known as Pontiac's War (1763–64). He enlisted support from many tribes to resist British power in the Great Lakes region of North America.

smaller numbers, the Iroquois-English alliance prevailed. Under the peace treaty, France turned over to England its colonies east of the Mississippi River. England now ruled a vast territory reaching from Hudson Bay to the Gulf of Mexico and from the Atlantic coast to the Mississippi River.

With English rule came a new flood of settlers. Like earlier emigrants, they often trespassed on native lands. Some Indians took advantage of the disorder near the end of the French and Indian War to attack the settlers. In 1763 the Ottawa leader Pontiac led a coalition of tribes in capturing several English forts near the Great Lakes. In response to Pontiac's War, the English issued the Proclamation of 1763, one of the most important documents in Native American legal history. The proclamation declared as Indian territory the land between the Appalachian Mountains and the Mississippi River and from the Great Lakes almost to the Gulf of Mexico. It forbade European settlement on this territory and ordered those settlers already there to leave. Nevertheless, thousands of settlers ignored the orders and moved into the reserved territory.

Disputes between the settlers and the British government eventually led to the American Revolution of 1775–83. In this war the English colonies won their independence. Many Indian tribes, under such leaders as the Mohawk known as Joseph Brant (Thayendanegea), fought for the British government, who posed as defenders of Indian land against the colonists. Indian aid provoked retaliatory campaigns by the colonial army, including one led by Gen. John Sullivan on the Iroquois of New York.

While the colonial wars raged in eastern North America, colonization continued in the western part of the continent. There the main imperial powers were Spain and Russia. In the Southwest the Spanish continued to dominate the Native Americans. The tribes there, particularly the Pueblo, continued to face severe punishment for any resistance to colonization. They publicly accepted some European ways while privately practicing their own traditions.

Spanish explorers had sighted California in 1542 but did not attempt to occupy it until 1769. Following the Pacific coast northward from Mexico, Spanish priests established 21 missions while soldiers built forts nearby. The arrival of the Spanish was disastrous for the California Indians. Troops forced these Indians to work as builders and farmers. As in the Southwest, resistance was often harshly punished. Nonetheless, many native Californians fled to distant areas to rebuild their lives.

Along the northern Pacific coast, Russia was the dominant power from the mid-18th century on. Russia sent Vitus Bering to explore the northern seas in 1728, and Russian traders reached the Aleutian Islands and the coasts of present-day Alaska (U.S.) and British Columbia (Canada) in the 1740s. The Russian occupation was brutal. The Native Alaskan men were forced to leave their villages for days to months at a time to hunt sea otters, which were valued for their fur. While the men were away, the Russians abused the women while

A Spanish missionary preaches to Indians at a California mission in the 1700s. The goal of the missions was to incorporate local Indian tribes into Spanish culture by persuasion if possible, by force if necessary.

also demanding food and labor. In the early decades of the 1800s, however, voluntary intermarriage between native women and Russian men began to soften colonial relations in Alaska. Both groups adopted some cultural traditions of the other.

EXPANSION OF THE UNITED STATES

After the American Revolution the new U.S. government hoped to maintain peace with the Native Americans on the frontier. The government promised that the Proclamation of 1763 would be honored. Nevertheless, as settlers continued to migrate westward, they built and farmed on Indian lands. The result of this expansion was decades of conflict between Indians and the U.S. government.

Wars in the East

By 1808–10 settlers had overrun the valleys of the Ohio and Illinois rivers. Game and other wild food were increasingly scarce, and settlers were actively trying to uproot native peoples. Tecumseh, a Shawnee leader, organized several tribes to oppose further ceding of Indian lands. A group of Shawnee led by Tecumseh's brother, Tenskwatawa, were defeated in 1811 by Gen. William Henry Harrison at the battle of Tippecanoe.

During the War of 1812, Tecumseh's coalition sided with the British and won a number of early victories.

Black Hawk led the Sauk and Fox Indians in defending their territory against white settlement. U.S. troops and the Illinois militia crushed the 1832 uprising, slaughtering many Indians in the final battle at the Bad Axe River in Wisconsin. The ruthlessness of the Black Hawk War so affected the Indians that by 1837 all surrounding tribes had fled to the far West, leaving most of the Northwest Territory to white settlers.

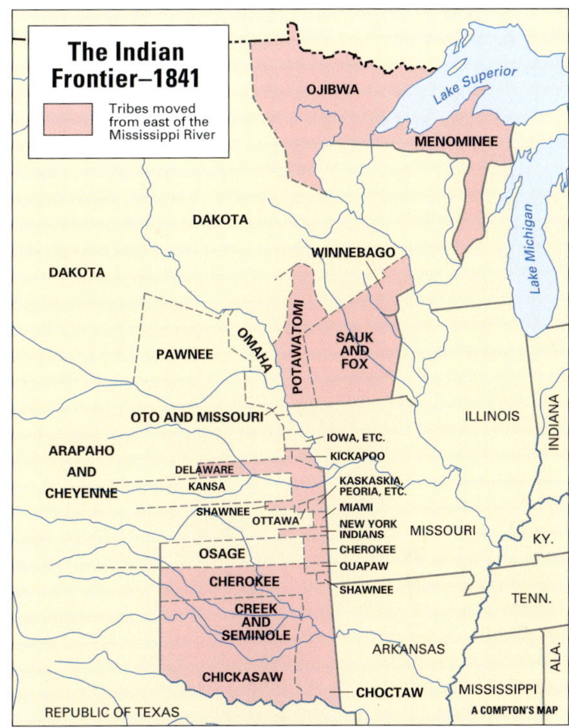

Under pressure from settlers hungry for new farmland, the U.S. government removed tens of thousands of Eastern Indians to the Great Plains during the 1830s and 1840s.

One of the most notable was the 1813 capture of Detroit. In the end, however, the war was a draw between England and the United States. Afterward, with the United States secure in its borders, federal policy focused on the removal of the Indians to areas west of the Mississippi River—to the so-called Great American Desert (the Great Plains), where, supposedly, no whites would ever want to live. To implement this policy, the Indian Removal Act was signed into law on May 28, 1830. It gave President Andrew Jackson, a dedicated foe of the Indians, the power to exchange land west of the Mississippi for the southeastern territory of the Five Civilized Tribes—the Cherokee, Creek, Choctaw, Chickasaw, and Seminole.

The removal policy led to a clash between Jackson and the U.S. Supreme Court, which had ruled in favor of the right of the Cherokee to retain their lands in Georgia. Jackson refused to enforce the Court's decision, and in

A painting depicts the Trail of Tears, one of the tragic events in American history. In the 1830s about 100,000 Cherokee and other Native Americans were forced from their homes in the Southeast and driven to areas west of the Mississippi River.

1838 and 1839 the Cherokee, like the other tribes before them, were forced westward to Indian Territory (later Oklahoma). Their bitter trek during the dead of winter has become known as the Trail of Tears.

In 1832 Sauk and Fox Indians under Black Hawk in Wisconsin had been defeated after refusing to abandon their lands east of the Mississippi. In the 1830s and 1840s the Seminole under Osceola unsuccessfully resisted removal from their homes in Florida. By the end of the 1840s, except for small segments of tribes who had fled to remote areas, the Northeast and Southeast Indians had been forced out of their original territories.

Wars in the West

By the 1840s the U.S. Army and the various Indian peoples in the Plains and parts of the Southwest and the Plateau were in a continual state of war. As white settlers encroached on Indian land, war would break out. Either the Indians would be defeated and transported elsewhere, or a treaty would be made in which the Indians and the U.S. government agreed to an exchange. Usually the Indians would trade part of their lands for a promise that the government would provide them with food, financial aid, health care, and schools. Because the land was to belong to others forever, the government was supposed to provide fresh supplies and services to the Indians forever. However, the government often broke these agreements after it had taken possession of the land.

Thousands of white settlers poured into the Oregon Territory after it was acquired from Great Britain in 1846. Numerous clashes erupted with tribes in the Northwest. In the 1850s wars broke out around Puget Sound after several small tribes were deceived into signing treaties

Geronimo led his people, the Chiricahua Apache, in the defense of their Southwest homeland against the military might of the United States. His final surrender came in 1886.

Library of Congress, Washington, D.C. (neg. no. LC-USZ62-36613)

Alone of all Native American leaders in the West, Red Cloud of the Oglala Sioux won a war against the United States when he forced the federal government to abandon forts in Montana in 1868. But Red Cloud then laid down his arms and spent the rest of his life on reservations.

Library of Congress, Washington, D.C. (neg. no. LC-USZ62-91032)

in which they gave up most of their land. But they were quickly defeated and were confined to reservations— tracts of land set aside for the Indians. Typically, the government created reservations on land that was difficult to develop economically.

In other areas of the Northwest, war continued into the late 1870s. In 1877 the Nez Percé people, led by Chief Joseph (Hinmaton-yalatkit), were defeated after refusing to agree to treaties ceding nearly all their land in the Pacific Northwest to the United States. Privations from loss of land, lack of food, and disease led to an unsuccessful uprising of the Bannock people of Idaho in 1878.

The Southwest came under U.S. control as a result of the U.S. victory over Mexico in the Mexican War of 1846–48. In 1847 Pueblo peoples rose up against settlers at Taos (later in New Mexico) and were defeated. But relations between settlers and the Pueblo, Pima, and Tohono O'odham (Papago) were usually peaceful. The Navajo and Apache retaliated when settlers seized their lands and destroyed their animals and gardens. The Navajo were overpowered in the 1860s and forced onto a reservation, but the Apache fought on. Even after they too were restricted to reservations, small bands continued to mount raids. When the Apache leader Geronimo (Goyathlay) finally surrendered in 1886, Indians in the Southwest ended their military resistance to colonization.

In about 1850 the tribes of the Great Plains had begun attacking wagon trains carrying settlers westward. They were angered by ill treatment from the settlers and by the driving away of bison herds on which they were dependent for food, clothing, and shelter. Efforts by the Army and the government to preserve peace led to the Fort Laramie Treaty of 1851. The Plains tribes promised to confine themselves to designated hunting grounds, and the government agreed to keep settlers out of those areas. But when the government violated the treaty in 1865 by starting to construct forts and a wagon road to mining camps in Montana Territory, the Oglala Sioux under Red Cloud (Mahpiua Luta) attacked and destroyed several forts. By the terms of a new peace treaty in 1868, the government stopped the road

The best-known event of the conquest of the American West was the battle of the Little Bighorn. On June 25, 1876, a combined group of Cheyenne and Sioux warriors annihilated Lieut. Col. George Armstrong Custer and his troops. The outcome of the battle so stunned and enraged white Americans that government troops flooded the area, forcing the Indians to surrender.

The Granger Collection, New York

construction, dismantled the forts, and again guaranteed the Indian reserve.

In 1871 Congress decided that Indian tribes were no longer to be recognized as sovereign (self-governing) powers with whom treaties must be made. Although existing treaties were still valid, violations continued to occur. The treaty of 1868 had made the Black Hills of the Dakota Territory part of a large Sioux reservation. The discovery of gold there in 1874 started a stampede of white prospectors. In 1875 the Sioux (an alliance of the Dakota, Lakota, and Nakota) refused to sell the land to the government, which then ordered them out of the area and onto reservations. When the Sioux refused, the Army, including troops under Lieut. Col. George A. Custer, was sent to enforce the order. On June 25, 1876, the government troops attacked a large group of Sioux and Cheyenne. In the battle of the Little Bighorn, the main body of Indians, under the Sioux leaders Sitting Bull (Tatanka Iyotake) and Crazy Horse (Tashunke Witko), wiped out Custer and his more than 200 men.

This was the last major military victory by the Indians. Gradually they were rounded up and confined to reservations. Sitting Bull and other Sioux soon joined a new supernatural cult that predicted that whites would be wiped out and the Indian way of life preserved if enough Indians would perform the ceremonies known as the Ghost Dance. The Ghost Dance movement was crushed in 1890 with the arrest and murder of Sitting Bull and the massacre by the Army of several hundred Indians at Wounded Knee Creek in South Dakota. Almost 400 years after Columbus' arrival, this massacre completed the military conquest of the American Indian. Across the continent, however, most groups continued to resist conquest in other ways, such as by maintaining their traditional languages and religious practices.

Government Policy

The first federal agency to oversee governmental promises under Indian treaties was placed under the secretary of war by Congress in 1789. A Bureau of Indian Affairs (BIA) was created within the War Department in 1824 and was transferred to the new Department of the Interior in 1849.

The BIA was supposed to enforce the restrictions against whites on Native American lands and to prevent the illegal sale of such lands. The BIA was also supposed to help Indians sell or lease their land when it was legal to do so and to keep track of land inheritance when the owner died. Money deposited in the U.S. Treasury to the credit of Indian tribes in payment for land was administered on behalf of the Indians by the BIA. Unfortunately, many BIA agents were corrupt. As a result, many Indian lands were illegally sold or even stolen.

Allotment and assimilation. Forcibly restricted to reservations, and finding it difficult to make them productive, Native Americans needed the government to fulfill its treaty promises of supplies and services. Many whites, regarding ownership of land as the basis of success, hoped that by owning their own farms the Indians would become independent farmers. Other whites, hungry for land, thought that too much land had already been reserved for the Indians. In addition, many whites thought that the government support of Indians was a kind of charity rather than a legal obligation.

All of these groups of whites urged the passage of the General Allotment Act of 1887. This act provided for dividing reservations, which had been held in common by the tribes, into parcels to be allotted to individual Indians. The "surplus" land, in at least one case a larger area than that divided among the Indians, was eventually sold to white homesteaders. Provisions of the act also granted citizenship to the Indians receiving parcels of land and to any other Indians who agreed to give up tribal life for "civilized" ways.

The General Allotment Act resulted in the seizure of tens of millions of acres of Native American land. Many Indians were unused to the idea of individual ownership of land and had little understanding of money. They

A group of Osage Indians poses with U.S. President Calvin Coolidge at the White House in 1925. A number of tribes sent delegations to Washington, D.C., in the 19th and 20th centuries to represent their interests in treaty negotiations and other matters.

Library of Congress, Washington, D.C.
(neg. no. LC-USZ62-111409)

sold their allotments at absurdly low prices, spent the money, and became destitute. Where land was retained, the amount possessed by each Indian became smaller as the land was divided through inheritance.

At the same time, the government tried to assimilate, or integrate, Indians into white culture. One method of assimilation was the boarding, or residential, school. From the mid-1800s until as late as the 1960s, native families were forced to send their children to these institutions. The instruction was designed to eliminate any use of traditional language, behavior, or religion. Upon arrival, for instance, the children were forced to trade their clothes for uniforms. Students often experienced cruel forms of punishment, verbal abuse, and—in some cases—sexual abuse. Assimilation policies were also enforced on reservations. For example, government authorities prohibited traditional religious practices such as the Sun Dance and the potlatch. However, just as the Pueblo had hidden their religious activities when pressured by Spanish missionaries, many Indians continued to engage in traditional practices in secret.

Reorganization. Eventually it became apparent to government officials that the programs forcing Native Americans to adopt an alien way of life had been largely

Children line up outside the Indian boarding school at Cantonment, Okla., in about 1909.

Library of Congress, Washington, D.C. (neg. no. LC-USZ62-126134)

unsuccessful. In 1926, just two years after U.S. citizenship was extended to the Indians, a survey found most Indians "extremely poor," in bad health, without education, and isolated from the dominant Euro-American culture around them. In response to these findings and other calls for reform, Congress enacted the Indian Reorganization (or Wheeler-Howard) Act of 1934, which ended the allotment policy. The new law's most important provisions reestablished tribes as political entities and partially restored their internal sovereignty. A revival of Indian culture and religion was promoted.

Under the new law many of the tribes set up governments patterned after that of the United States. The tribes wrote constitutions and bylaws, set up executive, legislative, and judicial branches, and proceeded to elect tribal officials by secret ballot. The new law appropriated money for buying back some of the "surplus" land that had passed out of Indian ownership. Money was also provided for better educational and medical facilities and for general economic development.

Termination. Tribes used the powers granted in 1934 to remove whites from their land and to assert their legal rights to its natural resources. But growing attacks on the Indian Reorganization Act finally bore fruit when in 1953 Congress declared that all federal relations with Indian tribes should be terminated as soon as possible. Congress also permitted the state governments to assume civil and criminal jurisdiction over Indian reservations without the consent of the tribes occupying them.

The results of the termination program were dreadful. Some very poor Indian communities had to shut down crucial services such as schools and clinics when the federal government stopped funding them, despite treaty obligations to provide such aid. The tribes fought strenuously against termination laws in court actions and in appeals to the American public. By the 1960s termination as a national Indian policy was dying. Subsequently, tribes that had been terminated worked to have their federal status restored. In the late 20th century American Indians became increasingly visible as they sought to achieve a better life on their own terms (*see* "Sovereignty and Activism," page 112).

CANADA

Early European interest in what is now Canada stemmed from explorers' reports of immensely rich fishing waters along the Atlantic coast. The English, French, Spanish, and Portuguese began fishing expeditions off Newfoundland as early as 1500. By the end of the 1500s, however, Europeans found that the fur trade could be more profitable. Fur trading spurred early colonizing efforts and led to a long rivalry between the French and English and their Indian allies. The expansion of Canada under British rule and then as an independent country forced the native peoples into a struggle for their land and rights.

French and English Rivalry

The French began to settle in the eastern part of what is now Canada in the early 1600s. Fur-bearing animals were abundant in the Subarctic, and the colonists profited from trading pelts with the native peoples. Because the traders depended on the Indians for their livelihood, they generally were friendly with them. The French and the native peoples frequently intermarried. Their descendants were called the Métis.

Indians trade furs with settlers at a Hudson's Bay Company trading post in Canada.

Stock Montage—Hulton Archive/Getty Images

In response to French expansion, the English established the Hudson's Bay Company in 1670. The company set up a number of fur-trading posts on the shores of James and Hudson bays. In the competition for control of the fur trade, the French formed alliances with the Algonquin and the Huron. The English sided with the Iroquois, who were enemies of the Huron. European firearms made warfare among the tribes much deadlier than before.

Starting in the late 1600s, the English and the French fought a series of wars for control of North America. The decisive conflict was the French and Indian War, which lasted from 1754 to 1763. The English and the Iroquois defeated the French and their Indian allies, becoming the dominant power on the continent.

Westward Expansion and Native Resistance

At the end of the French and Indian War, the British government issued the Proclamation of 1763. It designated as Indian land the huge territory bounded by the Great Lakes, the Appalachian Mountains, the Gulf of Mexico, and the Mississippi River. Later, in the 1830s, the British began setting aside reserve lands for Indians in Canada. But these measures failed to stop the westward push of white settlers, who regularly disregarded Indian land rights.

The events of the 1800s were greatly influenced by competition between the Hudson's Bay Company and another fur-trading enterprise, the North West Company. In 1811–12 the Hudson's Bay Company established a new colony, the Red River colony, in what is now Manitoba. This territory had long been the home of the Métis, a number of whom were officers in the North West Company. The Métis harassed the new settlers, sometimes burning their buildings and destroying their crops. In 1816 a group of North West Company men, almost all Métis, killed 20 Hudson's Bay Company soldiers in a conflict known as the Seven Oaks Massacre.

The hostility between the rival companies was not resolved until 1821, when the British government insisted that they merge. The resulting corporation retained the Hudson's Bay Company name and many of its policies. Among these policies was a refusal to hire native peoples for anything but the most basic labor. Many Métis lost their jobs as trappers and traders and began to move from the countryside into the Red River colony.

In 1867 the British government granted Canada independence through the British North America Act. The legislation did little to address the concerns of the Métis or other

Métis rebels battle the North West Mounted Police at Duck Lake, Saskatchewan, in March 1885. The short-lived uprising is known as the North West Rebellion or the Riel Rebellion, after Métis leader Louis Riel.

The Granger Collection, New York

native peoples. Two years later the Canadian government bought Rupert's Land (the land north and west of the eastern colonies) from the Hudson's Bay Company. Within this territory was the Red River colony. The Métis resisted the Canadian takeover. Led by Louis Riel, they seized Fort Garry (now Winnipeg), the headquarters of the Hudson's Bay Company, and established their own government. As president, Riel represented the Métis in negotiations with Canada. In 1870 the Canadian government issued the compromise Manitoba Act, which made the Red River colony into the province of Manitoba. The act also guaranteed many rights demanded by Riel.

Still, Canada's westward march continued. In the 1870s the Canadian government began negotiating treaties with the native peoples for lands in the west. Signed between 1871 and 1921, these 11 agreements are called the Numbered Treaties. In return for moving to reserves, the native peoples were often promised cash, farm equipment, livestock, and supplies as well as services such as health care and schools. The government, however, often failed to live up to its treaty obligations. Furthermore, the bison on which the Plains peoples depended were disappearing, largely because of slaughter by white hunters. Poverty, starvation, and disease spread among the western tribes.

In 1884, at the suggestion of the Cree leader Big Bear, more than 2,000 native people met on the reserve of another Cree leader, Poundmaker. Although tribal leaders had been quietly meeting for years to schedule bison hunts, this was by far the largest native gathering the Canadian Plains had seen. In response, Canadian government agents banned travel between reserves and began to withhold food as a method of control.

The government actions led to a crisis. In 1884, at the request of Métis leaders, Louis Riel returned to Canada from exile in the United States. He unsuccessfully pressed the Canadian government to grant the Métis a colony in Saskatchewan. In 1885 he led another armed uprising, known as the North West Rebellion. It was quickly crushed by the Canadian military. Riel was found guilty of treason and hanged. Big Bear and

Poundmaker, though they had acted as peacemakers, were sentenced to prison; both died within two years. The defeat of the rebellion subdued the native peoples of western Canada for decades.

Government Policy

The British Proclamation of 1763 marked the first time that a European colonial power formally recognized Indian land titles. It forbade all white settlement on Indian territory without the consent of the Indians and the Crown. It also established principles for negotiating treaties with the Indians.

After 1867, the new Canadian government drew on the British model in developing its own Indian policy. The treaties by which the government acquired western Indian lands were based on principles outlined in the Proclamation of 1763. A new Department of Indian Affairs negotiated the treaties and oversaw the reserves.

As in the United States, the Canadian government sought to assimilate the Indians into mainstream society. The main legislation promoting assimilation was the Indian Act, first passed in 1876 and expanded over the years. The original act established a legal definition for the word Indian. People legally defined as Indians were known as status Indians. They could live on reserves and had certain other rights. Indians who chose to give up their status rights were called nonstatus Indians. These Indians were said to be enfranchised. Indian women who married non-Indian men were automatically enfranchised until 1985, when the law was changed. Few Indians chose enfranchisement because they did not want to give up their tribal identity and privileges.

In 1969 the Canadian government tried to abolish the Indian Act and eliminate Indian status. Indian groups strongly protested the new policy and forced the government to withdraw its proposal, which had become known as the White Paper. The protest sparked a surge in political activism among Canada's native peoples. New organizations advocated for native rights, improved education, and economic development (*see* "Sovereignty and Activism," page 112).

MIDDLE AND SOUTH AMERICA

The primary European power from Mexico southward was Spain. During their explorations of Middle and South America in search of gold, silver, and precious stones, Spanish conquistadors plundered Indian villages and enslaved the inhabitants. The Spanish also worked to convert the Indians to their religion, Roman Catholicism. The largest part of this region that lay outside Spanish control was Brazil, which was colonized by Portugal. The Portuguese exploited the land and native inhabitants much as the Spanish did.

Exploration and Conquest

The Spanish realized the economic possibilities of the Americas only gradually. They had occupied the larger islands of the West Indies by 1512, finding the land nearly empty of treasure. On trips to the mainland, however, the Spanish heard stories about the wealth and splendor of the Aztec and Inca empires.

In 1519 the Spanish soldier Hernando Cortez reached central Mexico on an expedition to conquer the Aztec. Though he came with only about 500 soldiers and 16 horses, Cortez assembled a large army from among the Indian enemies of the Aztec. After a brief initial success at Tenochtitlán, the Aztec capital, the Spanish were driven out in 1520. They returned in 1521, however, to overwhelm the Aztec and destroy the city. This victory marked the fall of the Aztec Empire. Cortez established Mexico City on the site of Tenochtitlán.

Within a short time the Spanish conquered the rest of central and southern Mexico and much of Central America from their base in Mexico City. By 1525 Spanish rule had been extended as far south as Guatemala and Honduras. In northern Mexico and Costa Rica the Indians put up strong resistance, but they too were conquered later in the 1500s.

The conquest of the Inca in Peru was led by Francisco Pizarro, a Spanish adventurer who had settled in Panama. He sailed for Peru in 1531 with fewer than 200 men and about 40 horses. Taking advantage of a civil war among the Inca, Pizarro captured the last Inca emperor, Atahuallpa, in 1532. A year later the Spanish conquered Cuzco, the Inca capital.

Following the Inca conquest, the Spanish went out in all directions from central Peru. Pedro de Valdivia conquered Chile, and Francisco de Orellana explored the Amazon River. Other conquistadors entered the regions that would become Ecuador, Colombia, and Argentina.

The Portuguese explorer Pedro Álvarez Cabral reached the coast of Brazil in 1500. However, the new land was of little interest to Portugal until that country began to feel the threat of French or Spanish intrusion in about 1530. The Portuguese established their first settlement in Brazil in 1532.

Colonization and Its Effects

The impact of the European conquests varied among the native peoples of Middle and South America. Generally, the most severely affected groups were those who lived along major navigational routes. They suffered from nearly continuous exposure to the violence of conquest. In more remote regions, however, some Indians had

The Spanish soldier Hernando Cortez and his troops conquer Tenochtitlán, the Aztec capital, in 1521.

little or no contact with Europeans and managed to keep their cultures intact.

Some peoples, such as the Araucanian of southern Chile, fiercely resisted Spanish domination. Most groups, however, offered little resistance and quickly fell under Spanish rule. Many Indians were killed during the conquests. Others died from European diseases such as measles and smallpox, for which they had no immunity. The combination of disease and violence killed millions of Indians throughout the Americas. The Indians of the Caribbean virtually disappeared, as did some other groups. Central Mexico would not regain its pre-Columbian population numbers until about 1900.

In Middle America the Spanish overthrew the high civilization of the Aztec and destroyed the native culture. They substituted Spanish officials for the Indian nobility. The Indians were grouped into villages modeled on the European grid pattern, with a central plaza on which stood the church and town hall. The Spanish introduced new farming techniques and crops along with steel, horses and farm animals, mines, European crafts, and new forms of social organization.

In Peru the Spanish systematically took over the Inca Empire. Spanish forms of government replaced those of the empire, and land use and ownership changed radically. To some extent the Inca upper classes were absorbed into Spanish colonial society. The native nobles served in the colonial administration and adopted Spanish dress and other customs. The farmers who made up the bulk of the population, however, were treated merely as a source of labor for the colony. Inca agriculture underwent great change through the introduction of European crops that were demanded by the Spanish rulers.

Most of the native peoples in the Spanish colonies had their lands stripped away through the *encomienda* system. *Encomiendas* were estates granted to conquistadors and others who had provided service to the Spanish crown. In theory the receiver of the grant, the *encomendero,* was to protect the Indians living on the land and teach them Christianity in return for the Indians' labor. In practice, however, the landowner often abused and enslaved the Indians, forcing them to work the fields and to labor in mines. The landowner could also collect tribute, or payments, from the Indians. Later, *encomiendas* were gradually replaced by estates called haciendas. But the change did little to help the native workers, who were bound to the land by debts to the landowners.

In contrast to the Spanish, the Portuguese divided their colony in Brazil into pieces of land called captaincies. The government granted the captaincies to proprietors called *donatários*. The *donatários* in turn granted land to settlers. Plantation agriculture based on Indian slave labor quickly became the foundation of Brazil's economy. As increasing numbers of Indians died from European diseases, however, the Portuguese brought in African slaves to work on the captaincies.

To accomplish the goal of religious conversion, Jesuit priests set up missions and religious reservations. As the Europeans imposed Roman Catholicism, they tried to

The Mexican revolutionary Emiliano Zapata (seated, center) poses with his staff in a photograph from about 1912. Demanding the return of land that had been seized from Indian peasants, Zapata led a guerrilla war against the Mexican government from 1911 to 1917.

stamp out native religions. The missionaries were often violent. Beatings, dismemberment, and execution were common punishments for Indians who continued their traditional religious practices. Native beliefs and practices did not disappear, however. Rather, the Indians often incorporated elements of Roman Catholicism into their traditional rituals.

Marriage between European men and Indian women was accepted. The children of these marriages were called mestizos. After a few generations, a complex social order based on ancestry, land ownership, wealth, and noble titles had developed in the Spanish colonies.

The Postcolonial Era

Spain's colonies in Mexico, Central America, and South America gained independence in the early 1800s. Brazil declared its independence from Portugal in 1822. Yet even after the Europeans left, power remained concentrated in the hands of wealthy landowners. Many Indians remained poor laborers who were tied to the land by debt to the landowners. In most countries they still had to pay tribute to the landowners as well. The government of Bolivia, for example, received as much as 80 percent of its revenues from Indian tribute through the mid-1800s. Later in the 19th century, the Indians who had managed to remain relatively independent lost land as ranches and plantations expanded.

Native communities came together in opposition to land grabbing and anti-Indian policies. In Mexico Indian peasants rallied behind Emiliano Zapata to fight the government in the Mexican Revolution (1910–20). As a result of the revolution, the government began returning land to the peasants. Later, after World War II, other countries in Middle and South America introduced land reform programs. Among them were Bolivia, Chile, Peru, Colombia, and Brazil. Nevertheless, the standard of living for most Indians remained poor. By the late 20th century these conditions would spur Indians to political action in a number of Middle and South American countries (*see* "Sovereignty and Activism," page 112).

PART IV

NATIVE AMERICA TODAY

Depictions of American Indians are often frozen in the past. For many people, the prevailing images of Indians come from history books—mounted hunters chasing bison across the Great Plains or perhaps the forced march of the Cherokee along the Trail of Tears. Such depictions have led some people to believe that American Indians are extinct. In reality, of course, native peoples still live throughout the Americas. Some of them, especially in remote parts of South America, continue to live much as they did before European contact. Many others, however, have adapted to modern life and blend in with the general population. At the same time, many Indians have sought to preserve and revitalize their traditional cultures.

The largest American Indian populations today, as in the past, are found in Latin America. Some 45 million Indians and many more mestizos—people of mixed Indian and European ancestry—live there. In South America there are at least as many people of Indian ancestry as there were just prior to the European conquest. The vast majority of them live in the Andes. In Mexico Indians account for more than one sixth of the population, and mestizos make up nearly two thirds of the total. Almost all of the people of Guatemala are mestizo or Indian.

Since 1900 the Native American populations of the United States and Canada have recovered to some extent from the astonishing losses of the colonial period. In the early 21st century some 4.3 million people in the United States identified themselves as American Indian or Alaska Native. They represented 1.5 percent of the country's population. The U.S. government officially recognizes more than 560 tribes (federally recognized tribes are those eligible for government services). The most numerous U.S. tribes include the Cherokee, Navajo, Sioux, and Ojibwa. The states with the largest native populations are California, Oklahoma, Arizona, Texas, and New Mexico.

In Canada the number of people reporting Indian (First Nations), Métis, or Inuit ancestry surpassed 1 million in the early 21st century. They made up about 4 percent of the total population. The Cree are the most numerous of the more than 600 bands or tribes recognized by Canada's government. Native Canadian populations are highest in Ontario and the four western provinces—British Columbia, Alberta, Manitoba, and Saskatchewan.

For many American Indians, life in the contemporary world is very different than it was just a few generations ago. While in the past many native people had very limited educational and economic opportunities, by the turn of the 21st century they were members of essentially every profession available in North America. Many native people have also moved from reservations to more urban areas, including about two thirds of U.S. tribal members and more than half of native Canadians.

Despite these changes, American Indians continue to face numerous challenges. Many native communities are impoverished, and they often struggle with problems such as substance abuse. Native activists, however, continue to make progress in their efforts to achieve a better life for their peoples. Key to these efforts has been the pursuit of sovereignty, or self-government. When this right is secure, Native Americans are empowered to shape their communities on their own terms.

RESERVATIONS AND URBAN INDIANS

The lives of Native Americans today are shaped in large part by where they live. From the mid-1800s until well into the 20th century, most native peoples of the United States and Canada resided in rural areas. Many of them lived on reservations, or reserves—tracts of land set aside by the government for native use. The second half of the 20th century, however, saw a major shift of Native Americans from rural to urban areas. By the start of the 21st century, only about one third of the native peoples in the United States lived on reservations and in other rural areas; the other two thirds lived in cities or towns. In Canada, the number of native peoples living in urban areas surpassed 50 percent in the late 20th century and continued to climb thereafter. These changes have had lasting effects on the economic, social, and cultural lives of both native individuals and their tribes.

Reservations

In the United States, Indian reservations are concentrated in the West and in the Great Lakes region. The largest is the Navajo reservation, which covers some 16 million acres (6.5 million hectares) in Arizona, New Mexico, and Utah. Other large reservations include the Tohono O'odham reservation in Arizona, the Uintah and Ouray reservation in Utah, the Wind River reservation in Wyoming, the Fort Peck and Crow reservations in Montana, and three Sioux reservations—Pine Ridge, Cheyenne River, and Standing Rock—in the Dakotas. Most reservation land is owned communally by tribes, though some is held by individuals. Where land is communally owned, tribes generally grant pieces of land to individual members for their use.

Most reservations in the United States and Canada trace their origins to government policies of the 19th and early 20th centuries. The reservations dating from this period typically share some characteristics. For instance, they were generally created through treaty agreements or by colonial decree. They represented an area much smaller than, and often at a great distance from, a given group's traditional territory. In addition, early reserves were usually placed on land that was difficult to develop economically—that is, in areas that were very dry, wet, steep, or remote.

Considering these origins, it is not surprising that reservations have historically been limited in their economic opportunities. Often people seeking higher education or employment have to leave the reservation, which can make the economic hardship even more difficult for those left behind. Reservations have also generally lagged behind neighboring areas in terms of infrastructure and social services, most of which are government funded in the United States and Canada. In a notable example from the United States, census data show that rural electrification programs reached some 90 percent of farms by 1950. This was a tremendous increase compared to the 10 percent that had electricity in 1935. On U.S. reservations, however, the number of homes with access to electricity did not approach 90 percent until 2000.

In some reservation communities, these difficult living conditions have led to high rates of poverty, substance abuse, and violence. However, these tendencies have been countered by the efforts of a wide variety of Native American professionals and activists who have worked to

The Navajo reservation covers some 16 million acres in the southwestern United States. The region is mostly dry, however, and will not support enough farming and livestock to provide a livelihood for all of its residents. Thousands earn their living away from the Navajo country, and many have settled on irrigated lands along the lower Colorado River and in such places as Los Angeles, Calif., and Kansas City, Mo.

improve the economic, physical, and social health of their communities. Help has also come from people who left the reservations. Many of them continue to consider the reservation to be their true home and provide its residents with financial help and other forms of assistance.

Some reservations have also benefited from tourism. Highway improvements in the 1950s and '60s opened opportunities for tourism in what had been remote areas. A number of tribes living in scenic locations began to sponsor cultural festivals and other events to attract tourists. Beginning in the late 20th century, casinos on reservation land became an important source of income for some tribes (*see* "Economic Development," page 114).

Tribes have self-government, or sovereignty, over their reservations. This means that the laws on reservations can differ from state and federal laws. However, the U.S. government still sets limits on the authority of tribal governments on Indian land. Cases dealing with disputes between tribal and federal authority have come before the U.S. Supreme Court, with outcomes that have often threatened tribal sovereignty (*see* "Sovereignty and Activism," page 112).

Urbanization

Some American Indians lived in cities even in prehistoric times. The great cities of ancient Middle America—including Teotihuacán and those of the Maya—were home to tens of thousands of residents. In Northern America, the prehistoric Mississippian city of Cahokia had as many as 20,000 inhabitants. At the time of European contact, Tenochtitlán, the Aztec capital, may have had as many as 200,000 people. The residents of these early cities, however, were still only a fraction of the Native American population as a whole.

Urbanization did not have a major impact on the larger native communities of the United States and Canada until the 20th century. In the United States in 1900, less than 1 percent of the native population lived in cities and towns. By 1950 that number had risen to only 13 percent. By 2000, however, about two thirds of U.S. Indians lived in urban areas. U.S. cities with large native populations include New York City; Los Angeles, Calif.; Phoenix, Ariz.; Tulsa, Okla.; Oklahoma City, Okla.; Anchorage, Alaska; Albuquerque, N.M.; and Chicago, Ill. The number of native Canadians living in urban areas increased from 13 percent in 1961 to 30 percent in 1971 and eventually to more than 50 percent in the early 21st century. Canadian cities with large native populations include Winnipeg, Man.; Edmonton, Alta.; Vancouver, B.C.; Toronto, Ont.; Calgary, Alta.; Saskatoon, Sask.; and Regina, Sask.

The main cause of urbanization among Native Americans has been migration from reservations and other rural areas to cities. In the United States, this migration began largely as a result of a relocation program launched by the U.S. Bureau of Indian Affairs (BIA) in 1948 and supported by Congress from the 1950s on. The program was designed to transform the mostly rural native population into an urban workforce that was integrated into the mainstream culture. The BIA established offices in a variety of destination cities,

Lezlie Sterling—MCT/Landov

The Sacramento Native American Health Center in Sacramento, Calif., provides health services to the city's sizable native community. Staffed largely by Native Americans, the center uses traditional drumming as part of the healing process.

including Chicago; Los Angeles; Dallas, Tex.; Denver, Colo.; San Francisco, Calif.; San Jose, Calif.; and Saint Louis, Mo. The BIA promised to provide a variety of services to ease the transition to city life, including transportation from the reservation, financial assistance, and help in finding housing and employment.

Many Indians, who could find little work on the economically depressed reservations, tried the program. From 1948 to 1980, when the program ended, some 750,000 Indians are estimated to have relocated to cities (though not all did so under the official program). Some program participants fared well in the cities, adjusting to urban life and joining the middle class. This was true especially of those Indians with education and skills. Many participants were poorly educated, however, and thus ill-equipped to succeed in the cities. In addition, the distribution and quality of the services provided by the BIA were often uneven. Many Indians who failed to find work returned to their reservations. Some moved back and forth between reservations and cities following job opportunities.

Today, Native Americans who live in cities differ in some ways from their rural counterparts. For example, they are more likely to marry non-Indians and less likely to speak a native language. To keep from losing touch with their cultural traditions, many urban Indians make a point of keeping in contact with their extended families still living on reservations. In addition, they can seek out the American Indian centers found in many large cities. These centers host social events and provide services for urban Indians of all tribes in such areas as employment, housing, and education.

SOVEREIGNTY AND ACTIVISM

From the start of European colonialism, a central concern for American Indians has been sovereignty, or self-government. Although most Indians and scholars agree that historical injustices are the source of many of the problems facing native communities, they also tend to agree that the resolution of those problems ultimately lies within the native communities themselves. They believe that tribal well-being depends in large part on the tribes' authority to make their own decisions concerning the issues that affect them most. The pursuit of tribal sovereignty and related rights has often brought native communities in conflict with government authorities. These ongoing battles have kept the question of sovereignty at the forefront of contemporary Indian life.

United States

Although Native Americans had been fighting for their rights for centuries, they became increasingly visible in the late 20th century. During the 1960s, as African Americans campaigned for equality in the civil rights movement, Indians also drew attention to their causes through mass demonstrations and protests. The causes they championed included economic independence, revitalization of traditional culture, and protection of

In November 1969 American Indian activists occupied Alcatraz Island in San Francisco Bay. They demanded the deed to the island and refused to leave until they were forced off by federal marshals in June 1971.

AP

legal rights. Above all was control over tribal areas and the restoration of lands that they believed had been illegally seized.

The American Indian Movement (AIM), a militant organization formed in 1968, took part in many highly publicized protests. For 19 months in 1969–71 Indian activists occupied Alcatraz Island in San Francisco Bay (California), claiming it as Indian land. In 1973 about 200 armed AIM supporters, led by Russell Means and Dennis Banks, occupied the hamlet of Wounded Knee on the Oglala Sioux Pine Ridge Reservation in South Dakota. Wounded Knee had been the site of a bloody massacre of Indians by the U.S. Army in 1890. In a 71-day siege, two Indians were killed and one federal marshal was seriously wounded.

During the 1960s and '70s native peoples turned increasingly to the courts to press their causes. For example, the rights to forest and mineral resources on tribal lands became the subjects of many lawsuits. Perhaps the most famous case was United States *vs.* Washington (1974), more commonly referred to as the Boldt case after the federal judge who wrote the decision. This case established that treaty agreements entitled certain Northwest Coast and Plateau tribes to one half of the fish taken in the state of Washington. The far-reaching decision also had implications in other states where tribes had similarly reserved the right to fish.

Some native groups have pressed claims to land taken in the 19th century and earlier. In some cases the Indians want the land returned to them; in others they want cash reparations. The largest land settlement in U.S. history was the Alaska Native Claims Settlement Act, passed by Congress in 1971. It awarded approximately 44 million acres (17.8 million hectares) of land and almost 1 billion dollars to the Indians, Aleut, and Eskimo of Alaska. Even in cases where native peoples are victorious, however, land-claim issues can be difficult to resolve. In United States *vs.* Sioux Nation of Indians (1980), for example, the U.S. Supreme Court ruled that the government's 1877 acquisition of the Black Hills region of South Dakota from the seven Lakota tribes was not legal. Although the Lakota were offered a substantial sum of money, all seven tribal governments refused to accept payment. Instead, they insisted upon the return of the land they regard as a holy place. As far as the Lakota are concerned, the issue remains unresolved.

In the United States sovereignty and other rights issues can be very complex because of competing national, state, and local claims to authority. One area that demonstrates this complexity is criminal jurisdiction—that is, who has the authority to handle criminal matters involving Indians and their lands. Two examples help to clarify the interaction of tribal, regional, and federal authorities in this area of law. One area of concern has been whether a non-Indian who commits a criminal act

Thousands of Indians march in Bogotá, the capital of Colombia, in 2008 in support of indigenous rights.
William Fernando Martinez/AP

while on reservation land can be prosecuted in the tribal court. In Oliphant *vs.* Suquamish Indian Tribe (1978), the U.S. Supreme Court determined that tribes do not have the authority to prosecute non-Indians, even when such individuals commit crimes on tribal land. This decision was clearly a blow to tribal sovereignty. In response, some reservations closed their borders to non-Indians to ensure that their law enforcement officers could keep the peace within the reservation.

The Oliphant decision might lead one to presume that, because non-Indians may not be tried in tribal courts, Indians in the United States would not be subject to prosecution in state or federal courts. This issue was decided to the contrary in United States *vs.* Wheeler (1978). Wheeler was a Navajo who had been convicted in a tribal court. He argued that the concept of double jeopardy—which protects a person from being tried twice for the same crime—meant that he could not be prosecuted for that crime in federal or state court. In this case the Supreme Court favored tribal sovereignty—it ruled that the actions of the tribal court stood separately from those of the states or the United States. In other words, a tribe was entitled to prosecute its members. Additionally, however, the ruling meant that Indians could indeed be tried for a single crime in both a tribal and a state or federal court.

Canada

In the late 1960s the Canadian government tried to abolish the Indian Act and eliminate Indian status. Indian protests defeated the proposal and also led to a sharp increase in native political activism during the 1970s. New native organizations flourished in the provinces and territories. At the national level, Indians were represented by the National Indian Brotherhood (now the Assembly of First Nations), while Métis and people who lacked legal recognition as Indians, such as Indian women who had married non-Indian men, were represented by the Native Council of Canada (now the Congress of Aboriginal Peoples). Inuit interests were represented by the Inuit Circumpolar Conference (ICC), formed in 1977 by the Inuit of Canada, Greenland, and

Alaska. In 1983 the ICC was recognized officially by the United Nations.

The efforts of native Canadian activists led to significant progress. The Constitution Act (or Canada Act) of 1982 legally recognized native rights, including the right of self-government. In 1983 a government report recommended the establishment of new forms of self-government, and since then efforts to increase native sovereignty have continued. Land claims by the Inuit led to the creation in 1999 of Nunavut, a new province administered by and for the Inuit. The name Nunavut means "Our Land" in the Inuit language.

Middle and South America

The late 20th and early 21st centuries saw a variety of political and economic movements by the Indians of Middle and South America. The Indians often protested the loss of their lands to industry and agriculture. An Indian uprising in Ecuador in 1990 pushed the government to recognize native land rights and address the Indians' other concerns, but unrest continued into the 21st century. Amazonian Indians in Brazil and Peru have battled against the intrusion of mining and other companies. In 2009 clashes between Indians and police in Peru turned violent, and dozens of people were killed. In Guatemala Indian peasants fought repressive military governments in a 36-year civil war that ended in 1996. Brutal government tactics resulted in the deaths of about 200,000 mostly unarmed citizens. In Mexico a group called the Zapatista National Liberation Army rebelled against the government in 1994 to demand Indian rights. In later years that group staged massive protests and demonstrations throughout Mexico. In other countries, such as Belize and Costa Rica, governments responded to Indian activism by integrating Indians more completely into the national culture.

In some Middle and South American countries, native peoples have become a strong political force. They formed political parties to represent their interests and elected native representatives to office. The first Native American head of state, Juan Evo Morales Aymo, became president of Bolivia in 2006.

ECONOMIC DEVELOPMENT

Economic underdevelopment and poverty have been persistent problems for many Native American peoples. For a number of reasons, many of them historical, native peoples have generally had more difficulty in achieving economic success than non-natives. In the 21st century more than 25 percent of Indians and Alaska Natives in the United States lived in poverty, more than double the national rate. Studies of reservation income help to illustrate the situation: in the early 21st century, if rural Native America had been a country, it would have been classified on the basis of median annual income as a "developing nation" by the World Bank. Nevertheless, in the second half of the 20th century Native Americans began to make economic progress.

Causes of Underdevelopment

The causes of economic underdevelopment among Native Americans are many. One is the limitations of reservations. Reservations were typically established in rural areas that were considered to be too dry, too wet, too steep, or too remote to be economically productive. Later land losses increased the economic challenges faced by native peoples. In addition, the rural locations of reservations meant that for much of the 20th century farming was the only available employment for many Indians. During this time farming was declining as a source of employment and income in the United States as a whole. Thus, it is not surprising that Native American farmers and farm laborers struggled to make a living.

Another reason for economic underdevelopment among American Indian peoples is the historical lack of quality schools for native children and young people. These limited opportunities are reflected in measures of educational attainment. In the United States in the early 21st century, only 12 percent of the native population age 25 and older had a bachelor's degree, compared with 24 percent of all Americans.

Beginning in the mid-20th century, many Native Americans migrated from rural areas to cities as part of a relocation program run by the Bureau of Indian Affairs (BIA). It was hoped that the Indians would find work in the cities and improve their standard of living. However, they often lacked the skills and education needed to adapt to the urban setting. In addition, services promised to urban Indians by the BIA were often inadequate. For most Indians, relocation failed to improve their economic standing. (*See also* "Reservations and Urban Indians," page 110).

Economic Growth

During the late 20th and early 21st centuries native groups used a variety of methods to foster economic growth. Some of these had been in use for centuries, such as the filing of lawsuits to reclaim lost territory. Long-standing operations in mining, forestry, fishing, farming, and ranching also continued to play important roles in economic development on reservations that are rich in natural resources. For the Crow tribe of the U.S. state of Montana, for example, coal mining was an important source of income and employment. Some tribes

Native American vendors sell jewelry, pottery, beadwork, weaving, and other traditional arts and crafts in the central plaza of Santa Fe, N.M. They belong to the Native American Vendors Program, sponsored by the Museum of New Mexico.

Stephen Power/Alamy

In the late 20th and early 21st centuries gaming became an important source of income for some Native American peoples in the United States. Indian gaming includes a range of business operations, from full casino facilities with slot machines and Las Vegas-style high-stakes gambling to smaller facilities offering games such as bingo, lotteries, and video poker.

Joe Raedle/Getty Images

developed new industries, typically in light manufacturing or services. The Choctaw people of Oklahoma established particularly successful manufacturing enterprises, producing a variety of equipment for the military. Using the Internet, tribes in even the most remote areas could provide services such as information technology, accounting, and order processing.

Tourism has been a growing source of income, especially for Native Americans who live in scenic places. Tribal businesses such as hotels, restaurants, golf courses, water parks, outlet malls, and casinos have been profitable. Some tribes sponsor cultural festivals to attract tourists. Especially popular is the powwow, a festival of native culture that features traditional singing and dancing. These festivals also provide native families and individuals with opportunities to sell traditional and modern art. Some Native Americans have used their skills to find employment as hunting and fishing guides.

Some native communities have made money by agreeing to store materials that are difficult to dispose of, such as medical and nuclear waste. For the most part, these projects did not begin until the late 20th or early 21st centuries, and they have generally been controversial. Tribe members often disagree about whether the income is worth the potential dangers of storing or disposing of these materials.

Gaming

Although Native Americans have developed a variety of businesses, the most important tool of economic development for many U.S. tribes has been the casino. The first Indian casino was built in Florida by the Seminole tribe, which opened a successful high-stakes bingo parlor in 1979. Other native peoples quickly followed suit.

The Seminole and other tribes faced a number of legal challenges over the next decade. Many lawsuits argued that state laws regarding gaming should apply on tribal land. The issue was decided in California *vs.* Cabazon Band of Mission Indians (1987), in which the U.S. Supreme Court upheld tribal sovereignty. Gaming could thus take place on reservations in states that did not forbid gambling or lotteries.

The U.S. Congress passed the Indian Gaming Regulatory Act in 1988 to place some limits on the industry. The act divided various forms of gambling—such as bingo, slot machines, and card games—into categories and set regulations for each. It also required tribes to enter into agreements with state governments. These agreements guaranteed that a proportion of gaming profits—sometimes as much as 50 percent—would be given to states to offset costs related to the casinos. Among such costs are increased law enforcement and treatment programs for gambling addiction. Some of the profits are also distributed as assistance to tribes that do not have gaming.

Some Native American gaming operations have been very profitable, while others have been only minimally successful. The level of success depends to a great extent on location. In general, casinos in or near major cities attract more visitors and are much more successful than those in remote areas. Because many reservations are in remote areas, many Indian casinos have not made significant profits. For the tribes that run these casinos, gaming has failed to provide the economic boost needed to pull them out of poverty. Tribes with successful operations, however, have been able to use gaming income to improve the general health, education, and cultural well-being of their members. Some peoples have reached a level of prosperity that they had not seen since the first European contact centuries ago.

CULTURAL PRESERVATION

Since the arrival of Europeans in the Americas, Indians have embraced certain elements of Euro-American culture and resisted others. Many Indians of the 21st century participate in the same aspects of modern life as the general population: they wear ordinary clothing, shop at grocery stores and malls, watch television, and so forth. Yet at the same time many Indians fear that the acceptance of modern lifestyles threatens their traditional cultures. They believe that the beliefs, values, and knowledge of the past are vital to the survival of their communities. These traditionalists have worked for the preservation of native cultures.

The goals of cultural preservationists are best met in communities where elders and young people work together. Today many Native American youth show strong interest in traditional knowledge. In native societies that depend on the oral tradition, elders are still the main source of such knowledge. Some young people are learning to use new technology and other skills to develop new means for learning and maintaining that knowledge. The results may differ from the traditions known and loved by today's elders when they were young. However, they will serve the goal of carrying on those traditions to future generations.

Languages

A primary area of concern is Indian languages. European conquest and colonization ultimately led to

Students at the Nizipuhwahsin Center on the Blackfeet reservation in the U.S. state of Montana learn the Blackfeet translation for common English words. Almost all of the lessons at the center are conducted in the Blackfeet language. The center is widely recognized as a model for the preservation of Indian languages.

Joe Cavaretta/AP

the disappearance of many Indian language groups and to radical changes in the groups that survived. One third of the native languages spoken north of Mexico have become extinct. In the West Indies native languages have almost entirely disappeared. The situation is somewhat different in Middle and South America. Although there are no precise figures, a greater number of languages are still spoken, some of them by large populations.

Of the American Indian languages still spoken, many have only a few hundred speakers. They are spoken even more rarely by young people who are educated in English. In short, even though the Indian population north of Mexico is actually increasing, most of the native languages are slowly dying out. Only a few languages are flourishing: Navajo, spoken in New Mexico and Arizona; Ojibwa, in the northern United States and southern Canada; Cherokee, in Oklahoma and North Carolina; and Dakota-Assiniboin, in the northern portions of the midwestern United States. Even in these groups, many people speak English in addition to the native language. Some tribes have established schools in which all instruction is in an Indian language. This is creating a new generation of speakers.

In parts of South America and Middle America a number of language groups are still widespread and flourishing. One of these is Quechuan, which includes the language of the former Inca Empire. Scholars estimate that this group of closely related languages has several million speakers in Ecuador, Peru, and parts of Bolivia and Argentina. Yet even though Quechuan languages are still widely spoken, they are slowly losing ground to Spanish, which is the language of government and education. In Mexico and Central America, languages of the Uto-Aztecan, Oto-Manguean, and Mayan families have been preserved among many Indian groups. Like Quechuan, all of these were languages of Indian empires before the Spanish conquest.

The Tupí-Guaraní languages, spoken in eastern Brazil and in Paraguay, are a major pre-Columbian language group that has survived into modern times. Before the arrival of the Europeans, languages of this group were spoken by a large and widespread population. After the conquest, Tupí became the basis of a shared language that Europeans and Indians used to communicate with each other in Brazil. Guaraní similarly became a general language for much of Paraguay. By the 21st century Tupí was gradually being replaced in Brazil by Portuguese. Guaraní, however, remains an important language of modern Paraguay. The country's 1992 constitution made Guaraní an official language alongside Spanish, and since 1996 it has been used in schools. Paraguayans are proud to converse in Guaraní, which acts as a strong marker of their identity. The language is strongly represented through folk literature and festivals.

Participants in the Totah Festival, held in Farmington, N.M., reenact the movement of a warrior in a traditional dance.
Lucas Ian Coshenet—The Daily Times/AP

Religions

Religious oppression threatened the survival of traditional Indian beliefs and practices from the start of the colonial era. Though both the United States and Canada guarantee freedom of religion, their governments have historically banned many native religious activities. Pressure from native groups urged the U.S. Congress to pass the American Indian Religious Freedom Act (AIRFA) in 1978. AIRFA committed the federal government to protecting Indian religions and their followers. Today many forms of traditional worship are thriving. The most widespread native religious movement among North American Indians is the Native American Church. Combining Indian and Christian elements, the church is a unifying force for native peoples across the United States.

The passage of AIRFA also helped Native American efforts to control their sacred sites. Many places used for ceremonial purposes or believed to be the home of powerful spirits have been disrupted by recreational activities and commercial use. The Wyoming rock formation called Devils Tower, for example, is a national monument administered by the U.S. National Park Service. For many Plains peoples, however, it is a sacred site known as Grizzly Bear Lodge. Many Indians visit the monument during June, which is a holy month in their religious calendar. Some Indians believe that climbing on the formation should be banned at the site either permanently or at least during June. Some climbers, however, believe this would unfairly restrict their use of public lands. Since 1995 the National Park Service has asked visitors not to climb the formation during June. Although the restriction is voluntary, many people have chosen to follow it out of respect for native religious traditions.

A related concern among Indian preservationists is the control of human remains and sacred objects. For centuries scientists and curiosity seekers have collected the bodies of Indians from battlefields, cemeteries, and burial mounds. The scientists have claimed that the remains were essential to the study of human origins. Masks, carvings, and other sacred artifacts have also been taken, sometimes illegally, and held in museums and universities. Using both moral and legal arguments, native peoples have worked for repatriation—the return of these items to tribal control. The Native American Graves Protection and Repatriation Act (NAGPRA), passed by the U.S. Congress in 1990, created a process for the return of many remains and sacred objects to native peoples. NAGPRA allows tribes to press claims for the repatriation of certain types of objects from any institution receiving federal funds.

Music and Dance

Native Americans celebrate their traditional music and dance at events called powwows. Powwows take place over a period of one to four days and often draw dancers, singers, artists, and traders from hundreds of miles away. They are open to participants from all tribes. Spectators (including non-Indians) are welcome to attend, as participants seek to share the positive aspects of their culture with outsiders. Hundreds of powwows are held each year in North America, with some of the largest in cities.

The songs and dances performed at 21st-century powwows come mainly from those practiced by the warrior societies of the Plains Indians. These performance styles spread after World War II, when thousands of Plains peoples were relocated to cities in other parts of the United States. Modern powwows can be grouped into two broad divisions: "competition" (or "contest") events and those referred to as "traditional." Competition events offer substantial prize money in various dance and music categories. In contrast, traditional powwows offer small amounts of "day money" to all or some portion of the participants and do not have competitive dancing or singing.

CONTEMPORARY ARTS

Modern Native American arts often reflect the native heritage of the artist. In many cases they combine elements of traditional culture and modern Western styles. Many Native American writers have drawn on the folktales, myths, and histories of the oral tradition in their novels and dramas. Native painters and sculptors have reinterpreted traditional subjects, both in realistic and abstract forms. Musicians have combined Western and native instruments to create popular music, with lyrics in both English and native languages. Other Native American artists have adhered more closely to tradition, preserving and in some cases reviving centuries-old art forms. And still other native artists have chosen not to deal in native themes or styles at all. Rather than being defined as "Native American artists," they prefer to be known as artists who are also Native American.

Visual Arts

The influence of tradition on Native American visual art varies among different regions. In the southwestern United States, for example, the arts flourished in the past and are still active forces in the lives of the peoples who practice them. Almost all of the crafts practiced in prehistoric times are still practiced today, along with some newly introduced forms of expression. The masterful weaving, painting, and especially pottery making of the Pueblo peoples closely follow ancient forms. The Navajo are celebrated for their weaving and silverwork, particularly jewelry. The carved and painted kachina dolls of the Hopi and Zuni have become popular collectors' items (*see* sidebar, "Kachinas," page 64). To the south in Middle America, native artists have been able to

keep tradition alive by adopting ancient designs. Another area in which traditional art has held firm is California, where basket weaving and other art forms continue to be passed from one generation to another.

In contrast to these regions, some parts of the Americas have had to do considerable work in reinvigorating and reinventing their artistic traditions. In the Caribbean and in parts of Central America, for example, the European conquest wiped out native culture more completely than in other areas. The result is that virtually no traces of pre-Columbian traditions remain. In the southeastern United States, the stone sculptures for which the region was once famous, such as calumets, are produced by just a few artists. Modern pottery is quite different from the earlier styles, though wood sculpture and basketry have continued almost unbroken. On the Northwest Coast of North America, all but a few Indian carvers and basket weavers abandoned the arts over the years because those arts provided so little income. In the late 20th and early 21st centuries, however, several craft products that had all but disappeared were revived. Among these were the famed blankets hand woven by the Chilkat people. On the Plains the traditional art of quillwork—the use of porcupine quills in decoration—was replaced for a time by the use of glass beads. But in the late 20th century quillwork experienced a resurgence.

Contemporary painting by Native Americans has taken several new and positive directions. Many native artists have created remarkable works in acrylic, tempera, oil, and related media. They have gained recognition in the fine arts and established successful careers in the world at large.

Nevertheless, Native American art still occupies a peripheral role in the contemporary art world. Efforts to encourage and preserve native art have been made throughout the Americas, but especially in the United States. The Indian Arts and Crafts Board, established by the U.S. Congress in 1935, is one of the few governmental organizations set up to promote and revive native arts and crafts. The Institute of American Indian Arts in Santa Fe, N.M., provides higher education in native arts. In addition, many tribes, particularly the Navajo, Hopi, Cherokee, and Crow, have set up funds to develop crafts areas and museums to promote their traditional arts. The National Museum of the American Indian, established in 1989, was the first national museum devoted to the culture and history of North and South American Indians.

In other parts of the Americas, organizations similar to those in the United States have been established to promote native arts. In general, such movements find their greatest support in places where pride in native heritage is strong. The Latin American country that has taken the most effective steps is Mexico. Its National

The marble sculpture Apache *is an example of the modernist style of Chiricahua Apache artist Allan Houser. Houser is an internationally known sculptor and painter whose work has been exhibited in the Americas, Europe, and Asia.*

Chuck Pefley/Alamy

The music of Taos Pueblo musician Robert Mirabal combines traditional Native American flute with elements of rock, folk, hip-hop, and world music.
David Rae Morris—Reuters/Landov

Museum of Anthropology, built in 1964, stands as a monument to the country's native heritage.

Literature

Native American writers have made their mark on the national literatures of their countries. In the United States N. Scott Momaday, a Kiowa, won the 1969 Pulitzer Prize for fiction for his novel *House Made of Dawn*. It tells of a young man returning home to his pueblo after serving in the U.S. Army. Other successful Native American writers in the United States include James Welch (Blackfeet and Gros Ventre), Leslie Marmon Silko (Pueblo), Louise Erdrich (Ojibwa), and Sherman Alexie (Spokane and Coeur d'Alene).

In Canada numerous First Nations, Métis, and Inuit writers emerged during the 1980s and '90s. A recurring theme in their work is the troubled relation of native individuals to the dominant culture. Among the prominent native Canadian writers are Jeannette Armstrong (Okanagan), Beatrice Culleton (Métis), Tomson Highway (Cree), and Thomas King (Cherokee).

Music

While Native Americans carry on their traditional music at cultural festivals, they have also found a place in modern popular music. Native musicians participate in many genres, including jazz, rock and roll, blues, country, folk, gospel, rap, hip-hop, and reggae. Their lyrics express native issues and concerns in both English and native languages, and the music is appreciated by Indians and non-Indians alike. Some of the best-known Indian popular musicians are Buffy Sainte-Marie (Cree), Joanne Shenandoah (Oneida), Joy Harjo (Creek), Geraldine Barney (Navajo), Robert Mirabal (Taos Pueblo), and Jim Pepper (Kaw and Creek). Marlui Miranda, a Native American musician from Brazil, won international acclaim in the 1990s. Movements to revive and restore Native American traditional music had begun by the 1950s and were common throughout the Americas by the 1990s.

Dawn Villella/AP
The novels of Ojibwa writer Louise Erdrich deal mainly with life among her people in the Midwestern United States, often as they face the intrusion of Euro-American culture in their communities.

Native American composers of the 20th and 21st centuries produced symphonies, ballets, chamber music, choral music, film scores, and more. They included Carl Fischer (Cherokee), Jack Kilpatrick (Cherokee), Louis Ballard (Cherokee-Quapaw), and Brent Michael Davids (Mohican). Blas Galindo of Mexico (Huichol) and Teodoro Valcárcel of Peru (Andean) were also prolific 20th-century composers.

Film

Native Americans have produced, written, and directed feature films in all genres. Perhaps the most prolific native filmmaker in the early 21st century was Chris Eyre (Cheyenne/Arapaho), whose best-known work was the road movie *Smoke Signals* (1998). Valerie Red Horse (Cherokee), Randy Redroad (Cherokee), and Zacharias Kunuk (Inuit) also won acclaim as directors.

FURTHER RESOURCES

Arts

Braman, A.N. Traditional Native American Arts and Activities (Wiley, 2000).

Bruchac, Joseph. Our Stories Remember: American Indian History, Culture, and Values Through Storytelling (Fulcrum, 2003).

January, Brendan. Native American Art & Culture (Raintree, 2005).

Montgomery, D.R. Crafts and Skills of the Native Americans: Tipis, Canoes, Jewelry, Moccasins, and More (Skyhorse, 2009).

Porter, Joy, and Roemer, K.M., eds. The Cambridge Companion to Native American Literature (Cambridge Univ. Press, 2005).

Shea Murphy, Jacqueline. The People Have Never Stopped Dancing: Native American Modern Dance Histories (Univ. of Minnesota Press, 2007).

When the Rain Sings: Poems by Young Native Americans, rev. ed. (Smithsonian, 2008).

Civil Rights and Law

Johnson, T.R. Red Power: The Native American Civil Rights Movement (Chelsea House, 2007).

McCool, Daniel, and others. Native Vote: American Indians, the Voting Rights Act, and the Right to Vote (Cambridge Univ. Press, 2007).

Clothing

Brasser, Theodore. Native American Clothing: An Illustrated History (Firefly, 2009).

Her Many Horses, Emil, ed. Identity by Design: Tradition, Change, and Celebration in Native Women's Dresses (Collins/Smithsonian, 2007).

Early Civilizations

Bancroft-Hunt, Norman. Historical Atlas of Ancient America (Mercury, 2009).

Coe, M.D., and Koontz, Rex. Mexico: From the Olmecs to the Aztecs, 6th ed., rev. and expanded (Thames & Hudson, 2008).

Foster, L.V. Handbook to Life in the Ancient Maya World (Oxford Univ. Press, 2005).

Ganeri, Anita. Mesoamerican Myth: A Treasury of Central American Legends, Art, and History (Chartwell, 2007).

Green, Jen, and others. The Encyclopedia of the Ancient Americas (Southwater, 2001).

Montgomery, John. How to Read Maya Hieroglyphs (Hippocrene, 2003).

Phillips, Charles. Aztec & Maya: The Complete Illustrated History (Metro, 2008).

Silverman, Helaine, and Isbell, W.H., eds. Handbook of South American Archaeology (Springer, 2008).

VanDerwarker, A.M. Farming, Hunting, and Fishing in the Olmec World (Univ. of Texas Press, 2006).

Wood, Marion. Ancient Maya and Aztec Civilizations, 3rd ed. (Chelsea House, 2007).

General

Blaisdell, Bob, ed. Great Speeches by Native Americans (Dover, 2000).

Bowen, R.A. The Native Americans (Mason Crest, 2009).

Brennan, Kristine. Native Americans (Mason Crest, 2009).

Garroutte, E.M. Real Indians: Identity and the Survival of Native America (Univ. of Calif. Press, 2003).

Nardo, Don. Early Native North Americans (Lucent, 2008).

Sepehri, Sandy. Rourke's Native American History & Culture Encyclopedia, 10 vols. (Rourke, 2009).

Stonich, S.C., ed. Endangered Peoples of Latin America: Struggles to Survive and Thrive (Greenwood, 2001).

Waldman, Carl. Atlas of the North American Indian, 3rd ed. (Facts on File, 2009).

Waldman, Carl. Dictionary of Native American Terminology (Castle, 2009).

History

Gallay, Alan. The Indian Slave Trade: The Rise of the English Empire in the American South, 1670–1717 (Yale Univ. Press, 2003).

Holm, Tom. Code Talkers and Warriors: Native Americans and World War II (Chelsea House, 2007).

Jones, D.S. Rationalizing Epidemics: Meanings and Uses of American Indian Mortality Since 1600 (Harvard Univ. Press, 2004).

Josephy, A.M., Jr. 500 Nations: An Illustrated History of North American Indians (Pimlico, 2005).

Juettner, Bonnie. 100 Native Americans Who Changed History, updated and rev. (World Almanac Library, 2006).

Kennedy, F.H., ed. American Indian Places: A Historical Guidebook (Houghton, 2008).

MacQuarrie, Kim. The Last Days of the Incas (Simon & Schuster, 2008).

Montejo, Victor. Voices from Exile: Violence and Survival in Modern Maya History (Univ. of Oklahoma Press, 2008).

Moore, MariJo, ed. Eating Fire, Tasting Blood: Breaking the Great Silence of the American Indian Holocaust (Thunder's Mouth, 2006).

Nunnally, M.L. American Indian Wars: A Chronology of Confrontations Between Native Peoples and Settlers and the United States Military, 1500s–1901 (McFarland, 2007).

Rossi, Ann. Cultures Collide: Native American and Europeans 1492–1700 (National Geographic, 2004).

Rozema, Vicki, ed. Voices from the Trail of Tears (Blair, 2003).

Trafzer, C.E., ed. American Indians/American Presidents: A History (Harper, 2009).

Public Image

King, C.R., and Springwood, C.F., eds. Team Spirits: The Native American Mascots Controversy (Univ. of Nebraska Press, 2001).

Rollins, P.C., and O'Connor, J.E., eds. Hollywood's Indian: The Portrayal of the Native American in Film (Univ. Press of Kentucky, 2003).

Sheyahshe, M.A. Native Americans in Comic Books: A Critical Study (McFarland, 2008).

Religion/Medicine

Deloria, Vine, Jr. The World We Used to Live In: Remembering the Powers of the Medicine Men (Fulcrum, 2006).

Hirschfelder, A.B., and Molin, P.F. Encyclopedia of Native American Religions (Facts on File, 2000).

Jones, D.M., and Molyneux, B.L. The Mythology of the Americas (Lorenz, 2001).

Social Life and Customs

Berzok, L.M. American Indian Food (Greenwood, 2005).

Horse Capture, G.P., and Her Many Horses, E., eds. A Song for the Horse Nation: Horses in Native American Cultures (Fulcrum, 2006).

Mankiller, Wilma. Every Day Is a Good Day: Reflections by Contemporary Indigenous Women (Fulcrum, 2004).

McMaster, Gerald, and Trafzer, C.E., eds. Native Universe: Voices of Indian America (Smithsonian, 2008).

Patent, D.H. The Buffalo and the Indians: A Shared Destiny (Clarion, 2006).

Reyhner, Jon, and Eder, Jeanne. American Indian Education (Univ. of Oklahoma Press, 2006).

West, R.T. Penucquem Speaks: A Look at Our World from a Different Culture (BookSurge, 2006).

Sports

King, C.R., ed. Native Athletes in Sport and Society (Univ. of Nebraska Press, 2005).

Staeger, Rob. Native American Sports and Games (Mason Crest, 2003).

Vennum, Thomas. Lacrosse Legends of the First Americans (Johns Hopkins, 2007).

Whittington, E.M., ed. The Sport of Life and Death: The Mesoamerican Ballgame (Thames & Hudson, 2001).

Technology

Delgado, J.P. Native American Shipwrecks (Watts, 2000).

Ipellie, Alootook, with David MacDonald. The Inuit Thought of It: Amazing Arctic Innovations (Annick, 2007).

Kavin, Kim. Tools of Native Americans: A Kid's Guide to the History & Culture of the First Americans (Nomad, 2006).

Keoke, E.D., and Porterfield, K.M. American Indian Contributions to the World: Food, Farming, and Hunting (Facts on File, 2005).

Taylor, C.F. Native American Weapons (Univ. of Oklahoma Press, 2001).

INDEX

Page numbers in **bold** indicate main subject references; page numbers in *italics* indicate illustrations.

Page numbers in **bold** indicate main subject references; page numbers in *italics* indicate illustrations.